IRISH

A Reed Security Romance

GIULIA LAGOMARSINO

For Carol
Your idea brought to life

CAST OF CHARACTERS

Sebastian "Cap" Reed- owner
   Maggie "Freckles" Reed
   Caitlin Reed

Team 1:
   Derek "Irish" Cortell- team leader and part owner

Hunter "Pappy" Papacosta

Lola "Brave" Pruitt

Team 2:
   Sam "Cazzo" Galmacci- team leader and part owner
   Vanessa Galmacci

Mark "Sinner" Sinn
   Cara Sinn

Blake "Burg" Reasenburg

Team 3:
John "Ice" Peters

Julian "Jules" Siegrist

Chris "Jack" McKay

Team 4:
Chance "Sniper" Hendrix

Jackson Lewis

Gabe Moore

Team 5:
Alec Wesley

Florrie Younge

Craig Devereux

Training:

Hudson Knight- formerly known as Garrick Knight
Kate Knight

IT Department:

Robert "Rob" Markum
Becky

Chapter One

CLAIRE

*H*oly hotness, Batman. The man standing across the produce section was so drool-worthy that I had to wipe my mouth to be sure I wasn't actually drooling. He was tall with thick, dark brown hair that was just long enough that I could run my fingers through it. My fingers twitched at my sides as I imagined walking up to him and pulling him toward me by his shirt and then kissing him breathless. Of course, I wasn't actually that bold in real life. In fact, I was pretty sure I didn't possess any of the qualities of a strong, confident woman that took what she wanted. I was more of the 'sit back and stare at the gorgeous man' type. Which was exactly what I was doing.

I crept closer to him, feigning interest in the fruit in front of me. I picked up a half pint of blueberries, pretending to inspect the contents. I watched as he reached into a large bin and pulled out a large watermelon. It was like it weighed nothing in his large hands. He tapped the side of it and then put it in the cart. He grabbed another five watermelons, doing the same to each. I popped the top of the blueberry container and put a few in my mouth, slowly chewing the soft fruit as I imagined smearing blueberries over his hard abs and then licking them from his body.

He pushed his cart over to the cantaloupe and squeezed the melons as he picked them up. My nipples hardened as I imagined him squeezing my breasts. Good Lord, this man was sending my body into overdrive. When my container of blueberries was gone, I decided to get a better vantage point and I walked over to the grapes. Picking up the bag, I popped a few in my mouth and let the juices flow down my throat. Hmm. *I would let his juices flow down my throat*, I thought as I watched him quirking his eyebrow at the melons.

He moved on to tomatoes and then avocados. His cart was so full that he must be shopping for some kind of get together. Nobody ate that much fresh fruits and vegetables. He squeezed the avocado in his hand and put six of them in a bag. I ate a few more grapes as I walked around the corner of the produce stand and stood in the same aisle as him. He was now holding a cucumber and testing the firmness. I chewed faster as I glanced from the cucumber in his hand and imagined that he was gripping his own cucumber. Long, thick strokes as I watched from his bed where I was spread out for him. I moaned and the lady that was walking past me turned and gave me an odd look.

"Good grapes," I said as I popped a few in my mouth.

"You know you're not actually supposed to eat the fruit in the store, right?"

"I'm watching the show," I said, nodding to the man at the end of the aisle holding the cucumbers.

"Mmmm. That man is fine. I would totally wrap myself in cellophane and meet him at my door."

Sighing, I popped another grape in my mouth and held the bag in front of her. "Grape?" She took one and we continued to watch as the man went to the ears of corn and started stripping the husks down to see the kernels. "I'd let him strip me like that. Could you imagine his fingers skimming across your skin as he tore the clothes from your body?"

Another woman stopped beside me, trying to get through with her cart. "Excuse me, but you're blocking the- oh dear Lord. Look at that man."

"Grape?" I asked as I handed the bag over to her. She took one and grimaced.

"Why are we eating fruit? We need chocolate and a good bottle of wine."

"I was using the grapes as a distraction so he wouldn't see me ogling him."

"Honey, we're standing in the middle of the produce section and eating fruit as we all stare in the same direction. I'm pretty sure that if he looked over here, he would know exactly what we were doing."

"Ooh," the other lady said as she smacked my arm. "Look, he's helping that little old lady get down a bag for her vegetables."

"Oh, that's so sweet," I said sighing.

"I think I just got a lady boner." The lady on my right fanned herself as she grabbed another grape.

"One of us should go say hi," the woman on my left sighed.

"I'm married. As much as I would love to go flirt with a man like that, I'm pretty sure that would be considered cheating in my husband's eyes," the woman on my right replied.

"You're right," the other woman nodded. "I'm pretty sure my boyfriend wouldn't be too happy either. Stupid boyfriend. If we hadn't been together for over a year, I might be tempted to go talk to him. What about you? Do you have a boyfriend?"

"If I had a boyfriend, I wouldn't be stalking this man around the grocery store," I said around a grape.

The woman on my right sighed. "Well, I guess I'd better finish my grocery shopping. Good luck."

I nodded as she walked away, refusing to take my eyes off the delicious specimen that continued around toward the meat department. The woman on my left gave a half hearted goodbye and walked away, while I tried to work up the courage to go talk to the man. I followed him over to the cooler that held the steaks and pressed a cold pack of chicken against my chest to cool myself down.

I could do it. I could walk up to him and strike up a conversation about different steaks and the juiciest cut. I had no clue which was the best cut, but it sounded like an intelligent way to start a conversation. I took my bag of grapes and made my way over to the sexy man and popped a grape in my mouth.

"Hey." That was as far as I got before I started choking on the grape that got lodged in my throat when I sucked in a deep breath to summon the courage to talk to the man. I grabbed at my throat, trying to force the grape from my constricting passageway, but it wasn't helping. Shit, I was going to die in the meat department. The man must have heard my strangled gasps for air because he turned suddenly and his eyes widened. I could only imagine what I looked like. I could feel my eyes widen with each passing second and I knew that I was going to pass out if I didn't get air soon. The man didn't waste a second as he came up behind me and wrapped his arms around me. Even in my state of panic, I could still appreciate the feel of his strong arms wrapped around me.

My body flew off the ground as he gave me one strong heave and the grape flew out of my mouth and shot across the floor of the grocery store. I gasped in the fresh air that I wasn't sure I would ever breathe again and took in big swallows like I would be storing it up for later. Several claps sounded around me and I took in the people that were staring at us in awe. I turned slowly and saw my sexy savior staring at me in concern.

"Are you alright?"

Tongue tied, I couldn't think of one logical thing to say, so instead, I popped another grape in my mouth and chewed until it was well ground up in my mouth. The man continued to stare at me like I was insane and eyed the bag of grapes.

"Are you sure you should be doing that? You just choked on one of those. You really want to take a chance with another?"

I nodded vigorously, not wanting to open my mouth and risk word vomit that would surely leave my mouth. His eyebrow quirked at me and he crossed his arms over his chest. Finally, my brain came back online and I thrust my arm forward to shake his hand.

"Claire. I'm Claire," I said stiffly. He eyed my hand skeptically, but took my small hand in his and gave a firm shake.

"Derek."

"Derek," I said breathily. "That's such a sexy name," I mumbled.

"Excuse me?"

"I mean, McDreamy was a Derek and he was really sexy, but you're easily ten times more gorgeous than him. I mean, you've got strong arms," I said, reaching up and gripping onto his bicep. My eyes widened as I realized I couldn't even wrap my hand half way around his arm. "Dear Lord, that's amazing. Are your legs like this too?"

"Umm.."

Shit, more word vomit. The man saved my life and I was rambling on about the size of his muscles in his legs. "I just meant that you have really gorgeous arms and your legs are probably just as sexy. I mean..not that men have gorgeous legs. You wouldn't describe a man as gorgeous. Well, not you personally. I mean, men in general. Not that men describe other men. I meant that women don't describe men as gorgeous. Usually it's sexy or strong. Something along those lines."

I slapped my hand over my mouth to stop with the descriptions that were probably on the verge of sending this man running for the hills. Awkward was the only word I could use to describe this whole scene. I was beyond being able to save any dignity in this conversation.

"How about we start over," he said with a sexy smirk. "I'm Derek and you are?"

"Claire," I said, snapping my mouth closed before I could say anything else.

"That's a beautiful name. It's nice to meet you."

I nodded, not wanting to open my big, fat mouth and ruin this further. I could tell he was losing interest fast when I refused to say anything more. I could hear the words on the tip of his tongue and then he said them.

"Well, I have some shopping to finish up. You take care, Claire, and be careful with those grapes."

He turned and started to walk back to his cart. I couldn't let him go yet. This amazingly beautiful man was still in my grasp. I could still have a chance with him.

"I think you're totally sexy," I shouted. I shook my head. That was what came out of my mouth? I couldn't think of anything more intelligent? But he turned back to me and I figured I might still have a chance. "I would love to get to talk to you some more. You know, like actual conversation, not me spewing crap about your arms and legs. I'm sure if we met again when I wasn't choking to death on a grape that I was only eating to work up the courage to come talk to you, that we might get to know each other better. I mean, that's assuming that I haven't totally turned you off by now. Of course, after you've seen food fly from my mouth like that and then I hit on you and grabbed your muscles like I was going to devour them, I'm sure there's someone slightly less neurotic that you would prefer to go out with. On the other hand, there's something to be said for-"

His hand covered my mouth and he shook his head as he grinned down at me. "You just don't know when to stop, do you?" I shook my head as his fingers remained on my lips. "How about this? Let's get together for coffee sometime. We can try this again, without the choking, and see how we do."

I nodded, wondering if he was going to hold his fingers to my mouth the whole time we were on our coffee date.

"Can I have your phone?"

I handed it over to him and shrugged when he raised his eyebrow at me. Yes, I still had a flip phone. I had never upgraded to a smart phone because I didn't see the point. I didn't have the interest to sit around and play on my phone the way other people did, looking up random shit on the royals or whatever. He gave a short laugh and dialed his own phone. I was relieved when I heard it ringing, glad that he hadn't just pretended to put in his number.

"Are you free on Friday?" he asked.

"Um, well I have an appointment with my gynecologist in the afternoon." Oh, shit. Why did I say that? Now he's going to think I have herpes or chlamydia. "It's not for anything bad," I said quickly. "It's just a routine exam. You know, pap and regular check. Make sure everything works the way it's supposed to. I mean, I already know it does. You don't have to worry about that. Not that I'm suggesting that you sleep with me. I never sleep with someone on the first date. I'm not a whore. But it's not like I find you gross either. I'm not saying I won't sleep with you, just not right away. Then again, I guess you could be a totally terrible date and we won't get past coffee, so maybe we won't sleep together."

"Claire!" he practically shouted at me. I stopped talking immediately and turned bright red when I realized I had been rambling on about gynecologists and sex and we hadn't even been on one date. He was going to walk away. There was no way he would agree to meet me for coffee now. "How about we leave something to discuss over coffee? If we cover all this now, what will we talk about on Friday?"

My eyes grew big when my brain processed what he said. He still wanted to meet me. Holy shit. No man ever wanted to meet up with me after getting to know me. I nodded and started backing away. "Right. I'll just be going now. See you Friday."

I turned and started walking away, but he called me again. I spun around and watched him shake his head at me. "You didn't give me a chance to tell you where we were going to meet up."

"Just text me," I replied as I continued to walk backwards. I didn't want to take a chance that I would ruin this.

"Claire," he said and I watched his eyes widen.

I spun around, trying to get away from him before I was tempted to go back and lick his body. I mean, I had already talked about sex with him, why not take it a step further? Of course, had I been paying attention to where I was going instead of thinking about licking his body, I might have seen the giant display before I walked right into it and fell into a large pile of Little Debbie snack cakes. There had to be at least seventy-five boxes scattered around me on the floor. People were staring and I peeked over at Derek, who was shaking his head and laughing. Why couldn't I just behave like a normal person around a man? I quickly got up and grabbed my purse, walking toward the exit as quickly as I could. There was no way in hell I was sticking around to get my groceries when I had just embarrassed the hell out of myself.

"You're such an idiot," I berated myself as I stormed out of the grocery store. "You couldn't just say, 'Hi. I'm Claire. Would you like to get together for coffee sometime?' No, you had to go in there and completely embarrass yourself in front of the hottest guy you've ever met and the rest of the people in the store. You really need to get out more, Claire."

The sound of a horn honking had me looking up to see a car barreling out of control down the road. I stood frozen, unsure of what way to go. *Go left and the car will swerve left and hit you. I could go right, but he's already going right. You'll go right in the path of the car. There's no way out of this. I might as well just lay down and let the car hit me!*

Something hard hit me and I barely saw the car swerve out of the way before my skull cracked against the pavement, sending blinding pain through my entire body. My eyes fluttered a few times before I was finally able to open them enough to see a man's face with sunglasses covering his eyes. I wanted to know who had saved my life, but all I could think was that whoever it was had gotten to me really fast. *Super* fast. No person on the face of the earth could move the way he did.

"It's Superman," I said right before I passed out.

I wanted to see the eyes behind those glasses. I kept closing my eyes, hoping to get a few more details of his face, but I had been seeing spots after I hit my head and I couldn't remember the details. How was I ever going to find the man that had saved my life and thank him for what he had done for me?

"Claire, I'm telling you, there's no such thing as superheroes."

My sister, Lucy, was sitting by my hospital bed trying to convince me that I had completely lost my mind. "I'm telling you, there is no way that anyone could have gotten to me that fast. You know how time seems to stand still and you take in everything around you?"

"No."

"Well, it happened, and I'm telling you that no one was close enough to me to save me. He was Superman."

"Is this like the movie *American Dreamer?*"

"What are you talking about?"

"You know, she wakes up in the hospital after hitting her head and thinks that she's a character in a book. Is that what's going on here? Do you think you're Lois Lane or something?"

"I know I'm not Lois Lane, and no, I don't think I'm a character in a book. I just know what happened, and I'm telling you that it was Superman."

"I think I need to call the doctor back in and have him run some more tests. There's no such thing as a man with super powers. If there was, I would have multiple orgasms every night."

"I'm telling you, he was real!"

"I know he was real, Claire. The doctor told me that someone shoved you out of the way, but you're imagining the rest. There is no such thing as a superhero."

"There is too," I grumbled. "And I'm going to find him and thank him for saving my life."

It was obvious that she didn't believe me, so I wasn't going to push it. I didn't need her thinking I was crazy. But I knew what I saw and there was no way that man was close enough to shove me out of the way. I just had to find him and prove it.

She sighed and plopped down in the chair. "When are they going to get here with the paperwork? I want to get home."

"The nurse said she would be back any minute."

The door opened and the nurse walked in looking completely frazzled. "I'm so sorry it took so long to get back here," the nurse said.

"You can stuff your sorries in a sack, lady," my sister said. The nurse turned to her with a look of shock. "I was just joking," she said quickly. "Haven't you ever watched *Seinfeld*?"

"Who?"

My sister rolled her eyes, obviously irritated that the nurse didn't know what she was talking about. It was a great TV show after all. Who doesn't quote it?

"Am I ready to be discharged?" I asked.

"Right," the nurse said as she walked over to me with paperwork. "You have a concussion, so take it easy and make sure you get plenty of rest. Headaches, dizziness, and nausea are all common symptoms after a head injury, so try to avoid doing anything that could make that worse. Your symptoms could last for several weeks, so take the time you need to recover. You need someone to stay with you for twenty-four hours to keep an eye on you. Will your sister be staying with you?"

"Yes."

"Good. Well, here are your discharge papers," she said hurriedly. "Someone will be by in a few minutes to take you down."

"I'm ready now. We'll just head down on our own."

"Hospital policy-"

"Look, I can tell you're very busy and I don't want to be a nuisance, but I'm ready to get out of here. I have my sister and I promise she'll hold my hand the whole way down."

With that, I stood up on shaky legs and walked to the door with the nurse staring at me like I had lost my mind. Lucy and I were out the door and by the entrance doors before she came rushing after us. Luckily, she wasn't actually trying that hard to catch up to us. We slowed once we got outside, which was good because my head was pounding and that dizziness she was talking about was kicking in.

"*D*addy, I'm fine. I promise. It's just a little bump on the head. I hardly feel a thing," I lied. My dad still thought I was a little girl at times. He wasn't all there any more and it was easier to let him think that I was still his little girl than correct him and see him suffer through the confusion.

"Claire bear, I don't understand how you hit your head riding your bike. Didn't you have your helmet on?"

"I didn't tighten it all the way. It fell off when I fell off the bike."

He shook his head at me and walked over to the fridge. "I'll make some dinner. Why don't you sit down?"

"Daddy, I can make dinner."

"Don't be ridiculous. I'm your father. It's my job to take care of you, not the other way around. Just because your mother isn't alive anymore doesn't mean that you don't have a capable parent."

"I know. I think I'm in the mood for pizza. Can you put in a frozen pizza for me?"

"Anything for you, Claire bear."

I had a lot of frozen pizza. Daddy had Alzheimer's and didn't remember a lot at night, so he still thought that he had to take care of me. He wasn't a very good cook, and frankly, I didn't trust him at the stove. I could keep an eye on the pizza fairly easily without letting him know that I was watching over his shoulder. It was getting to the point where I wasn't sure how much longer Lucy and I would be able to look after him. He had started getting worse earlier in the day and we weren't always around to keep an eye on him. One day I found him outside trying to fix the roof of the shed. His balance wasn't that good anymore, but in his head, he was back fifteen years ago when he was younger and more capable.

I didn't want to put him in a home. It was my job to take care of him and make sure that he still felt loved. Lucy agreed to a point, but she was also the more pragmatic of the two of us. She had already started calling around to different nursing homes to find a spot for him. She knew that we wouldn't be able to keep this up too much longer. I just didn't want to admit that we wouldn't be able to take care of him soon.

"I made a call today to old man Wilson. He's selling his horses and I was thinking we could buy one off him. You and Lucy would have to share, of course."

"Daddy, that sounds great. You know Lucy and I have always wanted a horse."

"Well, things will be tight around here, but I think we can swing it."

I smiled at him lovingly. This had all happened twelve years ago. We never ended up getting the horse because we'd had other expenses come up. Lucy and I took it well, knowing that if Daddy had been able to get us that horse, he would have. Still, this was one of those times that I didn't mind when he slipped back in time. I loved seeing his eyes light up at the mention of getting those horses for us. He loved us so much and would do anything to make us happy. That was exactly how I felt about him and I'd do anything to keep him here as long as possible.

After dinner, I hopped on my computer and started researching people that had displayed extraordinary abilities. There was a man from Malaysia that could stick metal objects to his body like a magnet. He could also pull a car with his abilities. Interesting, but not quite what I thought my mystery man could do.

There was an 89 year old grand master of Kung Fu, Tai Chi, and Qigong that could generate heat through his palms. I wondered exactly how that was done, but it definitely sounded like a superpower to me. He was also able to stand on a thin sheet of paper without falling through. That sounded more like flying to me. Definitely a Superman quality. I would have to do more research on him.

Michel Lotito was a French entertainer who could eat everything. He even ate an entire Cessna 150 airplane. While that didn't seem like a superhuman quality, but more of an anomaly, I didn't want to rule it out.

Scanning the internet for other strange incidents, I came across a runner that could run continuously for more than three days and nights without stopping and without sleeping. Hmm. That also seemed a bit like Superman to me. I continued to write out a list, sure that one of them would lead me to what I was looking for. After two hours, my head was throbbing and I had seen more crazy things than I thought possible.

"This is crazy," I said, slamming my laptop shut. I crumpled up the piece of paper I had been writing on and threw it in the trash. "Superheroes aren't real. Whatever happened was some kind of weird fluke and now you're letting your imagination run away with you. Just stop!"

I got up and quickly showered, the whole time thinking about all the things that I had read online. Shaking my head, I got out of the shower and dried off quickly, getting in my pajamas and climbing under the covers.

"There's no such thing as a superhero," I muttered before I rolled over and went to sleep.

Chapter Two

DEREK

I stared down at the woman beneath me and watched as her eyes fluttered closed after she called me Superman. I wasn't going to lie, it made me feel ten feet tall to have a woman refer to me as the man of steel, which I was currently sporting at the moment with this woman spread out beneath me. I should have been thinking about the fact that she smacked her head on the pavement and not what she felt like beneath me, but my body was on a different track than my brain at the moment.

"Claire," I said, patting her cheek. She didn't respond. Luckily, I heard someone on the phone with 9-1-1, so they should be on their way soon. I shifted my body so I was no longer on top of her, but I stayed close to her. I wasn't ready to leave the warmth of her sweet, little body yet. She was a tiny little thing. Probably not any taller than 5'3". She had shoulder length brown hair and I had seen before she passed out that her eyes were a beautiful ocean blue.

When I landed on top of her, I could feel all her curves under me and they were damn good curves. She wasn't fat, but she wasn't thin either. When I was with a woman, I wanted something to grab on to. I didn't need a twig that I could snap if I fucked her too hard. By the feel of her hips under me, I could tell she would be perfect for gripping onto as I fucked her from behind. Exactly my kind of woman.

The ambulance showed up and checked her out before loading her in the back. They didn't allow me to ride with her since I wasn't family and had already admitted to them that I didn't know her. I jumped in my truck and followed her to the hospital, but they wouldn't allow me back to see her after she was stabilized. I was pacing the waiting room, hoping for someone to tell me something, but the last time I asked, the nurse told me that I should leave because they wouldn't allow me to see her or give out any information.

Since I had her number, I decided that I would text her tomorrow and find out how she was doing. I was just getting back to my truck when I finally checked my phone. I had dozens of missed calls and text messages. Shit. I was supposed to be getting the food for the party over at my boss's house and I had completely forgotten.

"Irish, where the hell are you? Maggie's over here bitching because she doesn't have the food you promised her you'd pick up!" Cap yelled at me through the phone.

"Sorry, Cap. I had a bit of an emergency."

"It better not have involved your dick."

I hesitated for a moment as I remembered the feel of her body under mine. "Nothing like that. A woman almost got run over at the store and I knocked her out of the way, but she ended up smacking her head. She's in the hospital."

"So, where's the food?"

"At the store," I gritted out, trying to hold back my anger. "Don't be such a dick. I wanted to make sure she was alright."

"And is she?"

"I don't know. They wouldn't give me any information on her. All I have is her phone number."

"How the hell do you have her phone number?"

"She picked me up in the store. She was following me around and eating grapes, trying to pretend like she wasn't watching me. It was cute as hell, but then she choked on a grape and I had to give her the heimlich."

"She sounds like a fucking mess."

"So did Maggie when you first met her, but now you're married and have a kid together," I snapped back at him.

"Jesus, we don't need any more crazy women surrounding us."

"Relax, we're meeting for coffee, not getting married. I'm on my way back to the store now. Give me a half hour and I should be there."

"Hurry the fuck up. I'm hungry."

"Yeah, yeah. I'm on it."

I hung up and went back to the store and reloaded a grocery cart with everything I needed. I didn't take my time this time around. I just threw shit in the cart and hit the road. When I got to Cap and Maggie's house, everyone was out back already, drinking beer and shootin' the shit. Mark "Sinner" Sinn came out to help me unload the truck and grinned at me.

"I heard you picked up a pretty little lady at the store."

"I didn't pick her up; she picked me up."

"Did you know she was after you?"

"Yeah. She was following me around. At one point, she stopped with two other ladies and they were watching me pick out corn."

"Did you put on a show for her?"

"Give me some credit. This isn't my first rodeo."

"So, that's a yes."

"Of course, it's a fucking yes. She's smokin'. Nice, round curves. Big breasts. Juicy ass."

"Did you get her number?"

I shot him a look, telling him he was off his fucking rocker if he thought I didn't. He held up his hands and grabbed his beer off the counter. "Alright, alright. So, you got her number."

"Yes."

"And you knew she was there."

"Yes."

"And you put on a show."

"Yes," I said in frustration.

"Then you picked her up. Tell yourself whatever you want, but you laid all the groundwork to score."

I went to tell him he was wrong, but then I realized that even if I wasn't trying to, I really had been reeling her in the whole time. I had seen her watching me and I wanted her to approach me. I hadn't realized how batshit crazy she was at the time, but then again, my body stood to attention from the first moment I saw her delicious body.

"Fine. I picked her up. Can we move on now?" I started chopping up the watermelon while Sinner started shucking the corn.

"Cap said she's in the hospital and you have her number. You should have Becky look her up. She's out back with everyone else." Becky was one of our computer techs and could find anything you wanted in a matter of minutes.

"Nah, I don't want to bother her today."

"Becky would have all her information in five minutes. Just do it so you aren't moping around the rest of the day."

"I wouldn't be moping around after a girl I just met."

"You keep telling yourself that," he grinned.

We finished cutting up all the fruits and vegetables and got it all set out. Freckles, Cap's wife, had been upstairs taking care of her daughter, Caitlin and just came down the stairs looking exhausted.

"I don't understand how women have more than one kid. Caitlin's been teething for weeks now and I haven't gotten any sleep."

"Why don't you just go to sleep now? You know none of us care. We'll take care of everything."

"But then I don't get to talk to anyone. Do you know how long it's been since I talked to an adult? I swear, my vocabulary has been reduced to talking about poop, farm animals, and food."

"We'll hook you up, Freckles. I promise, no talk of food, farm animals, or poop."

We walked outside and sat down around the bonfire that Cap had started. Julius was in the middle of a story about his latest conquest.

"So, I woke up the next morning thinking that things were going pretty good between us. I gave her orgasms and I figured it was only right that she make me breakfast," Jules said.

"What'd she make?" Burg asked.

"Protein smoothies," he grimaced.

"Not what I would have expected, but at least she made something good for you," Chance said.

"Not fucking good for me. Apparently, she was offended that I asked her to make breakfast and she put a shit ton of laxatives in the smoothie." A round of groans filled the air. We all knew what was coming. "I was on the fucking toilet with diarrhea for two fucking days."

Maggie stood suddenly, looking pissed off. "You know, I came out here to talk about something other than shit." She spun around and looked at me. "You promised," she yelled before marching off to the house. We watched her walk away and started laughing when the door slammed closed.

Cap was grilling out and we sat around bullshitting for a few hours. As much as I tried to enjoy the company, I couldn't stop checking my phone, wondering if Claire had been released from the hospital yet. I was pretty sure that she would be okay, but I wanted someone to actually tell me. Sneaking away, I dialed her number, hoping that someone would answer.

"Hello?" I breathed a sigh of relief.

"Hey, this is Derek." There was no response. "From the grocery store." Silence again. "Hello?"

"This is her sister, Lucy."

"Oh, hey. I was just calling to see if she was alright. They wouldn't let me in to see her at the hospital."

"She's doing okay. She has a concussion and she's supposed to take it easy."

"That's good. It looked like she smacked her head pretty hard."

"You saw it?"

"I was the one that pushed her out of the way of the car."

"Oh. Well, thank you."

"Listen, just have her call me when she's up to it."

"Will do."

I hung up and turned around to see Lola smirking at me. "What?"

"Another one bites the dust."

"What are you talking about?"

"I'm talking about another man at Reed Security who's going to fall to his knees over a woman."

"I'm not falling to my knees. I'm checking on a woman that was almost hit by a car."

She quirked an eyebrow at me and grinned. "The only women you check on are the ones currently warming your bed."

"That's not true. I check on you."

Her face turned darker and her eyes flicked away. "I don't need you to check on me."

"You sure about that?"

"Since when have I ever needed a man to check up on me?" she said angrily.

"Lola, you don't have to put on the tough girl act all the time. It's okay to tell us you need help."

"I don't need help. I'm fine and I don't need you and Hunter treating me like I'm going to break."

"We don't think you're going to break, but we've heard you screaming from nightmares. It's been years and you still haven't gotten any fucking help."

"Because I don't need it! Stop trying to fix me," she yelled.

"That's bullshit and you know it. Hunter and I both saw someone after that shit went down with Alex and Cole and we didn't deal with half the crap you did. It has nothing to do with you being a woman and everything to do with the fact that that fucker messed with your head. Literally and figuratively."

"I don't need this bullshit from you. You may be my team leader, but you don't run my life. Until I start fucking up on the job, you have no say in anything but my job performance."

Lola stormed off for the door and I did something real fucking stupid. "Yeah, go to the bar and pick up another one night stand so that you can sleep through the night," I shouted. She turned and glared at me, but behind the anger was hurt and I felt like a complete ass for using her coping mechanism against her. I just didn't know how to get through to her any more. Years later, we all knew Lola was still struggling with her demons, but she wouldn't allow anyone in to help her.

"Shit," I said, running a hand over my head in frustration.

"What happened?" I turned to see Hunter "Pappy" Papacosta standing in the doorway with a beer. Lola, Pappy, and I had been on a team together from the start and the people I trusted most in this world.

"Lola. I said some shit to her about getting help and she tore me a new asshole about trying to fix her."

"You can't keep blaming yourself for what happened, Irish. None of us knew what the fuck was going on. You did the best you could under the circumstances."

"I knew that something was fucked up. I could feel it in my gut. The same fucking thing happened when we were at the safe house with Knight. I knew that something was wrong with that whole situation and I went along with it anyway."

"What happened with Knight worked out for the best. Go outside and ask him right now if he would change a goddamn thing and he'll tell you that he's happy with the way everything turned out. Yeah, we were blindsided, but shit worked out."

"That's besides the point," I snapped at him. "When am I going to fucking learn? Every time my gut tells me that something's wrong, I don't do a damn thing to change the outcome. I should have fucking gone somewhere else with Cole and Alex. I should have just run with them. You wouldn't have ended up in a coma. I wouldn't have been shot in the leg. Lola wouldn't have been fucking terrorized. Cole wouldn't have been stabbed. And Alex wouldn't have had to face that psychopath again. Same fucking thing with Knight. I knew that something was off and I still didn't do anything. How the fuck do all of you put your trust in me?" I yelled.

"Because you're fucking good at your job. There's not a single situation you've described that you should have known to do something different. You could have run with Cole and Alex, but guess what? That asshole could have been following us and something worse might have happened. Same thing with Knight. They were tracking us. Running wouldn't have done a fucking thing for us. Bad shit happens. That doesn't make you a bad leader. That just means that we've had some shit luck. Now, go the fuck outside, grab a beer, and stop whining like a little bitch!"

"You're such an asshole, Pappy."

I was waiting at the coffee house in town for Claire. She told me that she was feeling fine and would meet me like we had planned. She was running late and that wasn't something I particularly liked. I was a person that was always on time to everything. It was something that was instilled in me during my military days. Even now, years after being discharged, I still had to be early for everything. I checked my watch again and saw that she was fifteen minutes late. I wasn't going to wait around any more. Maybe she didn't really want to meet me. I got up and threw down a few bills for the waitress, even though I hadn't ordered anything yet.

"Excuse me! Excuse me! I need to get through." I couldn't see her, but the voice was all her. She was so tiny that she got lost in the few patrons that were trying to leave the coffee house. She finally pushed her way through, tripping over her own feet and falling to the ground, her bag spilling out all over the ground. She quickly shoved an e-reader and another book back inside her purse. I shook my head, realizing that this woman was a damn klutz. Walking over to her, I bent down and gripped onto her arm and pulled her up. She stumbled into my arms before jerking back and adjusting her clothes.

"I'm so sorry I'm late. You must think I'm so rude. I was just refreshing the chickens' water before I left and then Beatrice flew at me and it freaked me out. I ended up stepping in the chicken feed and then I fell back into the roost. All the chickens went crazy, flapping their wings and trying to get away from me. By the time I got out of there, I was covered in chicken shit and feathers and I had to take another shower because if you've ever dealt with chickens, you'd know that you don't want to smell like them when you're going on a date. I mean, of course I would have taken a shower anyway, but I really had to scrub myself down after that one."

She stopped her rambling and I noticed that her ample chest was heaving from how much air she used in such a short amount of time. It made me wonder how much her breasts would be bouncing if I had her wound up in bed.

"Chickens?"

"Yes, chickens. I live on a farm. In the country. With my father.

He's not really all there any more so I take care of the farm for him with my sister, Lucy. It's not exactly what I would have imagined I would be doing with the rest of my life, but when your family needs help, you step up, right? It's not like there was anyone else to do it anyway, and my father loves his farm and his chickens. I couldn't just sell the farm and move him into a nursing home or something. I never really understood how people could do that to their loved ones. I guess there are times when the situation calls for it. Like if the person couldn't physically take care of themselves. Then I suppose it would make sense, but my father just isn't all there any more up top," she said, tapping her head. "So, yeah. I live at home on the farm with my sister and dad."

Did this girl ever stop rambling? She was cute as shit when she did it. It was like she had no filter and I wanted to kiss her silly when she got going, but we had just covered a shit load of stuff and we hadn't even technically started our date yet.

"Okay. Well, how about we save something to discuss with our coffee. Maybe how you feel about euthanizing animals."

"Are you kidding?" she said in shock. "I could never- oh. You were joking."

I grinned at her and slipped my hand around hers, thinking about how perfect her hand felt in mine. "Come on. Let's get some coffee before we get into anything deeper."

I pulled out her chair and helped her into it, then walked over to mine and sat down.

"How's your head?"

"Good. Well, as good as it can be when it's smacked against the pavement."

"Lucy said that the doctor told you to take it easy."

"Yeah, but I feel fine. I still get headaches, but the doctor said that could happen for a few weeks. It's nothing I can't handle."

She was fidgeting with her purse, obviously not comfortable with this date.

"Do I make you nervous?" I asked.

"What? No. Of course not. I mean, you're extremely handsome and you have muscles that match the fantasies I have about any book boyfriend that ranks in my top 100 list. You have this really sexy, deep voice that makes me want to squeeze my legs together and hope you'll take me home all at the same time. And I'm just me. I'm short and I'm just average looking. Especially compared to you. So, I guess I'm kind of wondering why you would even want to take me out on a date, but I'm not going to complain either. I mean, I would give my left arm to have you kiss me. But am I nervous? No. I'm totally cool with all this."

I wondered if she knew how much she just revealed about herself to me. She was obviously very insecure about herself and it was clear that no man had ever bothered to set her straight about exactly how gorgeous she was. Then again, maybe no man ever got the chance to tell her with how much she rambled. I leaned across the table and picked up her hand that was resting in front of her, intertwining our fingers.

"First of all, there's no such thing as you just being you. You're not average by any man's standards. You have an ass that any man would kill to get his hands on and don't get me started on the things I'd like to do to your breasts. I could see myself on top of you, fucking those tits and coming down your throat. And that has nothing to do with just wanting to fuck you and everything to do with how gorgeous you are. I'm thinking based on that you can come to the conclusion that I'm going to kiss you and I may not be enough of a gentleman to hold out until we've dated before I try to get you into bed. Because there's nothing I want more than to sink my hard cock inside that hot, little pussy."

Her eyes dilated and her mouth dropped open. I didn't normally get quite so descriptive with women, but she needed to hear just how bad I wanted her. I didn't want there to be any insecurities on her part or rethinking whether or not I wanted her.

"Close your mouth or I may be tempted to shove my cock in there and I don't give a fuck that we're in the middle of a cafe." Her mouth snapped shut and she blushed deep red. Damn, she was gorgeous. "So, besides working on your farm, what do you like to do?"

"Um.." She thought about it for a moment and smiled at me. "Well, I don't get much time to go out, so I usually just read when I have some down time."

"Why don't you get to go out much?"

"Too much work to do. The farm is my side job in the summer, but I'm also the town librarian. I usually close the library because it works best with my schedule on the farm, but sometimes that changes. I have another woman that opens the library for me in the mornings and then she leaves after lunch. I close the library every night and then I go finish up on the farm."

"Damn. That sounds brutal."

She shrugged like it was no big deal. "The farm doesn't make enough for me to stay home and I work with Lucy, so we both have to have other jobs. Honestly, if Dad didn't love the farm so much, I might consider giving it up just so that I didn't have to work two jobs."

"Do you not like doing the farm work?"

"I love it. I grew up working on the farm with Dad and I really enjoy the work, but it doesn't make enough income and it doesn't allow me to get a job with more nine to five hours, which is what's so great about the library. I have a little more flexibility."

"But that can't pay the bills."

"It does the job," she said cryptically.

I noticed that now that we were having an actual conversation, she had calmed down and wasn't quite so spastic. When she took the time to slow down, I could see the person she was beneath all that nervousness. She could have walked away from her family, but she was holding it together with her sister because her father loved the farm.

"So, what is it that you do, Derek?"

"I work in security."

"Like a bodyguard?" she said, eyes widening.

"Sometimes. I work for Reed Security. We do everything from installing security systems to protecting people in trouble."

"Wow. That's amazing. How did you get into that?"

She seemed a little eager to know more about my work and it made me a little wary. Usually women that were so curious were only looking for one thing: A roll in the sack with someone they considered dangerous. Not that it bothered me that much. That's what I was looking for too, but she hadn't struck me as that kind of woman.

"I was in the military and when I was discharged, I was looking for something to do that I could use the skills the military gave me. It's not the easiest to come back after being deployed and get a normal job."

"Because it's not what you're used to?"

"Yeah. I mean, when you go from watching your back and thinking that everyone is out to kill you, it takes time for that to wear off enough that you can act normal in public."

"I could see that. I've never met anyone in the military before. It's kind of cool to know someone that's such a badass," she grinned.

"When you're over there, it has nothing to do with being a badass and everything to do with making sure you don't get your ass shot off or any of your friends killed," I snapped. I hated when people thought that being a soldier automatically elevated you to God like status. The truth was, when you were over there fighting for your life and those around you, you didn't really give a shit what people thought of you, as long as they cared enough to welcome you home and be understanding during the adjustment period.

"I'm sorry. That's not what I meant," she said as her eyes widened in horror. She fumbled with her purse and pulled out some bills, throwing them down on the table as she shoved the chair back as she stood. "I didn't mean to offend you. I sometimes just word vomit all over everything and I'm really sorry. I'm just going to go," she said as she spun around and right into the tray of a waitress carrying several coffees. The drinks spilled down the front of her shirt, quickly making her white t-shirt see-through. Her head swiveled to mine and her beautiful face quickly morphed into complete embarrassment and I'm pretty sure there were a few tears in her eyes. I felt like such an ass, but before I could apologize, she was out the door and running down the sidewalk.

"Shit." I ran a hand roughly through my hair and tugged on the ends, pissed at myself for being such an asshole to her. She was obviously socially awkward as it was and I just made her feel like crap and then got her so worked up that she embarrassed herself further. I could be a real jackass sometimes.

Chapter Three

CLAIRE

*W*ell, I had just made a total ass out of myself in front of one of the hottest men on the face of the earth, again! There was nothing normal about the way I behaved around men. I didn't know how to carry on a normal conversation and the more I tried, the worse it got. I stomped out of the coffee shop, irritated with myself for being so spastic, throwing my messenger bag over my shoulder and across my body. It didn't matter, I told myself. I didn't need to worry about dating right now. I had to figure out who the mystery man was that saved my life.

Before I headed home, I had to stop at the bank and deposit my check from the library. I went to write out my deposit slip and then I waited in the longest line known to man. There was only one teller working and about ten people in line ahead of me. There were other tellers gathered around someone's desk and they were laughing and totally ignoring the rest of the people in the bank. I checked my watch and sighed. This was going to take forever and after my disaster coffee date, I just wanted to get home.

The doors of the bank burst open and five men dressed in head to toe black burst inside with guns. Three of them broke off to the sides of the bank and quickly went around to who I'm assuming they thought were the people they needed. The fourth person did something with the door and the fifth person, who I assumed was in charge, popped off a few shots with his large, extremely scary looking gun.

"Everybody get down and put your face to the floor! Hands above your heads!"

Everyone stood there in shock for a minute, scared to make a move. He shot his gun one more time and we all quickly obeyed. I was close enough to a table that I could half hide myself underneath. I hoped that because I was so small no one would notice. I saw someone across the bank on the phone and I prayed they were calling the police.

I watched as the man in charge walked up to the teller station and started demanding all the money from the drawers. The teller fumbled around, but started unloading the drawers. I glanced around the room and saw that the other men were disappearing into the back. The man in charge appeared to be talking to someone, maybe on some kind of radio and the other men were now out of sight. I pulled out my phone and pulled up Derek's number. He was in security and seemed like a good person to call.

"Claire-"

"Derek," I whispered. "I'm in the bank and there are five men that came in with guns ."

"Just hang tight," his voice all business. "I'll make sure the police have been informed. Is there anyone around you right now?"

"No. The main guy, he's having the teller get all the money from the drawers. The other four disappeared into the back. They've been back there about a minute."

"Okay. Where are you?"

The man in charge turned and looked out at everyone. I quickly averted my eyes and made sure my phone was out of sight. He paused on me for a second and I was sure he was on to me, but then he turned back to the woman behind the counter and urged her on again.

"Claire, are you there?"

I put the phone back to my ear and checked one more time to make sure I was clear. "I'm here. I'm hiding under a table."

"Good. Just stay there until the police get there."

"You're right down the road," I hissed. "You're in security, so come secure..something."

"Claire, the police will handle this. There's no way I could put together a team in time to handle this, not to mention that it's not my job."

"Time. Yes, you need time. Good. I'll create a distraction so that you can get in here and do your thing. What do you need? Like five minutes?"

"No! Claire, don't do anything. Just stay low and don't draw any attention to yourself."

"I have an idea. I'm not sure how well it'll work, but it should buy you enough time to get in here and take them out."

"No-" I hung up because I was afraid that someone would hear him yelling at me through the phone. He would come through. This was what they did after all. I stood shakily and raised my hand, which was ridiculous because I wasn't in school and they weren't going to call on me.

"Excuse me, but how long is this going to take?" I tried for snarky, but it came out nervous and I ended up laughing at the end.

The man turned to me and scowled, pointing his gun in my direction. "Lady, lay the fuck back on the floor."

I twisted my fingers, a nervous habit, and took a step forward. "I'm really sorry, but I've had a horrible day and I just want to get home."

"I don't give a fuck what kind of day you've had. Get your fat ass back on the ground."

My eyes welled with tears and I was sorry to say that I wasn't even acting. I hated being called fat as much as the next girl and it didn't take much to make me cry.

A man came jogging out of the back, his gun swinging lazily at his side. "Boss, we got a problem. We need a secondary code."

I took a step toward them, hoping to distract them a little longer and not get shot for it. The first man threw an irritated glance my way.

"Lady, I told you to sit down."

"I'm sorry. I know that you're busy. I mean," I waved my hand down the length of his black attire. "I can see that you're here for something very important, obviously or you wouldn't be dressed all in black looking like you're ready to kill anyone that gets in your way. Which could be me since I can't seem to keep my mouth shut. I tend to do that. Ramble. When I get nervous. I just can't stop the words from spewing out."

"Lady-"

"I'm sorry," I said, holding out my arms in a placating gesture. "I really don't mean to cause you any delays. I just thought I might be able to help you get whatever you need. Then we can all be on our way."

"Do you happen to have the codes to the safe deposit boxes?" the man sneered at me.

"No, but I'm sure one of us could help you," I said anxiously, hoping that I hadn't just put us all in danger.

"Who's the bank manager here?" the first man yelled.

A balding older man stood on shaky legs and raised his hand. "I am."

The first man walked over to him and grabbed him by the tie, dragging him over to the second man. "How do we get the secondary codes?"

"They're chosen by the owner of the boxes. We don't have those codes here and only a family member can get them through a series of questions. No bank employee can get those codes."

"Bullshit," the man jerked him. "You're fucking lying to me."

The man in charge shot the manager in the leg and got in his face while the man laid on the ground writhing in pain. "Fucking tell me what I want to know!"

"I am," the manager insisted.

The man spun around and grabbed me by the arm, pulling me tight to his chest. I could feel the man sweating through his clothes and wondered how close to the edge he was. He shoved the gun against my temple and my body shook with the realization that I had definitely made the wrong decision in getting involved. "You have one more chance."

"I swear. There's a number to call, but then you have to go through a series of questions and we don't have any of the answers on file."

"Shit!" the man yelled. He threw me to the ground and then started beating the man with the butt of his gun until the man collapsed in a bloody heap on the ground. I couldn't believe what I was seeing. I had started this and I was going to finish it. I couldn't allow this man to be beaten anymore because I had opened my big, fat mouth. I could do this. Distract them and save the day.

"I'm pretty good with numbers," I said with as much conviction as I could muster.

The first guy spun around and pointed his gun at me. "Are you telling me you can get in the box?"

I took a deep breath, knowing that I was probably sealing my fate, but I had to try something. "I don't know, but I can try. I've seen the boxes before and I'm good with codes," I lied.

The man jerked his head at me. "Go with him."

The second man walked over to me and hauled me up by my arm, yanking me in the direction of the back room. When we entered the room that looked like a jail cell, he shoved me toward the box that was currently standing open. Inside the small door was another door that required a code. I rubbed my fingers together, remembering my favorite scene from *Raiders of the Lost Ark*. I had to pretend like I knew what I was doing or they would shoot me too. The man stayed with me and jerked his head for the other men to head out into the lobby of the bank. I stared at the box, trying to figure out what the hell to do. Were there a certain number of times that you could enter a code before the box blew up or disintegrated?

"Get to work. Stop stalling," he said from behind me.

"I'm working on it. I have to figure out how many times I can enter a code before the box locks down. Based on this model, I figure I have three tries before we'll be completely locked out. What I really need is information on this person so I can rule out codes that would most likely be used."

I hoped like hell that I sounded convincing, which I must have because the man pulled a file from his bag and handed it over to me. Reading all those mystery novels was really paying off. I took the folder and skimmed through the notes, not really reading any of it, though I probably should if I had any hope of getting into the box and saving my own ass.

"You have two minutes," the man said, nudging me.

"Okay. I just need one more minute." I scanned the file again for any dates or numbers that might work and decided to try a birthday first, although that just seemed really obvious. With shaky hands, I entered the first set of numbers, only to have a red light pop up and start blinking at me. I looked through the file again, being sure to take my time so that I hopefully would give myself a little more time.

I saw that the man from the file was a United States Army Ranger, born and raised in Pennsylvania. Pictures of his house showed a flag outside. He also had what appeared to be the Declaration of Independence in a frame inside his house. I thought back to my conversations with Lucy and all her ramblings about the ratification of states. Pennsylvania was the second state to be admitted into the Union. Was it December 7th or the 12th?

"Come on, lady. We're almost out of time."

"Give me just a second. I've almost got it." I hoped to God that I was right because if I wasn't, I was pretty sure this guy was going to put a bullet in my brain. With no more time to delay, I punched in 1271787 and held my breath. When the light turned green, I squealed, jumping for joy that I had gotten it right. He shoved me out of the way and pulled open the box. The sound of gunfire had us both spinning around. It wasn't one or two shots, but a full on attack. I took advantage of the man being distracted and pulled my hardback copy of Leo Tolstoy's compilation of three novels from my bag and swung it into his head. He dropped to the ground like a brick, but groaned and rolled over. I picked up the book again and hit him several more times in the head to make sure he was out. I picked up his gun and ran out toward the lobby, stalling just around the corner.

Derek had shown up, along with other members of Reed Security. They were firing off round after round toward the other side of the bank where I could see two of the bank robbers hiding behind the teller station. Derek's team couldn't seem to get off a good shot, so I decided to help be a distraction once more. I crept toward the teller counter and aimed my gun toward the robbers. I was a pretty good shot, having been raised by a farmer that liked to hunt, but then I wasn't really trying to kill them. I just wanted to distract them enough so Reed Security could do what they needed to do.

I fired off a few shots, hitting just above where they were hiding. They ducked down, but then popped up and fired toward me. I quickly hid again and glanced over at Derek, who was yelling at me across the room.

"Get the fuck down, Claire!"

They were pinned down by more gunshots, so I took the opportunity to fire again. I saw one of Derek's men step out from his hiding spot and rush toward the other men. I fired off a few more shots to keep the men distracted. Derek's team did the same. The man who had rushed forward took a few shots and then was flung backward when he was hit in the chest. I covered my mouth to hold onto my scream when I realized that he wasn't wearing a bullet proof vest, but then he just stood up and ran toward them again.

I watched in utter fascination as he leapt over the counter and shot one guy in the head, then broke the other man's neck. When he turned back around, his eyes bored into me from across the room. I took a step back, a little terrified of the man that seemed to escape death so easily. He started to walk toward me, but then stopped when Derek stepped into his path and held up a hand.

I walked forward a little to check out the man and glanced down at his shirt, noting that he didn't even have a hole in his shirt. How the hell had he escaped unscathed? He rubbed at his chest a little, but other than that, showed no signs of the bullet even affecting him in any way. And then there was the way that he jumped over the counter and killed those other two men. They hadn't stood a chance. Could it be that this guy was my rescuer from the other day?

Derek and the man seemed to be arguing about something and I inched a little closer until I could hear their conversation.

"You shouldn't be here, Knight," Derek hissed. "No one should have seen you. What if someone talks?"

"Relax. No one's going to know anything about me."

"You'd better fucking hope so. You put us all at risk when you do shit like that. Get the fuck out of here before you get hauled down to the station. Sean's waiting in the back to make sure you get out."

I pretended to be fascinated with my own weapon when I saw Knight glance my way and then leave through the back exit. So, Sean Donnelly- badass detective, was obviously in on it. Of course, it made sense. Didn't all superheroes have someone in the department on their side? At least Batman did. It was the only thing that was making sense at this moment. No. Superheroes didn't really exist. Geez, I had been watching too many Marvel movies.

Cops swarmed the building, as paramedics entered and tended to the injured. The bank robbers were being cuffed and placed on gurneys and the witnesses were giving their statements to the police. Derek walked over to me with a swagger that I had to admit was damn sexy. My legs clenched the closer he came with an intense look on his face that promised danger. I swallowed hard and gasped when he stepped into me and then his hand slid down my waist. He looked into my eyes and my tongue darted out to lick my lips in anticipation of his kiss. My eyes drifted closed and I waited for his soft lips to touch mine. Then I felt his hand on my wrist and he was pulling the gun from my hand. My eyes flew open and I glared when he smirked at me.

"What were you doing over here with a gun?"

"I was causing a distraction," I said as his gaze drilled into me. I felt like I was on the witness stand. "The other guy-"

"Who?"

"The guy in the back room, he came out and said they got the initial door open, but needed a code for the second box. They started shooting, so I said that I was really good with codes."

"Why would you do that?" he asked as if I was a total moron.

"Well, it occurred to me that if they didn't get the answers they were looking for, they would just keep shooting hostages until they found what they were looking for. I thought I could at least buy some time for you by pretending that I knew what I was doing."

"You should have fucking stayed where you were," he growled. "If we hadn't come in when we had, they would have shot you."

"I know, but I got it open," I said smugly.

"You got the box open?"

"Yep."

"How?"

"I looked in the file they had on the guy and I put the pieces together. I could have been wrong and I probably should have been wrong, but I did get it open and if you hadn't shown up when you did, they would have it."

He gripped onto my arm and started pulling me back. "Come on. Show me."

I took him into the back where the bank boxes were kept and grinned when I saw that the man was still unconscious on the floor. "I did that," I said, puffing out my chest. He raised an eyebrow and nodded toward the box that was open.

"Show me."

I opened the box that I had unlocked and pulled out the contents. It was an old fashioned key, but I didn't have the slightest clue what it belonged to.

"That was the only thing in there?"

"Yeah. It doesn't look like any key that I've ever seen. It obviously doesn't go to a car or a house. It's too big for a lock box."

"Maybe for an old fashioned door?"

"No, look at the cuts of the key. This is too strange. This wouldn't fit in any door."

"How do you know so much about this?"

"I've worked in a library for years. I read a lot."

"Is that how you put together the code?"

I blushed and dropped my head. "Sort of. I just looked for clues and hoped I was right."

"And you learned how to do that from reading?"

"Well, I like mystery novels."

"Who are you? When I first met you in the grocery store, you were a nervous wreck. Now you're a gun wielding, code breaking librarian that is confusing the hell out of me."

I shrugged and winced a little at the pain that I felt in my neck. I could feel a headache coming on, most likely from the intense situation I had just been through.

"Are you okay?" Derek asked in concern. "Did you get hurt?"

"No. It's just..you know..everything. Just a headache."

"Let's go finish up and then I'll take you home."

I picked up the box, slipping the key into my pocket before putting the box back. I shut the door, knowing no one else would be able to get back in the box without cracking the code, and chances were, that wasn't going to happen.

Derek led me out to the lobby and we spent a good hour going over what happened with the police. Knight was long gone and by the time we left, I had met the other members of the team that were with Derek. The team had consisted of Derek, Hunter, Lola, and Knight. Apparently, Hunter and Lola were on a team with Derek and Knight trained with all of them. Derek informed me that occasionally they help out the police department for situations that are too big for them to handle. He said they normally wait for a request for assistance, but seeing as how I had insisted on causing a distraction, he made a decision to go in without permission, something that the police chief wasn't too happy about.

I was exhausted by the time we were done and I just wanted to go home and start researching the key I had taken, but when Derek led me to his truck, we didn't head toward my house.

"Where are we going?"

"Reed Security."

"Why?"

"Because, we're going to figure out why those men wanted the key that's in your pocket."

I stared at him in surprise. "How did you.."

He smirked at me. "I'm very observant."

We pulled into a garage several minutes later and then he led me through a series of scanners, key codes, and other security measures. He pushed me down into a seat in a conference room and sat across from me. I squirmed under his intense stare, feeling like I was about to be grilled.

"Listen, there are things that we need to discuss-"

"I know!" I shouted before I could think better of it. He narrowed his gaze at me and leaned forward in his seat.

"What exactly do you know?"

"That man, Knight. I know who he is, but you don't have to worry. I'm not going to say anything. Frankly, I think what he does is great and I'm not going to do anything to jeopardize what he has. I promise."

Derek's eyes searched mine and narrowed in on me with an intensity that had me shifting in my chair. Oh, shit. I should have kept my mouth shut. I was going to end up in a dungeon while they figured out how to keep me quiet. I would never see my dad and Lucy again. And what would happen with my job at the library? Would they allow some idiot to come in and take over? If I ever stepped foot in there again, I would see non-fiction books arranged by last name instead of the Dewey Decimal System. It would take me months to get everything back in order. I started wringing my hands together as the anxiety of my library being destroyed took over.

Derek nodded, seemingly appeased with my promises and waved in someone behind me. A tall, muscular man with short, dark hair walked into the room and sat at the head of the table. Hunter and Lola sat down as well. Knight was absent.

"Claire, I'm Sebastian. I'm the owner of Reed Security. Derek tells me that you were able to crack the code to open the box that the bank robbers were trying to get into."

"Yes, I cracked it."

"And then you took what was inside the box. I'd like to see it."

I looked at Derek and realized that it wasn't a request, but a command and all his team were expecting me to just give it up without hesitation. "Um, I'm not sure-"

"Don't fuck with us right now," Sebastian growled. "You have no fucking clue who those men were."

"Claire," Derek snapped. I looked over him and he gave me a slight nod. I turned back to Sebastian, swallowing hard, and pulled out the key that I had taken from the box, sliding it over to Sebastian. He picked it up and looked it over, seeming to realize right away that this wasn't your average key.

"Do you know whose box this was in?"

I nodded and thought back, hoping I was getting the name right. "Nathan Kent."

Sebastian leaned back in his chair and the rest of them started murmuring amongst themselves. "What the fuck do they want with him?"

"You know him?" I asked.

Sebastian nodded and turned to Derek. "Is he still overseas?"

"As far as I know. I haven't heard from him in a few months, but last he told me, he wasn't due back for another three months," Derek said.

"See if you can get ahold of him. I'll look into what's going on in his unit, see when he'll be coming home."

He stood and motioned for Lola and Hunter to follow. Derek stood and shoved his hands in his pockets. "I have to take care of something real quick. Just hang out here for a few minutes and then I'll take you home."

"Okay."

He walked around me and was gone before I had a chance to ask any more questions about what just happened. There were so many things that I didn't have a chance to think about until right now. Derek was gone for a good half hour and I really had to go to the bathroom. I poked my head out of the conference room to an empty hall. My bladder was screaming in protest, so I made my way down the hall to where I assumed the bathroom was. I paused outside a room when I heard Derek talking with someone else.

"I fucking told you that you shouldn't have been there. Claire just told me that she knew exactly who you are. What the hell am I supposed to do now?"

"How the hell does she know me? I've never met her before."

"I don't have a fucking clue, but now there's one more person that knows your true identity."

"Then you'd better make sure she doesn't talk or I'll deal with her."

I gulped and took a step back. I knew I shouldn't have said anything to Derek.

"You're not going to kill her. I'll make sure she knows that it would be a very bad thing to let on that she knows who you are."

"You'd better because it's not just my ass on the line. Everyone here would be put at risk. We'd all be exposed."

All be exposed. Did that mean that they all had these powers or whatever it was that Knight had? I backed up until I hit the door on the other side of the hall and slipped inside. Robotically, I went through the process of going to the bathroom and washing my hands. I had to figure out a way to get out of here before Knight made good on his promise. I couldn't trust that anyone would protect me when they all had something to lose.

I opened the bathroom door and ran smack into a hard chest. I looked way up into the scary eyes of Knight. I stumbled back against the door and tried my best to hold it together.

"Something wrong?" he asked.

"N-No," I stuttered. "Nothing at all. Everything's just hunky dory. I was just going to the bathroom," I motioned at the door. "You know, because I had to..go to the bathroom."

"You sure everything's okay?"

"Of course. Why do you ask?"

"Because that's the men's bathroom," he pointed out. I looked at the sign on the door and realized he was right. I had been in the men's bathroom and hadn't even known it.

"Maybe you should watch where you're going. It would be a shame if you..disappeared."

The threat was clear in the deep rumblings of his voice. My whole body started to shake when he lifted his hand and placed it right next to my head on the door. I tried to slink back against the door, but I couldn't move any further. He leaned into me and I was sure he was about to break my neck, but he pushed the door open and slipped inside the bathroom, leaving me a quivering mess in the hallway.

"You ready to go?"

Derek's voice made me jump and I stumbled against the door. "Uh..yeah. I'm ready. Ready as I'll ever be. Let's hit the road." Even I could hear that my voice was just a little too happy for what he was asking. He raised an eyebrow at me, but held out his hand, gesturing me ahead of him. I walked in front, trying not to look over my shoulder every five seconds. I was sure that he was having me walk ahead so that he could kill me, but then we made it down to his truck and nothing had happened yet. He ushered me into his truck and drove me home, barely saying a word as I got out and headed inside. As he pulled away, I breathed a sigh of relief that I had another day to live.

Chapter Four

DEREK

"What the hell was she thinking?" Sam "Cazzo" Galmacci asked me as we were training the next day. He was one of the other investors, besides me, in Reed Security. We left most of the paperwork to Sebastian because neither of us wanted that responsibility.

"I don't have a fucking clue. The woman is so infuriating. One minute she's stumbling all over herself and the next, she's wielding a gun and trying to take out bank robbers. Who the hell does that?"

"We do that," Cazzo said as he put away his weights.

"Yeah, we do that, but she's not one of us. She's a fucking librarian."

"A librarian that kept you from getting your ass shot off."

"Whose side are you on?"

"Yours, man, but you have to recognize that as weird as she is, what she did was kind of hot."

"You know who else pulls shit like that?" He quirked an eyebrow at me. "Freckles. And look at the trouble she causes."

Cazzo laughed and shook his head. "I don't think you have to worry about Claire pulling the same shit Freckles does. From what you've told me, Claire seems like the type of girl that stumbles into a situation, not causes it."

"It doesn't fucking matter. She needs to stay on her farm where she belongs."

"I wouldn't let Lola hear you talk like that. She'd kick your ass for suggesting that a woman has 'a place'."

"Not all women, but Claire? Fuck yeah. She belongs as far away from our lives as possible. She's a fucking walking disaster. She doesn't pay attention to her surroundings, she's totally fucking clueless about how dangerous people are, and she puts herself into danger so she can help others when she should stay the fuck out of the way."

"Introduce her to Vanessa. I'm sure they'd have a lot in common."

"How's Vanessa doing?"

"Good. She's finishing up school and trying to figure out her next move. I think she wants to work at one of the restaurants in town."

"You should talk to Cap about hiring her as Reed Security's own personal chef."

"Yeah, I'm sure that would go over real well," he chuckled.

"So, when's the wedding?"

"I haven't asked her yet."

"Seriously? I thought you knew she was the one."

"She is, but she's finishing up school this year and I don't want her to be stressed out over planning a wedding. Then there's the situation with her mom. They're talking, but they don't have the greatest relationship. I think she needs more time before she really involves her in our lives. A wedding isn't something you want a parent to miss, so I want her to have enough time to really decide if she wants her in her life."

"But you are going to marry her, right? I mean, after all that happened with you two-"

"I know. That's part of it. Everything was so intense with us. We need some normal before we take things to the next level. I will marry her, but I want it to be about us before anything else happens. I don't want her waking up one morning and wondering where the hell her life went."

After all that Cazzo had been through, we were all rooting for him and Vanessa to finally get hitched. He'd had a shitty year and we'd all felt like we'd let him down in some way. It felt like every time we had good news, something fell apart with one of us.

"Who knows, maybe you and Claire will be hearing wedding bells before Vanessa and me."

I reared back and set my weights down. "Whoa. There will be no wedding bells for me anytime in the future. I don't want a wife and I don't want someone nagging me to take out the garbage."

"Sure. You keep telling yourself that. I'm telling you though, once the love bug bites, you're fucked."

"What the hell is wrong with all you sappy ass mother fuckers? You find a woman and suddenly you're talking about 'love bugs' and 'wedding bells'. Where the hell are your balls?"

"Vanessa owns them, and let me tell you something. I wouldn't trade it for all the pussy in the world."

"There's something seriously wrong with what you just said. Give me your wallet."

"Why?"

"Because, I'm revoking your man card. You no longer belong to the club and all your privileges have been revoked."

"Just wait. It won't be long before you're coming to us 'sappy ass mother fuckers' for advice. And when you do, I'm gonna laugh my fucking ass off."

He turned and walked out of the weight room with a grin on his face. There was no way I could ever let that happen. I'd seen the way these guys let women control their lives and turn them inside out. I didn't ever want that from a relationship. Hell, I didn't even want a relationship. He could grow feathers and shit in a tree because there was no way I would ever be one of them.

---

*T*wo weeks later and I was still getting hard every time Claire crossed my mind. I wanted to get my hands on her hips and feel her body rocking against mine. Damn. I only had one reason to go see her and I didn't think that paying her a friendly visit to remind her to keep her mouth shut would be welcomed. I didn't have any other ideas though. Dating her wasn't an option. She was way too flighty for me and would probably expect some kind of relationship. I wanted to fuck her, I was sure of that, but I knew well enough that women like her got thoughts in their heads about more. And more was something I definitely didn't need.

Still, I had to see her again, so I headed to the library and took the chance that she was working. It was an older building and the inside was not well lit. My security spidey senses were going off at the thought of her being here alone late at night. The library was on two floors and looked more like a smaller version of the Library of Congress than a small town library. It even had those ladders that rolled across the bookcases. I could definitely see why she liked working here. It had a certain old fashioned feel that was reminiscent of a time where things weren't quite so chaotic.

I walked around the deserted library looking for her. When she wasn't at the desk or in the office, I started wandering the aisles until I spotted a cart with books stacked in it. At the end of the aisle, Claire was perched on a rolling ladder, standing at the top. I stopped dead in my tracks as I took in her gorgeous figure. She was every man's fantasy, wearing a calf length pencil skirt that showcased that gorgeous ass and a blouse that was tucked in. She also had on black high heel shoes that had a strap around the ankle. Her hair was pulled up in some kind of bun and she wore glasses that were perched on her nose. It was fucking sexy. I had no idea that Claire had this side to her. She always looked like a regular girl that I would see on the street. Not a girl, a woman, but she had never looked this damn sexy before.

She was stretching to put a book away and it was just out of reach. *Get down and move the fucking ladder,* I said in my head. Of course, she didn't listen. She kept stretching until she just barely had a toe on the ladder. Her other leg was stretched out as far as her tight skirt would allow. A piece of hair fell out of her bun and fell in her face. She blew out a breath, trying to move the errant strand, but it fell right back in her face. I knew it was going to happen. I could see it happening in front of me and I took off like a rocket down the aisle, sure that she was about to kill herself, or at the very least break something. I pulled out a baseball slide and held my arms out as she shook her head one last time and her foot slipped off the rung. She screamed the whole way down until she plopped right in my arms, *exactly where she was meant to be.*

I shook my head of those crazy thoughts and set her down on the ground, doing my best to not snap at her for being so stupid. She shoved her glasses back up on her face and straightened her clothes as best she could before she stumbled to her feet.

"Thank you, Derek. I didn't realize I was that close to falling."

"Really?" I asked, reigning in my temper as much as possible. "You were practically hanging off the fucking ladder. If I hadn't been here, you could have broken your neck. Shouldn't you be wearing something more practical than fucking high heels while you're climbing ladders? This isn't the 1950's, Claire. You're allowed to wear sensible shoes."

She looked down at her heels and then back up at me, flushing bright red under my glare. "I-I didn't know-"

"You did fucking know! Have some common sense next time. Those shoes are shoes you wear when you wrap your legs around a man's back when he's fucking you. Those most definitely are not shoes you wear when you climb ladders."

"I just-"

"Don't give me any fucking excuses. You're all alone in this fucking building and no one would have known you were hurt. Do you have any sense of safety for yourself?"

"Would you stop yelling at me for two minutes and let me explain myself?" she shouted. It was the most outspoken Claire had ever been with me and it was then that I realized, for the moment, we had switched positions. I was the one losing my fucking mind and rambling and she was the one trying to get a word in. I closed my mouth and gave a sharp nod. "I was at a meeting today about the library. I don't normally dress like this when I'm working. The woman that was working this morning got sick and needed me to come in early. I didn't have a chance to go home and change, so I wore what I wore to the meeting. She had gotten behind since she was sick and these books needed to be shelved. No, I'm not normally stupid enough to wear an outfit like this to the library."

I stood there speechless, partially disappointed that she didn't normally dress like this. It was fucking hot. I opened my mouth to say something, but found that I didn't really know what to say. Was this what it was like to be her?

"Did you have a reason for coming here other than yelling at me?"

"Uh, yeah. I just wanted to remind you that it's very important that you don't say anything about what you know. About Knight."

She stiffened and took a step back, almost like she was afraid of me. "Yes, I remember. Knight made sure I knew what would happen if I said anything. I swear, you have nothing to worry about."

"Fuck," I swore as I ran a hand over the back of my head. Leave it to Knight to go spouting off at Claire, threatening her if she didn't keep her mouth shut. Yes, it was important that no one ever found out who Knight was. It would mean a lot of people, myself included, would be in a shit load of trouble and Knight would end up in Leavenworth. Still, he didn't have to go threatening her. "Look, I'm really sorry that he said anything to you. He's very intense, but I swear, he would never hurt you."

"He referenced me disappearing," she said, crossing her arms protectively over her chest.

"Yeah, I'm not gonna lie. He could definitely make that happen, but he hasn't killed anyone in over a year."

Her eyes widened in shock and she quickly pushed the cart down the aisle like she was trying to get away from me. Her ass swayed from side to side as her heels clicked along the tile. I stood there confused for a minute, trying to figure out why she was running. I was trying to reassure her, but I seemed to make her even more nervous. I ran after her, catching up to her and gripping her by the arm and spinning her around to face me.

"Look, I'm trying to reassure you. He has a deal with Sebastian and one of the stipulations is that he keeps his anonymity as long as he doesn't kill anyone."

"But he did kill someone. In the bank. He shot someone and broke another man's neck. And you stood up for him. And Sean is in on it. I heard you," she said. "Why would I trust your word? I could end up strung up by my toes if he suspects I'll say something. I just don't understand," she looked down in confusion. "How could a man that does such great things be so evil?"

"What are you talking about?" I asked. "Sure, he has good intentions, but I don't know that I would go so far as to say he does great things."

"How could you say that? He saves people. Think of all the women and children that would suffer without him?"

Great. The woman I wanted to fuck had a thing for Knight. She was treating him like he was fucking Superman. And apparently, I was just an average Joe Shmoe.

"You're right. He's fucking great, but you've missed your chance to have him. He's engaged to someone else."

She shook her head and her brows furrowed. "No, I don't want him. I'm just shocked. He's not the man I thought he was."

"And what kind of man is it that you want?"

"I-What do you mean?"

"I mean that you seem so wrapped up in a man that can take a life as quickly as he saves another. Is that the type of man you want?"

"No. No, I'm just so surprised. When I found out who he was and finally met him, I was just so shocked that he wasn't quite the hero I thought he would be."

"Claire, none of us are fucking heroes." She nodded and dropped her eyes like that was disappointing to her. "We've all seen and done things that would curl that beautiful hair of yours. It doesn't mean we're bad, but we aren't the saints you're thinking of."

"I know. I realize that now. I know that Knight isn't the man I thought he was." My anger was spiking again. Every time she mentioned Knight's name, I wanted to punch something. What the hell was so great about him that she was fawning all over him? A little over a week ago, she was flirting with me in the grocery store. She was touching my muscles and stumbling all over herself. Now I was competing with fucking Knight, a man that wouldn't give her the time of day if she threw herself at him.

"He's not the man you're thinking of at all. If he's who you want, you'll be sorely disappointed. He wouldn't give you a second look."

Her eyes widened and she started shaking her head. "I don't." She shouted. "I didn't mean to give you the impression that I did. I mean, yeah, he has that sexy, broody look to him and he's definitely gorgeous, but I'm not interested in him..sexually. He doesn't have anything on you. As hot as he is, you actually smile and it's very sexy and you have these awesome muscles that just..whew! I mean, totally hot and a lot sexier than what he has going on. Plus, you have really great hair, which I've always thought was one of the best features on a man. I'm pretty sure my fingers could get lost in your hair. Definitely pull worthy, you know, in bed."

"Pull worthy, huh?"

"Yeah," she said as she shuffled from one foot to the other. "Anyway, I just..okay, well, I have to get back to work."

She quickly started walking away, obviously embarrassed by how much she had told me. I didn't care though. She had just told me exactly what I needed to hear. She still wanted me and now that I knew how much, there was no way I was letting her walk away until I had a taste.

I let her get back to work, sure that she didn't really want to talk to me any more. She was the kind of woman that sometimes you had to go slow with or you'd scare her off like a frightened deer.

Chapter Five

CLAIRE

t was the next day and I was beating myself up over how stupid I had acted in front of Derek. I had made him think that I was interested in Knight when all I wanted was another look from him. Then, I went and ruined it by telling him all the things about him that I found sexy, including his hair, which I had fantasized about pulling while he was fucking me. I shook my head at my stupidity as I pulled more weeds from the flower garden around the house. I was almost done and decided that this year I was going to put down mulch. I didn't normally do it because I didn't want to spend the extra money, but I wanted a nice garden this year and I was determined to have it.

I finished the garden and then got in the old pickup truck that we used around the farm, and headed into town. When I reached the garden center, I found the cheapest mulch that I could and put in my order. While I was waiting for them to get my order together, I wandered around and looked at the different flowers that were sitting out. It had been so long since I had planted anything new and I had an old flowerbed that hadn't been used in years under the trees in the back yard.

Twenty minutes later, I had Hostas, Heuchera, Brunnera, and

Japanese Painted Ferns picked out for the start of a new garden. I was pretty pleased with my selection and was about to ask an employee to help me get everything up front when I heard his deep voice. I looked up and there he was, talking with a salesman about hosing or something. He was deep in thought, so I ducked down behind some of the plants and watched from my spot on the floor. I sighed, taking in his handsome features and wondered why the hell my big mouth had blown it between us.

He picked up something off the shelf and was just turning to leave when someone tripped over me, knocking the plants down that I was hiding behind and sending us both sprawling into some lawn ornaments. I scrambled to sit up and get away, but the old man that had tripped over me started yelling at me.

"Why the hell were you sitting down there? I could have killed myself." He spit when he talked and I took a closer look, seeing that the man didn't have any teeth.

I looked over quickly at Derek, hoping that he had already walked away, but he was looking right at me and smirking. Dammit. I had hoped to get out of here without him seeing me.

"I'm really sorry, sir. Let me help you get your stuff." I weeded through the plants, picking them up and moving them to the side and grabbing the cane the man had been using. I spotted a pair of dentures on the ground and grimaced. Disgusting.

"Here are your teeth, sir." I picked them up and held them out to the man, but he didn't take them.

"What in the cotton pickin' hell am I supposed to do with that? They're covered in dirt!"

I wiped them on my shirt and only then realized how dirty my clothes were. I hadn't changed before I came here and then I had landed in a pile of plants. My hands were filthy and so were my clothes. The man's dentures now had streaks of dirt on them.

"I'm so sorry, sir. I can take them in the bathroom and wash them off-"

He snatched them from my hands and pushed them back in his mouth. "You'd probably dunk them in the toilet. I'll take my chances with the dirt."

He stomped off, leaving me mortified and hoping that Derek wasn't still standing there, but he was. I started putting all the plants back, ignoring the sexy man across the aisle from me. No matter how hard I tried to ignore him, I could feel his stare boring into me, which only made me fumble more.

"Are you always this accident prone?"

"I'm not accident prone. You just show up at the wrong time."

He walked over to me and helped me pick up the last of the plants on the ground and then held out his hand for me to take. I couldn't help but notice how his hand wrapped around mine and enclosed it completely. When this man touched me, I felt zaps spread through my body. It was a shame that I had screwed it all up.

"Thanks for the help. I mean, technically you only picked up one or two plants. I did most of it by myself. If you really had wanted to help, you would have come over right away, which suggests that you only did it to appear to help me when you really just wanted to gloat."

"Do you ever stop rambling?"

"Not really. I can't help it. I don't have very good social skills and I usually end up saying the wrong thing. Then, I get nervous and I just can't seem to stop, and I make an ass out of myself. I'm pretty sure you've already seen that a few times from me. Either way, it doesn't matter. I'm just going to grab my stuff and go."

I turned around, not wanting to say anything else to make this worse.

"Wait," he said, halting me with his hand wrapped around my wrist. "I don't give a shit about your social skills. I find it cute when you ramble. Most of the time. I find out a lot about you when you go on one of your tirades," he said with a grin. I blushed deeply and shook my head, not sure if he was mocking me or if he was serious.

"Well, I don't mean to do that. It just comes out sometimes."

He nodded and smiled at me again. "Do you need some help with that stuff?" He pointed to the flowers that I had set aside.

"No, thank you. I'm just going to pay and then load up my mulch."

"Doesn't an employee do that?"

"They do, but I think they're really busy today. It's easier if I just do it myself."

"I'll help you."

"That's really not necessary. I do this all the time."

He loaded up the plants into his cart and grabbed my hand, pulling me along behind him. "I want to help. Stop busting my balls over this and just accept it."

I paid for the flowers and then drove around to where the mulch was sitting out back. As I thought, they hadn't had time to pull it yet for me and said they were fine with me loading it myself. When I stepped out of the truck, Derek was waiting for me and I was suddenly aware of how stinky I was since I had been working out in the heat all day. I ran a hand over my head and felt the frizz setting in. I quickly pulled my hair out of my ponytail holder and slicked my hair back as best I could, throwing it into a messy bun. There was nothing I could do about all the dirt I was covered in, so I went to the mulch pile and started loading, trying to pretend like I wasn't totally self-conscious about my appearance.

"How about I follow you home and help you unload all this?"

"Oh, um.." *Quick, come up with an excuse so he can't follow you home. There's no way I want him to come home with me when I look like this. Just say anything.* "Tampons!" I shouted out. Crap. I blushed bright red, but decided to go with it. Men were usually squeamish about that stuff. "I have to stop at the store for tampons. You know, that time of the month and all. If I don't get to the store, we could be facing the flood," I laughed nervously. God I was so bad at this. There was no way he would ever be interested in me after this. I should have let him just follow me home.

"Cool. I'll go with you. What kind do you use? Tampax? Playtex?" He grinned at me and in that moment I knew he was fucking with me. He didn't believe me for a minute that I needed tampons, but he wasn't going to let me get away with it. Might as well play along.

"Okay. Uh, sure."

I walked to my truck and got in, wondering if I could just hit the gas and head home. But then he would win. It looked like I was going to buy tampons, even though my period had just ended. I pulled up to the store and got out, wondering if I even had enough money with me to buy what I needed. I checked my purse quickly and saw that I only had two dollars left. I breathed a sigh of relief.

"You know, I just saw that I don't have any money left. I'll just come back later in the day for what I need."

"Nonsense. I can buy whatever you need." He grabbed my arm and started pulling me along. I tried to dig in my feet, but he was too strong and before I knew it, we were in the feminine products aisle staring down every different kind of tampon I could ever need.

"So, what's your poison?"

"Uh, I just need a small box," I said, reaching for the ten pack that would fit in my purse.

"I don't believe you. You told me you were preparing for the flood. Here." He grabbed box after box of tampons off the shelf and loaded up the cart. There was enough for at least two years. Then he started grabbing different packages of pads and tossing those in also. There was a little old lady walking past us with a package of Depends and she eyed me skeptically. I gave a small wave and she hurried past us.

"I think that's enough, Derek."

"Right. Well, we should also grab some Midol for you. That's what you use for cramps, right?"

"Uh.."

He took off down the aisle before I could say anything and was grabbing a box of Midol, along with a few other pain relievers.

"What are you getting all that for?"

"Just in case. I would hate for you to be in pain because one of these doesn't work. Better safe than sorry."

We left that aisle and I thought we would check out, but he went to the candy aisle. "What are we doing here?"

"Chocolate. I know women get cravings when they get their period. We'll load you up so that you have everything you need. Better grab some ice cream too. Maybe some chips."

Pretty soon, the cart was full of chocolate, ice cream, chips, and every feminine product that the store carried. There was no way I was going to let him go through with this. I decided to come clean and save him the embarrassment.

"Look, I don't really have my period. I just didn't want you to come home with me because I'm stinky and dirty because I've been working outside all morning. Let's just put this all back. You've made your point."

He looked at me for a minute before a sly grin spread across his face. "No, I don't think I'm going to let you get off that easily." He pulled me along with him to the checkout line and wrapped an arm around my shoulders. "It's okay, honey. We'll check out and then we'll get you home. You'll be feeling better in no time."

The check out lady practically swooned right on the spot. I glared at her and she instantly pulled back and tried to ignore us. Derek started unloading the cart and I watched as the girl's eyes widened at the conveyor belt full of tampons and pads. She started swiping them across the scanner, but kept glancing at me like I was deformed.

"Bad month?" she asked.

"Monsoon season," Derek said with an apologetic smile.

The girl nodded, but wouldn't look at me the rest of the time. After Derek paid hundreds of dollars for all the crap he bought, the lady looked at him with a sad smile. "You are such a wonderful man. Take care of her."

"I will and thank you."

I almost threw up right there on the spot. He was playing a joke on me and the cashier acted as if he was the most wonderful man in the world. When we got to my truck, he loaded the bags into my truck and smirked at me.

"So, are you going to let me go home with you and help you out or are we going to run another errand."

"Fine. You can help me."

"I thought you'd see things my way."

"You always get what you want, don't you?"

"Always," he grinned and then walked over to his truck. Stupid sexy man.

*T*he car in front of me was swerving all over the road, so I hung back, not wanting to get in an accident. My phone rang, but I didn't answer. My truck was older, so I didn't have that fancy hookup with my phone and my speakers in the truck. It rang several more times, but I still didn't answer. Derek came speeding up behind me and passed me, then turned right down a side road, waving me over as he turned. I followed and pulled over to the side, not sure what he wanted. He got out and came to the driver's side of my truck.

"Why didn't you answer your phone?"

"Because I don't have any kind of hookup thingy."

"Hookup thingy?"

"You know, how people can answer their phones through their speakers?"

He laughed, "Well, then I'm glad you didn't answer. I'm pretty sure the person in that car in front of you is drunk or texting. I didn't want you to get in an accident."

"I was hanging back."

"I know. I'd just feel better if–"

A loud crash had us both whipping our heads around to see a mangled heap in the middle of the road ahead of where we had been driving. It must have been the car. Derek ran to his truck and did a U-turn, taking off toward the wreck. I quickly followed, not sure if I could help, but for some reason, I didn't want Derek to be alone. When I pulled up behind him, Derek was already out of his truck and running to the accident. The car had collided head on with a pick up truck, which was on fire and turned on its side. Derek somehow got through the flames and minutes later, pulled the man from the wreckage. How the hell had he done that? His clothes didn't catch fire. Were all the men at Reed Security blessed with superpowers? Were they some kind of superhero coalition? First, Knight was shot and the bullet bounced right off him. Then Derek ran into a burning truck and came out completely unscathed. It just didn't make any sense. Had I walked into some alternate universe?

When the man was out and a safe distance from the truck, Derek yelled for me to call 9-1-1. I pulled out my little flip phone and called emergency services while Derek checked on the person in the other car. The police, ambulance, and firetruck pulled up not too long after and took over the scene, thanking Derek for his quick thinking. They called him a hero, which he was. A hero. I wondered if the firemen suspected anything. Nobody could have gone into that fire and come out unscathed. He wasn't even fazed by what had happened.

When Derek walked back toward me, I looked him over and saw that sure enough, he didn't have a mark on him. Even his clothes didn't appear to be any dirtier. I thought back to what I could remember of the man that had saved me from being hit by the car. He had sunglasses on, so I couldn't tell if his eyes were the same, but in general, he had the same shaped face.

"Derek, when the car almost hit me outside the grocery store, where were you?"

He looked at me funny. "I was the one that pushed you out of the way. Don't you remember?"

"No," I whispered, shaking my head slightly. "I don't remember a lot from that day."

"I came out of the grocery store to talk to you and you were walking right into traffic. I called out to you, but you didn't hear me."

I knew he was lying. I had looked around before that car came at me. I remembered trying to figure out which way was the safest to go and no one was close by. Obviously, Derek didn't want me to know that it wasn't just Knight that needed his identity kept a secret.

We unloaded my truck and I was ready for Derek to hit the road. I'd had enough embarrassing moments today and now I was ready to go lick my wounds in peace. There was only so much a girl could take in one day. I didn't have the first clue how to talk to a guy like Derek and it didn't help that every time he looked at me, I felt like he was undressing me with his eyes. Which was fair because I was doing the same to him.

"I have some time. I can help you get this all laid out."

"No. That's fine. I'm pretty tired. I think I'll save this for another day."

"Come on. With the two of us doing this, it'll be done in no time."

I was sure that he could do it faster on his own. I bet if I walked in the house for five minutes, the mulch would be all spread out and he would say that he was just super fast at yard work. He was obviously faster than a speeding bullet. That was the only way to explain how he had not only saved me, but got into a burning vehicle and out before the fire could burn him.

No, this was silly. There wasn't such a thing as superheroes. I was letting my imagination run away with me. There had to be a logical explanation for everything that had happened. Knight could have..I don't know..had something under his shirt that protected him from the bullet, like dog tags or something. Except, there was no hole in his shirt. And then Derek, maybe the fire wasn't as bad as I thought. Even though the flames were shooting from the truck. There had to be something I was missing. There was no such thing as superheroes. I just had to spend more time with Derek and I would see that he was a perfectly normal man.

"Fine."

He picked up two bags of mulch and started spreading them out between the flowers around the house. I joined him and we were worked in silence for a few minutes.

"So, you work at the library in town. Is that fun?"

"It's pretty great. I love to read, so I get to do a lot of that when the library is slow."

"What kind of books do you read?"

"Uh..Romance, mysteries, thrillers."

"Romance," he said with a grin. "Kinky stuff?"

"I read all kinds of romance," I said noncommittally. "Although, paranormal really isn't my thing, but I love historical romance and contemporary romance, but my favorite is...*Pride and Prejudice*."

"Would that happen to be because she's poor and falls in love with a wealthy man?"

"Maybe a little, but mostly because it's honest. Mr. Darcy and Ms. Bennett have a very frank conversation and really get to understand each other before they decide to get married. They fall more in love with each other because they understand each other so well. Their preconceived ideas were wrong and they were both big enough to admit that."

"That doesn't usually happen in real life."

"Which is why it's my favorite romance novel. If people could only learn to get past their initial opinions of others and really get to know them, imagine how many people wouldn't feel misunderstood."

"Is that how you feel?" He was staring at me intently and I felt like he could read all the bullshit that I tried to hide behind. I pushed my glasses up on my face and got back to work.

"I think it's obvious that I have some issues with speaking before thinking. I'm definitely odd in most people's eyes and that's what they see. I have very bad social skills and many people just expect everyone to behave a certain way in public. I just don't seem to have that same skill and I can socialize to a certain point, but when I get nervous, my brain goes out the window and things just start pouring out of me. I wish it wasn't that way, but I can't change who I am either."

"So, people judge you based on their first impression of you."

"That's the way it usually goes. I mean, I'm sure when you met me you were thinking that I was totally spastic, and I can be. But it's not because this is my personality, but that I just don't know how to talk to people. It just doesn't come naturally to me."

"Well, that explains a lot. I thought you were just quirky."

"Quirky? I guess I am. I'm definitely not normal like other people, not that I'm abnormal. I just don't do things or see life the way others do. I guess that makes me odd."

"I like odd. Being normal gets boring."

I smiled and tried to hide how happy it made me to hear that he was okay with me the way I was. Then again, if he was as..odd as I suspected, he would appreciate a woman that could see past normal. I didn't want to get my hopes up that a man so sexy and smart would be interested in me. I knew that I was a smart person, but after so many people making me feel like I was a freak, it was a lot easier to see myself that way than the way Derek appeared to see me.

"So, how did you end up as the town librarian?"

I looked at him, trying to figure out where he was going with this. "What does that mean?"

"Well, farmer by day, librarian by night. It's just all very different. I was wondering how you got into it."

"When I was in high school, I had an after school job working at the library. When everything happened with my dad, I decided to take night classes and get my associates degree in library science. When the town librarian retired, I was hired to take over. I've pretty much worked there my whole life. I can't imagine working anywhere else. Besides, what better place to work than a place you can immerse yourself in all those wonderful stories?"

"Really? Doesn't it get boring? I mean, not many people use libraries any more."

"No, but I try and find different ways to draw people in. We have certain days that are dedicated to little kids coming in and we usually have themes that go along with some books I've chosen. I also have reenactments of my favorite novels that I ask the high school drama club to put on for me. We spend a good month reading a certain book and we sort of have a book club set up for the drama students. Then on Mondays at 1:00, we have a cooking class featuring recipes from different cookbooks. The chefs from the different restaurants in the area come in to give lessons. It promotes the library, the restaurants, and gives a chance for people to get in some cooking lessons. It's been great so far."

"So, was that what you always wanted to do?"

I spread out some more mulch and tried not to stare at his ass as he bent over to spread more right in front of me. I cleared my throat and did my best to concentrate on what we had been talking about.

"I had planned to go to school, but I didn't really know what I wanted to do. I met a woman that was studying the same thing as me, but she transferred to a four year school. She works at the Library of Congress. I always figured that would be pretty cool. Dad got sick right around the time I was going to go to school, so I stayed at the library and it all just kind of worked out. Lucy is in school finishing up her masters degree. She wants to be a history professor."

"If I hadn't gone into the military, I'm not sure what I would have done. I didn't really have any direction."

"Is that why you joined?"

"No. I didn't go to college because I didn't have a clue what I wanted to do. I was just working whatever jobs I could find, but then when 9/11 happened, I just couldn't see working menial jobs when I could be doing so much more. I wanted to do something to help, something important."

"What branch did you join?"

"Army. When I retired, I was an Infantry Team Leader."

"Why did you retire?" He got quiet and continued to spread mulch. "I'm sorry. I didn't mean to push. I was just trying to get to know you."

"It's fine. I just don't like to talk about it. I loved being in the army, but it ended badly and..." He sighed and ran a hand through his short hair. "This looks pretty good," he said as he looked around.

"Yeah. Thank you for your help today."

"You're welcome. I have to get going."

He started to walk away and I smiled to myself. The more I was around him, the more comfortable I got. I was so confused though. Nothing about the way he acted today led me to believe that he had special powers. In fact, he seemed like such a normal guy. I was really losing my mind. I needed to get out of my books and back to reality. I turned for the house, brushing the pieces of mulch from my clothes and started walking up the steps to the porch when I was swept off my feet. I squealed and quickly wrapped my arms around Derek's neck. He was slick with sweat and had the distinct smell of a working man. My eyes connected with his and my whole body lit on fire. I wanted him to kiss me so badly, but then I remembered how gross I was and started squirming to get out of his arms.

"Stop moving," he said forcefully.

"I stink and I'm dirty. I haven't brushed my teeth since this morning and I'm pretty sure you wanted to kiss me, but I guess I could be wrong on that. I'm not always the best at reading people. Either way, we're so close that you can probably smell my breath, which is probably disgusting at this point. Not to mention that-"

"Claire," his eyes darkened and I swore I heard a rumble in his chest. "Shut up."

His lips crashed down on mine and his tongue slid inside my mouth as I stared at him in surprise. My brain finally kicked in and I let my eyes drift closed as I melted into his kiss. His mouth moved more urgently against mine as he deepened the kiss. I ran my hands up the back of his neck until they were tangled in his dark locks. I couldn't get enough of him, but just as I was really getting into it, he pulled back and quickly set me down, taking a step back as he ran a hand over his face.

I took a step toward him, but he held up a hand and shook his head. "Don't."

"Why?"

"Because. Just don't."

"I thought-"

"I have to go."

He turned around and stalked off to his truck, leaving me confused and horny as hell. I stood at the base of the porch steps and wondered why the hell he had pulled back. It was a good kiss, wasn't it? Maybe I was wrong. Maybe my breath really was as bad as I thought and I had turned him off. Shit. I knew I shouldn't have let him kiss me. Now I would go down in his books as the crazy lady with bad breath.

Sighing, I climbed the steps to my house and went upstairs to clean off the day. I may have pleasured myself in the shower as I thought about the kiss and I may have imagined him doing more than just kissing me. That was probably the only thing I would get from him based on the way he ran out of here like his pants were on fire.

Chapter Six

DEREK

"*I*f you keep throwing punches like that, I'm gonna get pissed. This is training, jackass," Chris said from across the ring. I had been in the ring with him for going on a half hour and not one punch I'd thrown had lessened the tension in my body. All I could think about was how good Claire felt against me and how badly I wanted her in my bed. I'd never wanted a woman the way I wanted her and I was sure that if I had her, I'd be a goner.

Chris came at me hard and I was too wrapped up in thoughts of the kiss I had with Claire two days ago to react to him. A few punches to the face later, I was on the ground as he swept my legs out from under me. I was lying flat on my back and staring up at his ugly face as he rested an elbow on me like I was a fucking armrest. He slapped my face twice, right over the cheek he had just punched the shit out of. I winced and rolled my head to the side to get away from him.

"Get your head in the game. Your team doesn't need you pussing out on them."

"Get the fuck off me."

"Why don't you tell me what the fuck the problem is?"

"I don't have a problem other than you leaning your big ass body on me like I'm a fucking pillow."

He picked at his nails like he had all the time in the world. Meanwhile, his weight was starting to make it difficult to breathe. "I got all day, man. What's the problem? Not getting laid?"

"Fuck off," I wheezed.

"So, definitely about a girl. Must be pretty good looking too if she's distracting you at work."

"I'm not fucking distracted."

"Sure, sure. I just kicked your ass in less than ten seconds because you were thinking about what you were going to make for dinner. I like meatloaf, by the way."

"You're such a dick."

"No, that would be Cazzo."

"Get the fuck off me."

"She has to be new or one of us would have heard about her by now."

"Hey, Jackass-"

"No, Just Jack. My nickname is Jack, not Jackass."

"I don't give a fuck what your nickname is. If you don't get the hell off me, I'm going to-"

"What? Kick my ass? Sorry, I already have you pinned. Now where were we? Oh yeah. Your lady friend. Is this the one from the grocery store?"

"Fuck you."

"Thanks, but I get plenty of pussy. Now, this lady friend of yours, is she what's got your head all fucked up? Cause I gotta tell you, you need to either hit that or go get fucked by someone else or you're gonna get your ass shot off."

"She's none of your fucking business."

"Well, she's about to be everyone's business because they all saw me kick your ass and they're wondering where the hell your head is," he said as he tapped my head with his finger.

"If I tell you, will you get the fuck off me?"

"Of course, why didn't you say so?"

He lifted his elbow off my chest and I took in a deep breath, relieved that the fucker wasn't crushing me any more. I sat up and saw that Pappy, Sinner, Cazzo, and Ice were sitting on the side of the ring staring at me with humor.

"Fuck off," I growled.

"I don't think so, Irish. We all want to hear about this girl," Pappy grinned. That fucker. He'd known ever since the party that there was a girl distracting me.

"She's just someone I met at the grocery store. She was almost hit by a car and I knocked her out of the way. She ended up in the hospital. That's all."

I tried to walk away, but Chris grabbed onto my arm to stop me. "Whoa, you're not getting off that easy. What has you so wrapped up in her that you can't concentrate?"

I looked around at the guys and sighed. There was no way they were going to let me get away without an explanation. At least Lola wasn't here to bust my balls. She was the worst.

"I really like this woman."

"So, fuck her," Ice said, like it was just that easy.

"You don't get it asshole, I mean I like her, like her."

"Say what?" Ice grinned. "This is a good thing, man. You don't have to work for it so much once you have them locked down."

Cazzo and Sinner snorted. "You got that dead fucking wrong," Sinner said. "They only make you work harder for it once you have them."

"But it's worth it," Cazzo pointed out. "When you have that one woman that worships the ground you walk on, you make sure you hold on with both hands." He rubbed his hands together and grinned. "I told you you'd be coming to us for advice." I rolled my eyes in annoyance. I hated that he was right.

"You two are fucking crazy," Pappy shook his head. "One woman to be tied down to the rest of your life sounds boring as hell. Don't get me wrong, Cara and Vanessa are great, but that shit's going to get boring after a while."

Burg walked in the door and Pappy turned to him with a nod. "Tell them, Burg. Tell them what a pain in the ass it's been with Meghan."

"Shit. I'm not gonna lie. It's fucking brutal. One minute, everything's fine and the next, I don't know what the fuck I did wrong."

"See? Why would you want that?" Ice asked me.

"On the other hand, I fucking love her and I couldn't imagine not fighting with her. I like that I can go home to her and she just gets me. I mean, the way a good woman can."

Sinner nodded and slapped me on the back. "You remember how I was with the ladies before Cara. I haven't looked at one woman since I met her."

"That's not true. You were with Vira when you and Cara broke up," Cazzo said, grinning.

"Shut up, fucker." I had a feeling we were missing some of the story when Sinner got so defensive.

"She forgave you for that?" I asked.

"She knew. Vira told her," Cazzo told us. "Apparently, our man couldn't get it up with her. She said he was the worst fuck of her life."

"I was too hung up on Cara," Sinner said defensively. "At least I didn't almost fuck a man."

"Not cool," Burg said, pointing a finger at Sinner. "I may have been misguided, but that shit stopped as soon as I found out she was a he."

"You still almost fucked a dude," Cazzo laughed.

"At least I didn't sit around my house watching chick flicks after my woman left," Burg growled at Cazzo.

"Those were fucking good movies," Cazzo said defensively.

"I'd have to agree with him," I stepped to Cazzo's defense. "There's nothing wrong with a man letting off some steam at the end of a hard week with a beer and a good movie."

"I'm with Burg on this one," Chris interjected. "There's nothing manly about watching chick flicks with a bunch of guys."

"Says the man that wore a pink, frilly apron to cook dinner," Cazzo scoffed.

"I'd like to see you prove it," he growled.

"I don't need proof. I have witnesses," Cazzo smirked.

Chris sneered at Cazzo and stepped into his space. "That shit doesn't leave the house. We swore we weren't gonna talk about that shit."

"Alright, alright. This is getting a little out of hand," Pappy said.

"Let's all just step back and agree that anything that happens on the job or in someone else's house-"

"Or in my own fucking house," Burg jumped in.

"Or in your own house, stays between us. We don't need to rehash all this shit," Pappy said.

"Can we get back to the problem at hand?" Chris asked. "Irish has himself a bit of a lady problem and if we don't work it out, he's gonna get us all killed."

"Don't be so dramatic," I said in irritation.

"So, you really like this chick. What's the problem?" Sinner asked. "She doesn't want to put out?"

I shook my head. "It's not about that. I kissed her a couple days ago and it was fucking amazing. Like it almost blew me off my fucking feet."

"Aw, fuck. You are so screwed," Chris muttered. "Why do all you fuckers have to go and fall in love?"

"Whoa, I didn't say anything about love," I said defensively. "All I said was that it was a really good kiss."

"Why don't you ask Cazzo about earth shattering kisses?" Sinner grinned. "He had one kiss with Vanessa and that was it for him. He was sunk and we all could see it."

"Yeah, and we all saw how it turned out for you and Cara. The only man I know to walk away from his job for a woman," Pappy said.

"Not true. Cazzo almost walked away from everything," Chris said grimly.

"Look, this is fucking great, walking down memory lane and all, but what the hell am I supposed to do about my situation?"

"Fuck her and get it out of your system," Ice said flippantly.

"I don't think I can do that."

"So, what's the problem?" Cazzo shrugged. "Just see how things go with her."

"When you met Vanessa, did you just know that if you took things to the next level with her that shit would never be the same?"

Cazzo's eyes went wide and he swore. "You're screwed. If you know that already, then you're fucked. Might as well bite the bullet and accept your fate, man."

Cazzo clapped me on the shoulder and headed for the door. Sinner grinned and pulled me in for a man hug. "Welcome to the club, man." I felt like I had just been issued a death sentence. I hadn't been in a relationship in..well, ever. I didn't do relationships. I liked my life the way it was. I didn't have a strong desire to get married and have kids. I wouldn't mind a steady relationship as long as those other things weren't expected. What the hell was I supposed to do?

"Wait," I shouted to Sinner. He turned around and looked at me quizzically. "That's it? That's all the sage advice you have for me?"

"Why fight it? You're fucked and there's no way around it?" He said with a shrug.

"No. That's not it. You don't just all the sudden know that the person you're with is the one. That's not the way this shit works."

"Look, maybe I'm wrong about all this. With Cara, I just knew that shit was different with her. There was no second guessing with her. Things just clicked and I knew I would do anything for her. Believe me, when we broke up, it wasn't because I wanted to. I tried to get her back, but it just wasn't meant to be at the time. It all worked out in the end though. My advice? Just go with the flow. If it feels right, don't let your head get in the way of what your heart is telling you."

"You've turned into a sappy fucker, you know that?"

He grinned. "Yeah, it's great."

He turned and walked out the door, leaving me with the only sane men left in the room. "So, any words of wisdom?"

"Get out now," Ice said as he passed me. "Before you get nailed down and can't get out of it."

Chris shook his head and slapped me on the back. "Have fun, but remember to suit up. The last thing we need is a little Irish running around."

"Pappy? Please tell me you have something better than what these fuckers came up with."

"I've watched as Knight, Sinner, Cazzo, and Cap have all fallen to their knees for a woman." I nodded, understanding exactly what he was saying. "There's nothing wrong with it, if that's what you're looking for. If you're not, walk away, man. The last thing you want to do is lead her to believe it could be something more and then break her heart."

That was about the only sound piece of advice I had gotten. I wasn't sure if I wanted more with her, but I wasn't sure I wanted to walk away either. The only thing I could do was go out with her again and see how things went. Then I would really know if I was imagining things or not.

*S*ince coffee was a bust last time, I decided to go a different route this time. I wanted to do something fun with her and see if I could loosen her up a little. However, after I walked away from her with no explanation, she was probably confused and I wasn't sure she would want to see me. I showed up at her house in the morning, deciding that surprising her was the best way to get her to do things my way. After today, hopefully I would have a better idea if I wanted more with her or not.

I knocked on the door to her house, but there was no answer. Walking around the property, I saw that she was in the chicken coop arguing with the chickens.

"Beatrice, I'm not going to tell you again. Stay away from the hens! Henry, you've already eaten. Let Harriet have a turn."

She was shooing away chickens and roosters, and coming awfully close to falling in the water bucket that she had just been using to fill the water trays. A chicken flew off the roost, flapping its wings and smacking her in the face. She stepped back into the feeder and then crashed into the nesting area. Wood shavings covered her from head to toe and what looked like chicken shit. I grimaced and wondered if maybe I should come back at a different time, but then I saw the tears in her eyes and I knew that I could make her day better by following through with my plans.

"Do you need a hand?" I asked as I approached the coop.

Her head whipped up and she quickly wiped at her face, smearing something across her cheeks that I was sure I didn't want to know what it was.

"What are you doing here?"

"I came to take you out. I figured if I came here, you would be more likely to go out with me."

She held up her hands as if showing me her surroundings. "Well, as you can see, I'm a bit of a mess right now. Unless you like women that smell like chickens and are covered in their shit."

"I'm not so much into the smell, but I'd be willing to let you take a shower before we head out. Besides, you look like you need a break."

"Look, you don't have to give me some pity date."

"This isn't a pity date."

"Really? You kissed me the other day and then ran out of here as fast as you could. I told you my teeth needed to be brushed. Nobody wants to kiss someone that's stinky." She huffed and wiped at her clothes. "You always seem to be catching me when I'm a disaster."

There was something different about her this morning. She wasn't her nervous self and it made me wonder if it was because she looked so defeated. I went over to her and pulled her to her feet. "I'm taking you out for the rest of the day. Go get cleaned up. Everything else can wait until later. I'll even help you when we get back."

Two hours later, we were at the beach, relaxing in the sun. I loved her figure in a swimsuit. The way she filled it out was spectacular. She had a beautiful, curvy figure with big breasts that were almost spilling out of the little triangles. I was tempted to give her my shirt to cover up just so the other fuckers walking along the beach would stop staring at her. I couldn't take my eyes off her the entire time and a few times, I had to look away quickly so she wouldn't catch me staring at her.

"Come on. Let's go for a swim," I said after laying out in the hot sun for about an hour. I was sweating and this was a great excuse to get my hands on her. She quickly got up and made a mad dash for the water. Chasing after her, I picked her up just as she was stepping into the water and hauled her up over my shoulder. I ran into the water as far as I could and then flung us both into the water while she screamed and slapped at my back. When we came up, she wrapped her body around mine and crawled up me until most of her body was by my neck. She flung herself backwards, taking me into the water with her again. The woman was kind of crazy, but I was digging it.

We spent more than a half hour swimming and doing our best to dunk each other. She was laughing like crazy and I found that I was smiling more than I had ever in my life. There was just something about her that was so intoxicating and had me craving more of her joy.

"Oh, God. I'm so tired now. You're going to have to carry me," she said as she wrapped her body around mine. I gripped her around the ass, pulling her in close to me. She was so small in my arms and she felt so right. I started walking out of the water, but then she buried her face in the crick of my neck and squealed.

"You have to put me down. I can't have everyone on the beach seeing my ass."

"They won't see. I have my hands covering it."

"Which is even worse. I don't need anyone seeing you grab my ass. Just put me down."

"Not a chance in hell. I happen to like my hands wrapped around your juicy ass."

She reared back and looked at me in horror. "You think my ass is juicy?"

"Uh, you've seen it, right? It's big and perfect for me to grab onto."

She struggled to get down and then pushed me away and stalked out of the water. "I can't believe you just said my ass was big," she yelled over her shoulder.

I stood there a minute trying to figure out what the hell I said that was so wrong. She had the most gorgeous ass I'd ever seen. Didn't all girls want a big ass like that Kardashian woman? I ran after her and gripped onto her arm, swinging her around to see me.

"I like that your ass is big."

She burst into tears and I stood there with wide eyes, wondering what I was supposed to do. There was a reason I didn't date women. I didn't know what the hell to say to them on the best of days. Sex was easy. Please them and they'll be screaming your name the whole night. This...this was totally foreign to me.

"Having a big ass is a good thing. Men like to know they have something to grab onto. Besides, we want to know that you're sturdy enough that we won't break you when we fuck you."

She looked up at me through her tears and cried even harder. "So, now I'm sturdy? Like a tree? Next thing, you're going to tell me I have big thighs."

"Big? No, definitely not big. They're thick and muscular."

"Thick?" She spun away from me and ran for the beach blanket, grabbing her stuff and throwing it in her bag.

"I like that you're not a stick," I said, trying to fix this before I totally fucked up the rest of our day. "If I wanted a model, I would go find one. But those women are all beauty and no brains."

She sniffed and wiped at her face. "Well, I'm glad to know that I'm thick like a tree, I have a big ass, and apparently I don't have beauty, but I have brains."

She grabbed her bag and threw it over her shoulder, stalking back to the car. I went over what I had said in my head and ran a hand through my soaking wet hair. Shit. I had really fucked that up. I ran toward her, leaving everything behind so I could catch up to her. Scooping her up in my arms, I took her down to the ground and laid my body over hers. Fuck, I was hard seeing her sprawled out beneath me.

"You misunderstood everything I was saying. Yes, you have a big ass, but that's what turns me on. I don't want someone with a flat ass that I can't appreciate. Yes, you have bigger thighs and I like that, too. I don't want a stick thin model that watches what she eats and can't enjoy life because she's too concerned about counting calories. And I did say that I wanted a woman with brains, but I never said you weren't beautiful. If I wasn't getting so fucking confused by your reaction, I would have finished telling you that you were the whole package. You're the most gorgeous woman I've ever met and what makes that even better is that you're fucking smart. I see the way you run the farm and not just anyone could do that and work another job to keep the house running."

I ground my hips against hers and watched her eyes widen. "And to top it all off, you make me fucking hard. I've never wanted a woman as badly as I want you. Now, I have more shit planned for today and I'd like to finish our date."

She swallowed hard and licked her lips. I couldn't resist getting a taste. I leaned down and ran my lips along her jaw until I met her lips and felt her tongue glide against mine. My hips had a mind of their own and I had to remind myself that we were in a public place before I tore her swimsuit off and fucked her right here in the sand.

"Come on. I have one more thing for us to do today."

I stood and held my hand out for her. She took it and brushed the sand off her body, giving me a great view of her ass again. I'd have to remind myself in the future to avoid saying things that made her feel fat. I didn't want to touch that bag of worms again.

"*Um*, you didn't say anything about going on a boat."

I looked at her green face and tried to figure out how this was possible. She loved the beach and we had fun playing in the water, so what was the problem?

"It'll be fine. We have someone taking us out. I completely trust him."

She chuckled nervously and gripped onto my hand so tight that I thought my bones would be crushed. We walked over to the boat and I pulled her aboard with me. The captain greeted me and told me about the weather and where he would be taking us, but all I could concentrate on was how terrified Claire looked.

"Hey, we don't have to do this if you don't want to," I said as I looked at her with concern. She was actually shaking in my arms.

"No, I'll be fine. It's just a boat and like you said, the captain knows what he's doing. We'll be fine. And you'll be right next to me the whole time, right?" I nodded. "Yeah, we'll be fine. Totally fine."

"You mentioned that. It's really okay if you don't want to go."

She shook her head wildly. "I'm fine." I laughed and pulled her into my arms for a hug. "Really. I've just never been on a boat before."

"Never?" She shook her head again, like she didn't actually want to say anything. "I promise, you'll love it. Come on."

I sat down on a bench next to her and pulled her tight against me.

Her body was shaking as we headed out onto the lake. I ran a hand up and down her arm and she started to relax. "I guess this isn't so bad."

"See? What did I tell you?" She smiled and relaxed into me some more. "When was the last time you took a day off and really just had fun?"

"I can't remember. I've been so worried about keeping up the farm, taking care of my dad, and working to keep us eating that I don't really have time for anything else."

I kissed the side of her head and wished that I could make life easier for her. It was a strange feeling to want to help another person and get nothing out of it but satisfaction in knowing she would be smiling. I still had my doubts that I would be interested in the long term. I just didn't think I was up for that, but for right now, I was enjoying the day with her.

That all changed about an hour later when the weather turned and the lake got choppy. In all actuality, it wasn't that bad, but the slightest roll seemed to send her running for the side of the boat to heave. The captain was doing his best to get us back, but we were already pretty far out on the lake.

"Claire, it's okay. Just breathe," I said as I spun her around to make eye contact with her. She looked like she was going to throw up on me at any minute. "Keep looking at me. Take a deep breath..that's it. Another one." She did as I said and her eyes went wide right before she threw up down the front of my shirt. I stepped back in disgust, never having been thrown up on before. I probably should have been more sympathetic to her plight, but all I could think about was the smell and how close I was to throwing up now that I could see and smell it on me. I quickly whipped off my shirt and threw it in the water. There was no way in hell I was ever wearing that shirt again. No amount of soap could tempt me to.

"That's fucking disgusting," I muttered as I took a towel and tried to clean myself off. I looked up to see Claire huddled next to the side of the boat with her arms wrapped around her legs and tears in her eyes. Fuck, I was such an asshole. Here I was worried about having puke on me and saying how disgusting it was and she was over there sick and trying to get through this little excursion without embarrassing herself further. "Claire-"

"Don't. Just leave me alone," she whispered. I sat down next to her and pushed my hand through my hair.

"I'm sorry. I was being a jackass. I knew that you didn't want to come out here and I should have taken you somewhere else as soon as I knew." She didn't say anything, which made this even worse. I didn't know how to fix things if she wouldn't talk to me. "Claire, I'm new at all this. I've never really dated anyone before and I'm bound to screw up a time or two."

She finally looked at me, but what I saw wasn't hope. "It doesn't take knowing how to date to know how to be kind to someone. I should have known better."

She turned away from me and right then and there, I didn't feel like a man, but a jerk that had just destroyed the woman in front of me.

---

*B*y the time we got back to shore, the weather had cleared and Claire wasn't looking quite so sick. She didn't speak to me as we gathered our stuff from the boat and headed back to the truck and she completely ignored me on the drive home. When I got to her house, she stormed out of the truck and up the steps to her house, not sparing me a backwards glance. I had no fucking clue what to do and there were only a few people I could go to, though it wouldn't be pretty when I told them how bad I fucked up.

Sending texts off to Cazzo and Sinner, I told them to meet me at my place, saying that beer would be waiting. I picked up a case on my way home and pulled in just after Cazzo and Sinner were parking their trucks. Sinner eyed the beer and then looked at me.

"Is there some reason we're gonna need a whole twenty-four pack?"

"I fucked up."

"Yeah. We've all been there," Cazzo said as we walked into the house.

"No, I really fucked up. Like, I should be kicked in the balls and then drawn and quartered."

"That bad, huh?" Sinner popped a beer open and sat down on the couch with Cazzo as they waited for me to tell them what happened. It took me a few minutes to get it out. I was ashamed by the way I acted and I knew they were gonna lay into me. Even if I couldn't get her to go out with me again, I needed to at least find a way to let her know how sorry I was.

"I took Claire out today. I wanted to do something nice for her, so I took her to the beach for the day."

"I don't see the problem," Cazzo said.

"Well, it was fine at first, but then I guess I called her fat. I hadn't meant to, but she took it that way and every time I tried to fix it, I made it worse."

"Like what? How exactly did you call her fat?"

"I told her she had a juicy ass." They both made pained faces and drank down their beer. I opened my own and took a big gulp before I continued. "I also told her she had thick thighs."

Sinner spit out his beer, covering me for the second time today in someone else's mess. "What the hell possessed you to do that?"

"I didn't mean for it to come out that way. I was meaning to tell her that she wasn't stick thin and I liked her that way. It just came out differently than I planned. Then I said that if I wanted a model I could go find one. That models were all beauty and no brains."

Cazzo shook his head at me and laughed. "You fucked up."

"I know. But I fixed that part. I explained what I was trying to say and she seemed okay with it."

"You never comment on a woman's body unless you're telling her how great she looks," Sinner retorted.

"That's what I was trying to do."

"Then learn to do it better," he said. "So, what else did you do?"

"I took her out on a boat. I was thinking it would be romantic and shit, but it turns out she's never been on a boat."

"Ooh," Cazzo shook his head. "I don't like where this is going."

"She ended up getting sick and she threw up all over me. I may have said that it was...fucking disgusting."

Cazzo and Sinner just stared at me in shock. "You did what?" Sinner asked.

"You fucking heard me. Don't make me repeat myself."

"I couldn't have heard you because only a total douchebag would say something that fucked up to a woman he liked when she was sick." Sinner's face was practically lethal, but I already knew I had fucked up. I just needed to know how to fix it.

"You fucking heard me right and I realized what a fucking asshole I was as soon as I saw her face, but it's not like I could take it back. That's not the worst part."

Cazzo ran a hand across his forehead as he leaned forward and grabbed another beer. "You should have bought something harder. I'm pretty sure we're all gonna need it by the time you're done with your story."

I sighed and sat back as I told them the worst part. "When I was trying to apologize to her, I told her that I was new to dating and she told me it didn't take knowing how to date to be kind to someone."

"Fuck. I hope you're not planning on ever seeing this woman again," Sinner said. "You screwed the pooch big time. I don't know if there's any amount of begging that can ever get you back in her good graces."

I stood and paced the room. "Come on, guys. There has to be something I can do to make this up to her."

"Dude, neither of us fucked up like this. Sure, we both had our issues, but we never did anything like that," Sinner scoffed.

"I gotta agree with Sinner. I mean, I fucked things up pretty bad with Vanessa, but it was about my own issues and had nothing to do with her. You made her feel like shit and that's not easy to come back from."

"I get it. I fucked up so bad that I should be called every curse word in the book, but there has to be something I can do."

"Beg," Sinner said. "You get down on your knees and you fucking beg for her to take you back. You take things slow with her and make sure that she knows how much you want her for her. If you do get lucky enough that you get her back, you don't fucking sleep with her right away, but you make sure she knows how bad you want her."

"And whatever happens, don't ever fucking comment on the size of her thighs again. Or her ass," Cazzo threw in.

"I get that, but what exactly do I do?" Both of them stared at me, completely clueless. "You guys are fucking useless."

"Says the man that insulted his woman on the second date," Sinner pointed out. Fuck, he was right.

Chapter Seven

CLAIRE

I stormed into the house and straight up to my room, quickly changing into some work clothes. I didn't work tomorrow, so it was a great opportunity to get some extra stuff done around the farm. Normally, I would take the night off and watch a movie, but I needed to do something to clear my head after the fiasco on the boat. Why did I have to be so goddamn spastic?

"Hey," Lucy said as I walked downstairs. She was munching on a snack and drinking some iced tea, probably taking a break before she headed back out to get some more work done. "How'd the date go?"

"It went in the shitter. He called me fat and I threw up on him."

"Good job, Claire bear. Sounds like you made a great impression."

"It's my specialty. I could write a book on how to push away a guy that's insanely hot and totally out of my league."

"He's not out of your league. You just don't realize what a catch you are."

"Either way, I'm pretty sure that he won't be calling me again. Why do I have to be such a spaz?"

"You're not like that with everyone. Just the totally hot guys that make your panties wet."

"Those are the ones I'd prefer not to scare away."

"I guess you'll just be stuck with the old, fat ones unless you can figure out a way to not fuck it up."

"Maybe I just need practice. Do you know of any insanely hot men that would be willing to give me tips on how to pick up men, but wouldn't expect me to sleep with them?"

"I do know of one guy. He's insanely hot."

"How hot are we talking?"

"Think Dwayne Johnson. He looks exactly like him and he's just as ripped."

"Do you really think he would help me?"

"I think I could persuade him," she smirked.

"Ugh. More apologies," I said as I cleared the text from my phone. It had been nonstop for the past week, Derek messaging me and apologizing profusely for his rudeness when I hadn't been feeling well. Seriously? I couldn't believe that he thought apologies would make up for the way he treated me on the boat. Sure, it was disgusting and I wished like hell that I could take it back, but to treat me like I had done it on purpose or that I was a piece of trash was beyond embarrassing. There was no way I was going to give him another chance.

I heard a vehicle pull in the driveway and I didn't know of anyone that was coming over, so I walked to the front door to see who it was. A woman stepped out carrying the most beautiful bouquet of flowers that I had ever seen and a basket of some sort. I raised an eyebrow, sure that this woman was lost.

"Can I help you?"

"Claire Grant?" I nodded. She smiled and handed me the vase of flowers. Wildflowers, I noted. There was also a large basket that was wrapped and I couldn't see what was inside. The woman smiled wistfully and headed back for her car.

"Wait. I didn't get a chance-"

She waved me off as she turned back around. "It's all been taken care of. Enjoy!"

That was odd. I went inside and set the vase of flowers down on the table, searching for a card. When I found it, I was a little taken aback by what it said.

These are not from the hothouse.

There was no signature, but I figured there was only one person that would have sent me flowers and knew of my love for Jane Austen. Derek. I opened the basket that had been carefully wrapped and gasped when I saw what was inside. *Pride and Prejudice, Memoirs of a Geisha, Jane Eyre, The Notebook, Gone With The Wind, Sense and Sensibility, A Walk to Remember, Outlander, Beautiful Disaster, The Thorn Birds, Northanger Abbey, Emma, The Tangled Ivy Trilogy, and Rebecca.*

Inside the basket, on top of the books, was an envelope. I opened it up and saw Derek's messy script.

I'm sure in one of theses books you can find a situation in which someone needs to be forgiven for something they said without thinking. Let me point you in the right direction. Emma. I'm sure you remember the scene well. Emma dismisses someone's nonsensical ramblings and embarrasses the woman in front of all their friends. It took awhile, but she eventually was able to get forgiveness for her harsh words. I'm hoping that one day you will be able to do the same for me.

I read the note several times, wondering if he had actually read the books or if he had just looked up things about the books that might relate to what had happened. The more I thought about it, the more I realized it didn't really matter. He went to the effort to find a way to relate to me on my terms and I appreciated it. Even though it was clear that we weren't suited for each other, I was glad that I could at least walk away without being angry any more.

"*Y*ou're sure he's okay with this? It's weird for him to do this. How many men do you know that would come help a girl figure out how to pick up men? It's just weird. Besides, he works with Derek. I think we should leave." I told Lucy as we sat in The Pub at a high table while Hunter grabbed our drinks.

"Would you relax? He wouldn't have met us if he wasn't okay with it."

"How did you meet him? He's so good looking."

"I met him here, actually. He bought me some drinks and we've had a sort of...friendship since then."

I looked questioningly at her. "What kind of friendship?"

"The mutually beneficial kind."

"Like he comes and takes care of your car for you when it's broken?"

"No, like the 'I need to fuck and you're available' kind." I stared at her, completely dumbstruck by what she was saying. I mean, logically I knew that happened. I was here to learn how to achieve that. Well, not that exactly, but how to get a man to notice me. She shrugged and threw a flirty wave his way. "It works for us."

"Ladies, your drinks."

He set down two beers and a gin martini for Lucy. I took my beer and chugged it, hoping that it would loosen me up a little before we got on with my lessons.

"So, Claire, what's the hardest part for you when you meet a guy?" Hunter asked.

"Um..talking in general."

He stared at me for a second before he burst out laughing. "Okay, I can see how that would be a problem. It's okay to be shy. Guys don't always want a woman that has the confidence of a seasoned hooker."

"Hey," Lucy said indignantly.

"Not you, babe. I like your hooker ways," he grinned. Lucy ran a hand down his arm suggestively and her hand disappeared below the table for a minute. I caught Hunter's eyes widening and then darkening as he whispered something in her ear and then kissed her silly. I felt like a gawker and blushed as I turned away, checking out the rest of the bar. When they finally came up for air, I turned back to Hunter.

"It's not that I'm shy. I just don't have a filter. I never know what's appropriate to say and I always end up saying the wrong thing. I'm just..I don't know what I'm doing."

The truth was, I had always been socially awkward. Mom always thought it was a phase I would grow out of, but that didn't seem to happen. I got worse when I hit puberty and started spilling my thoughts to every boy I met. I even got sent to the principal's office a time or two for inappropriate behavior.

"Well, in order to help, I think I'm going to need to see you in action. Why don't you finish your beer and then go up to that guy at the bar? I'll watch you and then I can give you pointers."

"You want me to go up to that guy and hit on him?"

"You don't have to hit on him. Just strike up a conversation and see where it goes. Remember, not every guy has to be someone you would date."

I nodded and finished my beer. "Okay, I can do this." I stood up and walked over to the bar where a good looking guy in a suit was sitting. I sat down next to him, staring straight ahead as I waited for the bartender to come get my drink order. I kept looking at him out of the corner of my eye, but then looked away quickly when I thought he might be looking at me. The bartender stood in front of me with a sexy grin on his face.

"What can I get for you, sweetheart?"

"A beer. Whatever's on tap."

My hands were shaking with nervousness and I just wanted to get this over so that Hunter could tell me how the hell to act around men. The bartender slid my beer over to me and I tipped him, giving him a smile. I took a sip of my beer, choking when I inhaled the foam on the top of the beer. The man next to me patted me on the back gently and I caught him smiling at me as his touch turned from a gentle pat to a back rub. It seemed a little too familiar, but I went with it.

"Thank you. Too much foam. Went down the wrong pipe, which would be very bad because food that goes down the trachea and into the lungs can lead to pneumonia."

He smiled good naturedly at me, which I took as a sign that I hadn't totally blown it before I got his name.

"It happens. I'm Mike."

"Claire." I said, breathing a sigh of relief.

"What's a beautiful woman like you doing here by yourself?"

"Oh, I'm not here by myself. I'm here with my sister and her friend," I said, pointing over to the table I just came from.

"Ah," he said grinning. "Sisters. That sounds promising."

I looked at him oddly and then caught on to what he was hinting at. "No! No. It's not like that. I'm not into...that. I mean, especially not with my sister. That would be just weird." His smile started to fade and I got the feeling that I had offended him. "Not that there's anything wrong with that. I mean, if you like having sex with two women, or another man for that matter, you should definitely do it. Just not with me. But I'm sure you'll find someone else out there that would love to do that. With you."

"Lady, I just came to have a beer."

"Right. Well, I'm sorry about the whole...menage a trois thing. I'm sure there's another lovely lady or gentleman here that would be into that sort of thing with you. Look," I pointed to a woman across the room playing darts. "That woman looks like she might be into that sort of thing. She definitely has the dirty girl vibe going on. You should talk to her about your situation. She'd probably be willing."

"That's my sister," he growled. "And she's not into that sort of shit."

I stumbled off the stool and practically fell on my face as he stood to his full height. "I'm so sorry. I'm sure she's not a hooker or into threesomes."

He took a step toward me and I backed up, only to step into a hard body. I spun around and was relieved to see Hunter standing behind me with a menacing look on his face.

"Back away," he snarled at the suit. Mike took a step back and his eyes flicked to me. "You should keep your bitch on her chain," he said before turning and stalking out the door.

"What the hell did you say to him?" Hunter asked as he guided me back to the table.

"He thought that I was into a threesome with you and Lucy and I corrected him that I wasn't into that and then suggested he find another woman who might be interested. I pointed to the woman by the darts and suggested he try her, that she looked like she was up for a good time. It turns out she's his sister," I said with a grimace.

Hunter shook his head and chuckled. "You weren't kidding about saying too much. Okay, we can work on that." Hunter looked around the bar and found another guy, pointing him out to me. The guy looked pretty laid back and was just hanging out with some friends.

"I don't know. I mean, he looks normal, but I don't want to interrupt his time with his friends. Isn't that annoying?"

"Not if the girl is smoking hot," he grinned.

"Oh," my face fell. "Well, then I definitely shouldn't go over there."

Lucy rolled her eyes at me. "You're hot, Claire bear. You just don't realize it."

"Go on over there, only this time, I want you to really think about what you want to say before you open your mouth. Remember, less is more when it comes to men."

"Right." I nodded and drank the rest of my beer and walked over to the man at the table. He was sitting with two other guys and a woman who was snuggled up to one of the other men. "Hi," I said and then stood there awkwardly as I tried to decide what to say next. "I'm Claire."

"Adam."

I could feel my face flushing as I stood there trying to remember to think before I spoke. What was the next thing I should say? The more time that passed, the more I realized what a terrible idea this was. His friends were staring at me, so I just went for it, hoping I didn't make a total ass of myself again. "I was wondering if I could buy you a drink."

His eyes sparkled at me and he glanced to his friends with a smirk. "Sure, Claire. I'd love another beer."

"Oh, okay." I stood there for another minute before heading to the bar to order two more beers. I glanced over at Hunter, who was giving me a 'what the fuck' look. I shrugged and ordered the beer, then walked back to the table to deliver them.

"Thanks, Claire." He turned back to his friends and they started talking, completely ignoring me. I got the distinct impression that I had just been played. Instead of hanging around to be humiliated further, I went back to my table and thumped my head against the table.

"So, what did you say to this one?" Hunter asked.

"I asked him if I could buy him a drink."

"Claire, you never offer to buy a guy a drink. If he's interested, he'll buy one for you."

"Ugh, I'm so bad at this."

"Did you say anything else to him?"

"You said less is more."

"Well, yeah, but you have to see if the guy is interested first."

"You know, I think I'm done for the night. I'm completely terrible at this."

"No way," Lucy said. "You wanted help and we're not leaving until you've successfully hit on a man."

"At this rate, we'll be closing down the bar."

"Maybe you need something stronger, you know, really loosen you up." Lucy walked over to the bar and ordered shots for all of us. I drank two down and felt my head get fuzzy. This probably wasn't a good idea. I really only drank beer, so shots were going to really mess me up.

"Okay, Claire. Your turn to pick."

I looked around the bar and sighed at the prospects. "I don't think this is a good idea. At this point, I'm pretty sure everyone has seen me and they know what an easy target I am."

"Alright, you can practice on me."

I looked to Lucy, thinking she would be pretty pissed, but instead, she was nodding her head vigorously and grinning.

"Umm, okay."

"Alright, let's start with the basics. Why don't you go to the bathroom and then come up to me like it's our first time meeting."

"Okay, I'll be back." I went to the bathroom and spent a good five minutes trying to figure out a good opening line. I couldn't come up with a damn thing, so I decided to go out there and just wing it. Lucy was nowhere in sight and I imagined it was so it all felt more realistic. Approaching Hunter, I blushed when he winked at me and gave a sexy smirk. Lucy wasn't lying when she told me about his good looks. He was devastatingly handsome and his muscles had my lady parts fluttering.

"Hi, I'm Claire," I said robotically. It was the one line I could think up to say that wouldn't be saying too much.

"I'm Hunter. Can I buy you a drink?"

"Sure." I forced myself to not start listing off all the drinks that I wanted to avoid and smiled.

He waved over the waitress and I took a seat across from him, trying to keep my yap shut and let him do the talking. He ordered two Captain and coke's and grinned at me.

"So, Claire. Tell me a little about yourself."

"Well, I'm a Gemini, though I don't really know anything about astrology. It's not really something I'm into. I work on my family farm because my dad is getting old and can't do it by himself anymore. I'm also the town librarian and-"

I stopped when he held up his hand. "First, you don't want to do an information overload when you first meet a guy. Keep it simple. If he really wants to know more, he'll ask. But if you say too much all at once, it's like trying to push two dates into the first meeting."

"Okay. Should we try again?"

"Let's work on body language. The way you approached me was hesitant and you were wringing your hands like you were going to squeeze water from them. Just come up to me like I'm one of your friends. The worst that can happen is I tell you I'm not interested."

I took a shot and walked away, coming back with more confidence this time. He was right. What was the worst that could happen? "Hi, I'm Claire." I held out my hand and smiled big for him. I was rewarded with a handshake and a sexy smile.

"Hi, Claire. I'm Hunter. It's nice to meet you."

"It's nice to meet you too. Is anyone sitting here?"

I was surprised at how casually it all came out, but all I could think was that it was the alcohol talking.

"Nope, please join me."

I took the seat and smiled at him, hoping he would continue the conversation from here. I didn't know what to say.

"Do you come here often?" he asked.

"Sometimes. My sister and I love to-" I paused, wondering if he was actually interested or if it was just a casual question. "Was that a pick up line or a real question?"

"It's a real question," he laughed. "I come here a lot and I've never seen you."

"Well, I don't come all that often. I work two jobs, so I don't have a lot of time off." I almost started rambling on about working on the farm again and working at the library, but I snapped my mouth shut, remembering what he said about too much information.

"Two jobs? That's kind of crazy. What do you do?"

I paused and considered what I should say so I didn't start rambling. "I work on my father's farm and I'm the town librarian."

"Librarian, huh? Do you wear your hair up in a bun and wear tight pencil skirts to work?"

"No. I usually wear pants and yes, I do like to wear my hair up, but I have no clue how to put it in a bun."

He laughed a little and I hoped it wasn't at me.

"Working on the farm and working in town full time sounds like a lot of work."

I nodded, but refused to say anything else about it. I could do this. Hunter was making this seem easy for me. It was a shame that Lucy was already sleeping with him because he made it seem like something was actually happening between us.

"So, what is it you do, Hunter?"

"I'm in security."

I paused for a second, trying to decide if I should break the play acting thing we had going. "Is this weird?"

"What?"

"I mean, because I know Derek."

"Why would that be weird? Are you dating him?"

"Uh, no I don't...no. I mean, he saved my life and he kissed me, but then things got all icky when I threw up on him and-"

"Wait. You said he saved you. Are you talking about in the bank?"

"Well, that too, but I meant outside the grocery store. He pushed me out of the way of a car."

He threw his head back in laughter and slammed a fist down on the table. "That's fucking hilarious. You're the woman from the grocery store."

"You don't have to laugh about it," I grumbled.

"No, this is really good. You've got nothing to worry about. He's totally torn up about you. Doesn't want to pussy out and take the next step, but he can't get you out of his head."

"I doubt that's true after our last date."

He raised an eyebrow at me. "One of the guys kicked his ass in the ring because he couldn't concentrate. He was too busy thinking about you. I'd say that you have nothing to worry about."

"I threw up on him a week ago, so I'm pretty sure he won't want to see me again."

He hissed in a breath and grimaced. "Yikes. Well, it's not like you can't come back from that."

"Really? Because I don't really see how I could throw up on someone and they would come running back to me for more. Besides, after I threw up on him, he said it was fucking disgusting, which it is, but that's not what a girl wants to hear after she was dragged out on a boat and got seasick."

"Trust me, Derek is completely clueless sometimes, but he's a good guy. I'm sure he realized right away that he fucked up and he's probably trying to figure out how to undo the damage as we speak."

"You didn't see his face."

"I'll let you in on a little secret. Guys are fuck ups like 90% of the time. We say and do stupid shit because it doesn't cross our minds that you don't think the way we do. Shit flies out of our mouths and then we realize afterwards that we totally fucked up. But even then, sometimes you still have to explain shit to us."

"I threw up on him," I said slowly. "That's going beyond fucking up or saying something stupid. I vomited all down the front of him. How the hell would he still want to be with me?"

"Because you're a total catch. You just don't see it. The only thing you see is that you're a little socially awkward. The right guy isn't gonna care about that. Don't let what happened get to you. Let's get some more drinks and have fun. You don't need to waste any more time trying to learn how to pick up a guy. If I know Derek, he felt like an asshole as soon as you left."

Hunter and I drank for a good two hours and I had lost my self-consciousness at some point during the night. When I asked where Lucy was, he told me she went home with someone else. It didn't seem to bother him at all. Hunter was a lot of fun to hang out with and he didn't make fun of me when I started rambling or when I said stupid stuff. He was like a protective older brother and I was happy that I had met him.

"Claire, just go with me on this and trust me, okay?"

"What?"

Before I could get an answer out of him, he was out of his chair and had pulled me in for a deep kiss. At first it was awkward, especially feeling like he was an older brother and all, but the way he kissed me was hot and I decided to just go with it and think about the rest later. When he pulled back and winked at me, I blushed hard, not sure what to think about what just happened. It was a hell of a kiss, but there was no spark between us. But Hunter was looking at me like I was his next conquest and it made me feel special.

"What the fuck is this?"

I broke out of the spell Hunter's kiss had me under and spun around to see Derek standing right behind me. He was glaring at Hunter and I quickly looked at Hunter for some kind of sign of what I should do. He just smirked at Derek and pulled me in close to him. This was definitely a situation I had never been in before and I wasn't sure how to handle it. Not to mention, the alcohol was making my head fuzzy and suddenly I found this whole situation hilarious. I started laughing and I couldn't stop. It was just so odd that I couldn't handle myself around a man just this morning and now I had two men that looked like they were going to come to blows.

"Hey, Irish. What's going on?"

"Do you want to tell me why you called me here?"

I looked up at Hunter in confusion. He had called Derek? Why would he do that? Hunter squeezed my side, like he was telling me to keep my mouth shut.

"Just thought you'd want to hang out, man."

"And you just happened to be here with Claire?"

"Do you two know each other?" Hunter asked as if I hadn't just mentioned earlier that we knew each other.

"Um.."

"Claire and I are dating. I didn't realize that she was meeting you tonight, though."

"It wasn't planned," I blurted out. "I was telling my sister that I suck at dating after our thing on the boat. She suggested that Hunter give me some pointers on how to meet men. I thought I'd give it a try since I totally blew it with you. But I totally suck at hitting on men." His face was growing angrier by the second, so I thought I should try to explain some more. Maybe he was misunderstanding me. "I went up to the first one that Hunter picked out and I somehow led him to believe that I wanted a threesome and then I accidentally called his sister a whore. Then the next guy Hunter picked out, I bought him a drink and he ignored me after I bought it. I was just trying to get some tips on how to pick up men so that I can actually get laid sometime this century."

"Is that what all that was about? You just wanted to get laid?" He said angrily.

"No. I mean, not totally. Of course, I want to get laid. Who doesn't, but after I totally blew it with you, I just figured I needed some guidance so I didn't screw it up with the next guy."

"The next guy?" He scoffed and sent a chilling look to Hunter. "And I suppose you're the next guy."

"You snooze, you lose." Hunter grinned and wrapped his arm around my neck, pulling me in close. I was really confused by what was going on. Derek grabbed onto my arm and pulled me away from Hunter. I knew that if Hunter wanted to, he could have kept me by his side, so I wasn't sure what he was playing at.

"Let's get one thing clear. I may be a dumb fucker at times and screw this up with you, but you are mine. You don't need to learn how to flirt with other men or how to pick them up because there won't be anyone else. Not until we see where this thing goes. Do you under-stand that?"

"But, last week you said-"

"I know what I said and I was an asshole. It seems that I have some socially awkward moments too when I say shit before thinking about it. I'm so fucking sorry that I was such a jerk to you when you were sick, but I can't take it back. I can only try to make it up to you. I don't know what the hell is going on between us, but I'm sure as hell not going to let you get away until I know for sure whether or not this could be something more."

I swallowed hard and stared up at the sexy man before me. There was nothing I wanted more than to kiss him and take him home with me. Well, we probably shouldn't go to my home. I had my father and sister there with me and I didn't need everyone knowing my business.

"Are we clear?" he asked. I nodded and squeaked out a yes. "Good." He looked at Hunter and glared. "You can remove your hands from my woman. Now. And don't ever think of fucking touching her again."

Hunter grinned and tipped his head at Derek. I didn't understand it. They had some weird man language that I just didn't understand. I needed to get out more and maybe study them. Kind of like how scientists study apes. Derek pulled me to the exit of the bar and dragged me over to his truck, shoving me inside and going around to the other side.

He slammed the door once inside and stared out the windshield for a few minutes. I sat there uncomfortably, not knowing what to do or say. I decided to keep my mouth shut so that I didn't say something to screw this up after he just called me his woman. When he finally looked over at me, there was a mixture of rage and lust on his face. I wasn't sure what to make of it. Was he going to fuck me angrily? That would be kind of hot.

"You don't ever go to a bar to find a man again. If you need something, you come to me."

"The only reason I would look for a man in a bar is to have sex with him. Anything else and I would look in the yellow pages," I said before I could think better of it. I slapped my hand over my mouth as my eyes widened.

"You won't be looking for sex from men in a bar anymore. You have me to take care of all your needs. Understand?"

I nodded, not able to say anything else at the moment. I actually had a lot of questions. Like, was I able to call him at any time for sex? Was this just a mutually beneficial relationship, as Lucy had called it? Would I be able to call him at any time or were there only certain times of the day he could be reached?

He gave a curt nod and started the truck up, pulling onto the road. I didn't know where we were going and I was afraid to ask right now. I hoped that he was going to take me to his house and have his way with me, but when he headed out of town toward my house, my heart sank. I had already said that I needed to get laid and now he was dropping me off. I didn't want to come out and say it again. What if he wasn't in the mood for me? Had I misread what he was saying? I wished that I understood men better.

He pulled into my driveway and parked the truck. "Do you want to come in? I mean, my dad's here, so that could be awkward. He tends to wake up at night and wander the house. And since he hasn't met you, he might pull a gun on you in the morning. Unless you weren't planning to stay until morning, in which case-"

I stopped talking when Derek placed his fingers over my mouth, essentially cutting off my rambling.

"Next Saturday."

"Next Saturday what?" I said slowly.

"I'll pick you up at six and we'll go to dinner."

"Wait. That's it?"

"What did you expect?"

"Well," How did I say this? That I wanted to have sex with him and that he told me to go to him, so he'd better pay up? "You told me if I needed anything that I should go to you."

He draped his arm across the seat back. "And what is it you need from me?" His deep voice struck me down in my core, sending shivers racing through me.

"I need you to..."

"Say it," he rumbled.

I blushed furiously and was grateful for the dark. "I need you to fuck me hard. It's been way too long and I'm horny. You can't leave me hanging after you just told me that I couldn't get it anywhere else. Not that the men are lining up to take me to bed, but..."

He smirked and scooted across the seat to me. Wrapping his hand around my neck, he pulled me in close to him and brushed his thumb across my cheek. "You can bet that sweet ass that I'm gonna fuck you hard." His other hand slid down to the apex of my thighs and skimmed across my heated core. I gasped and waited for him to undo my pants and slip his hand inside. He leaned in and whispered in my ear. "But when I make you come, it won't be because I've dragged you out of a bar after you were getting tips on picking up men. When I take you, you'll only be thinking about me and all the things I'm going to be doing to you." His fingers pinched at my clit through my pants and I almost came on the spot. "I will have you, but it'll be when you're all mine."

He pulled back and gave me a deep kiss that made my body constrict. I tried to pull him in closer, but he untangled me from his arms and slid back to his side. "Go, before I change my mind and take you right here in the truck."

"I wouldn't complain," I said breathily.

He shook his head slightly. "That's not how it's gonna go with us."

I fanned myself a little and pried the door open, getting out on shaky legs, and made my way to the house. I turned and gave him a wave before heading inside and flopping down on the couch.

Chapter Eight

DEREK

I was nervous as hell, which was a new feeling for me. I was never nervous about a date, but I was so scared of screwing things up with Claire that I couldn't seem to get a grip. It was all that talk Sinner and Cazzo had done about being screwed and knowing that she was the one. It was freaking me out, but at the same time, deep down, I knew they might be right. I was generally okay with the idea of her being the one. I already knew that she drove me crazy, in a good way, and that I like being with her. It just freaked me out to have thoughts of marriage and family running through my head when just two weeks ago, I had thought I would be a lifelong bachelor.

I climbed out of my truck, determined to break away from my nerves and just go with the flow. I knocked on her door and waited for her to open the door. Only it wasn't her that pulled the door open, but a man that I could only assume was her father. I held out my hand, but he just glared at me.

"Sir, I'm Derek."

"So."

I cleared my throat and pulled my hand back. "I'm taking Claire out tonight for dinner."

He reared back and pulled something from behind the door. It was a Remington twelve gauge, pump action shotgun. Part of me wanted to take a step back because, well, he was pointing a gun at me. But logically, I knew that I was better off close to him where I could grab the gun before he could shoot me. Which, I could. I wasn't new to this, but I also didn't want to piss off Claire's dad. I had a feeling he wouldn't think more of me for taking away his gun.

"There's no fucking way I'm letting you anywhere near my daughter, you sick fuck."

"Have we met before?" I asked in confusion.

"I don't need to have met you to know that there's no way I'm letting you anywhere near my daughter."

Did my reputation precede me? "Uh, sir-"

He shoved the gun in my face and I quickly knocked the gun away so I didn't get hit in the face. I grabbed the barrel of the gun and yanked it out of his hands before he could threaten me again. Unloading the gun, I shoved the ammunition in my pocket and leaned the gun against the side of the house.

"Why don't you tell me what the fuck the problem is before you decide to threaten me again? I don't particularly like having a weapon pointed at me."

"My problem is that you're too old for my daughter, you fucking pervert."

I looked at him in confusion. What the hell was he talking about? "Sir, I couldn't be any more than ten years older than her. And all due respect, your daughter can make her own decisions."

"My daughter is just a child, not even old enough to date."

"Daddy!" Claire came running up behind her father looking like every man's wet dream. She had her hair down in soft waves around her shoulders and a tight black dress that accentuated all the curves that I loved so much. She also had on heels, which made her legs look longer than they were. I wanted her to turn around so I could see what her calves looked like. I was a leg man and nothing made me harder than seeing beautiful, shapely legs.

My eyes snapped back up to Claire's face and saw the concerned look on her face. Something was definitely wrong here. Sure, Claire was short, but there was no way that I had misjudged her age.

"Daddy, this is my tutor. He's not taking me out on a date. We're going to the library and then I have a date with that nice boy that you met last week."

Her father eyed me skeptically, but nodded. Claire stood on her tiptoes and kissed his cheek. "I'll be home before midnight, Daddy."

She walked out to the truck, completely avoiding all contact with me and got in her own side. I took her lead and went to my own side, trying my best to appear like I was her tutor. As we drove down her driveway, I looked over to see her staring out her window and wiping at her eyes.

"Do you want to tell me what that was all about?"

"Remember I told you that my dad wasn't all there any more?"

"Yeah."

"Nights are the worst. He thinks that I'm still a little girl. He's usually pretty good during the day, but there are times that he gets confused early in the day."

Now it all made sense. I slid my hand over the seat to hers and gripped her hand in mine. She squeezed my hand back and I got the feeling that this had been weighing on her mind for way too long.

"Hey, you okay?"

She turned to me with a shaky smile and nodded. "Yeah. Let's just go have some fun."

I nodded, understanding that she didn't want to talk about it right now. I took her to dinner at the local Italian restaurant. I had reserved their most private table, hoping that it would help her relax. I figured that if people were watching her, it would only make her more nervous and bring out more of her awkwardness.

After dinner, we walked along the streets downtown to a local ice cream shop. Claire had been quieter tonight and I wondered how much of it had to do with what happened with her father.

"How long has your father been that bad?" I asked as we licked our ice cream, walking down the sidewalk.

She blew out a breath and took another lick. I wanted to be that ice cream. The way her tongue slid across the creamy goodness made my cock harden. I cleared my throat and looked away. It would be difficult to listen to her if I kept picturing the things I wanted her to do to me in the bedroom.

"It's been getting gradually worse over the last few years, but the last few months have been really hard. Not every day is a good day for him. Some days he wakes up thinking that I'm still a young teenager."

"That's gotta be hard."

"Some days aren't so bad. Sometimes he goes back to a really good memory and it feels so good to have that part of my dad back, but most of the time, he's just confused. I know that Lucy and I need to think about our options, but it's a hard decision to take him away from everything he knows."

"I know this isn't the same thing, but I had this dog, Barkley, that I'd had since I was a kid. My parents watched him for me while I was serving and they called me up one day saying that he wasn't doing so well. He was getting too old and the doctor said that he had really bad arthritis and he was in a lot of pain. My parents didn't know what to do. They didn't want to put him down when I wasn't home, but they didn't want to make the dog suffer either. They called me and asked me what I wanted. I told them they should put him down. It was fucking brutal. That dog was like my best friend growing up and as much as I wanted to be there for him, I didn't know when I would be able to get home. They don't exactly give leave for your sick dog."

"Did they do it?"

I nodded. "Yeah. We all knew it was the right thing for him. I'm not saying that your decision about your father is anything like mine, but you have to think about what's best for him. He could get hurt if he gets too confused and tries to do something he shouldn't be doing. I'm not saying now's the time, but try to remember that you're not giving up on him, but helping him the only way you can."

She was silent and I wondered if I had stepped over the line. Maybe she wasn't ready to face reality yet.

"Where do your parents live?"

"North Carolina. They moved out there a few years back after my dad retired."

"Do you ever go visit them?"

"Not really. I'm usually pretty busy, so they come back here and stay with me for a few weeks every year."

"What were you like as a kid?"

I laughed and rubbed my hand across the back of my neck. "You know, rough and tumble kid. I got into a lot of trouble growing up."

"No, you?" she mocked me.

"I know. It's hard to believe, right? My parents had their hands full with me and my brothers."

"How many brothers do you have?"

"Six."

"Six? Six brothers? Oh my gosh. Your poor parents."

"You have no idea. Eric is the oldest. He's the most straight laced out of any of us. I'm the second oldest. Will is the third. He's very book smart. Robert is next. He's a lawyer and given his name, you could definitely picture his name on a billboard. Josh is fifth and.." I swallowed hard, ashamed at this next part. "We don't really know where Josh is. He's had some trouble and no one's heard from him in a few years. Andrew is the sixth son. He's really into technology and music. And last is Joe. He's kind of the wild child. Last born and gets away with everything."

"And I thought it was bad that my dad had to put up with me and Lucy."

"Let's just say that we were sort of notorious in my hometown."

"Where did you grow up?"

"A small farming town south of Chicago. There are about three thousand people that live there. I had twenty-eight people in my graduating class. Everyone knew everyone and no one had any privacy unless you lived in the country."

"And did you?"

"Yeah, but that didn't stop us from being well known in town. We caused so much trouble that my parents pretty much just started shaking their heads when they heard another story. I mean, we didn't do anything illegal, but it was still embarrassing to my parents."

"What kind of stuff did you do?"

"Uh, promise you won't use it against me?"

"I'm pretty sure I've given you plenty of ammunition against me."

"True. Alright, well there was this one time that Joe convinced us to stage a bank robbery."

"Hold on. Like an actual bank robbery?" she asked in amazement.

"Yeah. It wasn't such a great idea, but at the time, we thought it was a pretty cool idea."

"How old were you?"

"I was about fourteen. The younger brothers weren't tall enough to pass as bank robbers yet, but that didn't stop us. We had on masks and everything. The problem was, we only had our winter ski masks and at the time, they had designs on them. At first the employees were freaked out, but then the bank manager recognized Joe's Spiderman mask and he played along. He called the cops and they showed up, sirens blaring and we were all hauled off to jail after a short standoff."

"I thought you said you didn't do anything illegal?"

"Well, it was a different time. Small town and all, the cops kind of expected it from us."

"So, did you get in trouble?"

"Not really. It was kind of like a town performance. Once everyone kind of clued in that it was the Cortell brothers up to their tricks, they all played along. It got quite dramatic. The cops warned us about making sure we didn't take things too far. Mom and Dad were a little pissed, but they laughed when we got home."

"It sounds like you guys were really close."

"We were. Not so much any more. We're all kind of scattered at the moment. Eric is still back home with Joe and Andrew. They stayed in the house after Mom and Dad moved to North Carolina. Robert works in Chicago, so he's not too far away. William teaches a few towns over."

"And you're here."

"Yeah."

"What was Josh doing the last you heard from him?"

We stopped walking and sat down on a bench by the park. With my elbows resting on my knees, I decided that I would tell Claire what happened that made me lose touch with my family.

"I, uh, I don't really know. I was so wrapped up in my own life and starting over after I left the military that I didn't pay attention to the rest of my family. My last mission, my whole team died and I knew we shouldn't have been going in. I knew that something was off. I was the team leader and I should have spoken up, but I didn't. Two of the guys were wounded, but they survived while we were waiting for a rescue. We were running to the extraction point when they were killed. I was the only one that made it out of there that day."

I stared at the ground as I remembered Burk taking a bullet as we boarded the helicopter. Fisher shoved me in and then was climbing in behind me when he took a bullet to the back. I tried to catch him and pull him in, but his body was dead weight and he fell back to the ground. We were under heavy fire and we couldn't go back right away. Their bodies were recovered later, but there wasn't much left for their families to bury.

"Anyway, I was a mess when I was discharged. My family wanted to help, but I didn't know how to let them. I got ahold of Cap and started working with him. It was easier to work with people that understood than to go home and have people look at me like I was damaged."

"When was the last time you saw your brothers?"

"A few years. I've wanted to go back, but there's been so much shit happening around here that I just keep making excuses not to."

"It seems like we both make excuses not to do things."

I didn't sleep with her that night or any of the other nights over the next two weeks. It was killer because every time I saw her, I wanted her even more, but I wanted to take things slow with her and make sure that I didn't fuck things up with her. I had already made some major mistakes and once I slept with her, I knew things would completely change between us. I needed to be sure I was ready to give her everything she deserved because I didn't want to hurt her. She had different plans though.

"I want you to fuck me tonight," she said as she leaned over the armrest in the movie theater. We were sitting in the back watching some stupid romantic comedy that I didn't want to see, but I did anyway for her.

"Watch the movie," I whispered. She huffed and crossed her arms in front of her chest. After a few minutes, she started messing with her purse and I thought she was going to get up and leave, but instead, she got down on her knees between the seats and grabbed onto my cock through my jeans. I sucked in a deep breath and glanced around, relieved that we were sitting in the back and no one was paying attention.

"Claire, get off the fucking floor."

She undid the zipper on my jeans and my hips lifted against my will as she started to yank them down so she could reach my throbbing cock. When she pulled out my cock, I knew I should stop her, but I just couldn't bring myself to say the words. This wasn't the way our first time was supposed to go. I was going to take her back to my place and make it special for her. That was what she deserved.

She started stroking me and then licked the tip. I had to bite down on my fist to keep from groaning and letting the whole theater know what we were up to. She started stroking me harder and faster and I just couldn't hold back. I had been dreaming of her lips wrapped around me for weeks now and I exploded down her throat, barely holding back a shout. She looked up at me smugly, but there was no fucking way it was ending there. I hauled her up and set her in her seat and got down on my knees in front of her, smirking at her shocked face.

Of course, I didn't fit down there the way she did, but I made it work for me. It just so happened that a sex scene came on just as I started licking her pussy. I saw her watching the screen and then flicking her eyes to mine. She was turned on and it drove me wild. I sucked her clit hard and thrust a finger inside her, covering her mouth with my other hand as she started to whimper. I could feel her body tightening around my fingers and after a few flicks of my tongue, she was coming in my mouth. I made sure to lick her clean so she didn't have cum running down her legs for the rest of the movie.

We had missed a bunch of the movie, but I didn't give a shit. Tonight I was going to take her home and make her mine. There was no more holding back with her. There was no denying that she was mine in every way and nothing could tear her away from me now that my head was on board with everything.

I dragged her out of the theater and drove to my house, making it in half the time. When we pulled into my driveway, I pulled her across the seat, not wanting to waste the time it would take to walk over to her side and let her out. I threw her over my shoulder and smacked her ass when she squealed in laughter. Digging my keys out of my pocket, I quickly let us inside and kicked the door shut behind us, carrying her down the hall to my room and tossing her on the bed. I was on her seconds later, tearing at her clothes, needing to taste her on my tongue. Her skin was salty and I couldn't stop lapping at the flavors that burst from her skin and had me begging for more.

"Derek," she moaned. "Please, I need you inside me."

"Tell me, did that turn you on when I ate you out while you were watching two other people fucking?"

I already knew the answer. I didn't need her to tell me, but I wanted to hear the words leave that fucking amazing mouth. "I-I don't..I mean..."

I dragged her pants off her and latched onto her pussy, flicking my tongue over her clit and then sucking her hard until she was on the verge of breaking. "Tell me. Tell me that I was mistaken. That it didn't make your heart pound out of your chest to see some other man fucking someone while I was sucking you."

Her breathing went out of control and I shucked my pants, gloved up, and sank inside her in one swift move. "You can say it," I said as I pounded into her. "You can tell me that it turned you on." I lifted her legs over my shoulders and fucked her harder. "You can tell me that you want to do that again. I'll find the dirtiest thing for us to watch and I'll fuck you until you're screaming from being split in two."

"Yes! Yes, I want that," she shouted. I thumbed her clit as I thrust inside her a few more times. When she tightened around me, I shouted out as she strangled me to the point of near pain. I could have sworn the condom exploded from how hard I came, but I was happy to see it still intact. Discarding it, I got a washcloth from the bathroom and cleaned up her limp body. She was on the verge of falling asleep and suddenly, I didn't want her to go to sleep unless it was in my arms. I climbed in beside her and pulled her in close to me, stroking her back as she fell asleep.

———

I woke her with kisses and had her passing out from multiple orgasms. It was that explosive between us. In fact, I was surprised that I was able to hold out long enough for her to reach three orgasms. The way she squeezed my cock, it took all my willpower to keep from blowing my load inside her. Day after day, I dragged her back to my place when she got off work and woke up inside her. It was rough because she had to leave early to get back to the farm before she headed off to work for the day. Which meant that if I wanted my morning wood taken care of, I had to get up extra early.

She also tried to get home before her dad woke up in case he wasn't all there first thing in the morning. She had Lucy to help her out, so I didn't feel so bad about keeping her out all night. She deserved a break too.

"Derek, I can't take any more."

She squirmed under me as I tried to get one more out of her. It was my new goal in life to see how many orgasms I could get out of her each day. "One more. Give me one more."

"I can't. Please..." Multiple fart sounds came from her and she looked at me with wide eyes, her face filling with embarrassment. I tried to hold back the laughter. I really tried, but she looked so fucking cute as she hid her face in her hands. "Oh my God! I can't believe that just happened. Please tell me you didn't hear that. Please tell me this is a nightmare and I'm going to wake up."

I pulled her hands from her face and leaned in to kiss her. "Relax, you queefed. Who gives a shit? It happens."

"Queefed?"

"Sex farts. Every woman gets them at some point. It's not like you can prevent it."

"I fucking farted in your face!"

"You did not. Vaginal farts aren't real farts. It's just air."

"But it was in your face!"

"Could have been worse."

She scooted back against the bed frame and pulled the blankets up high around her neck. "In what way could it have been worse? Please tell me what would have been worse."

I thought of something really gross that would have been a game changer for me. It had to be something terrible or she would never get over it. "You could have shit all over my face while I was tonguing your ass hole. That would have been much worse."

"Tonguing my...do people actually do that?"

"All the time."

"That's disgusting. People shit from that hole."

"And yet, it wouldn't stop me from sticking my dick there."

"That's different. You can wash that off. Your mouth...Ick. That's just too disgusting to even think about."

That's what she said, but her eyes were wide with desire. "I bet you'd like it if I did it."

"No...No I wouldn't like it and I would never let you do it. It's totally..."

"Disgusting?"

"Exactly." I pulled her legs out from under the blankets and dragged her toward me. I flipped her over to her stomach and pinned her down as she squealed. "What the hell are you doing?"

"I'm giving you what you need."

"I don't need that!"

"But you want it. I could tell that as much as it repulsed you, you wanted to know what it would be like to have my tongue fucking that tight bundle of nerves. You want my tongue to lick every inch of you," I whispered in her ear.

"No," she said weakly. "I don't."

"Shh. Just let me do this. If you don't like it, I'll stop."

She shook her head, but said nothing as I slid down her body, kissing down her spine until I reached the little dimples in her back. I massaged her cheeks as I moved down to her crack and spread her cheeks, looking at the tight hole that I was about to make mine. When my tongue took the first lick, she flinched and jumped a little, but by the third lick, she was moaning and squirming. I slid a finger down to her cunt and felt wetness dripping from her. There was no denying that my girl was a dirty girl. I hadn't watched any dirty movies with her yet, but now that I knew what she liked, what turned her on, I would get on board with whatever she wanted. I spread her cheeks further, slipping my tongue inside her, flicking it in as far as I could. She bucked up into my face and I grinned as I slid a finger inside her pussy.

"Oh, God! Derek, don't stop."

"Not a fucking chance in hell."

I fucked her over and over with my tongue until she was on the verge of coming. I slid my finger out of her pussy and back to her other hole, sliding it deep inside. She came seconds later, squeezing around my finger. Tremors wracked her body as she fell apart with my finger inside her. Damn, that was the sexiest thing I had ever seen. And she thought she wouldn't like it. I grinned as she laid her head down on the bed, blushing from what I had just done to her. I crawled up her body and laid over her, trying not to put my full weight on top of her.

"That was the fucking sexiest thing I've ever seen. Now that I know how much you like it, you can be sure we'll be doing it again." She blushed even harder, but didn't say a word. "I'm going to go make us breakfast. The chickens can wait today."

I smacked her ass and pulled on some pants, making my way to the kitchen. I hadn't been able to make her breakfast in bed yet and I really wanted to. I didn't want to tell her that she should put her old man in a home, but part of me was selfish and wanted all of her whenever I could get her. He really was going downhill and as much as I didn't want to see her hurting from how bad he was getting, I also didn't want to see her giving up her whole life to take care of someone that she couldn't really care for any more. I knew she was running herself ragged trying to keep up with everything and I didn't really know what I could do to help. Her dad didn't know me and didn't recognize me when I came over. Claire told me it was probably best if I didn't come over because he would just get confused.

I was just about to start breakfast when someone knocked at my door. I made my way over and groaned when I saw that Pappy was standing on the other side. I really didn't want to deal with him when Claire was still in my bed. I flung the door open and glared at him.

"What the fuck do you want?"

"Good morning to you, too, Sunshine. Is Claire bear here?"

"What?"

"Claire bear. That's what Lucy calls her."

"To you, she's just Claire. You don't need a pet name for her."

"Aww. Is someone jealous? Still got that stick up your ass from when she went drinking with me?"

"Shut up, fucker."

He grinned and went into the kitchen, taking a banana and peeling it like it was his house. I stood there watching him with my arms crossed over my chest, wondering what the hell he wanted. When he turned to me, he smiled as he slowly chewed his banana.

"Did you come here for something or did you just come to show me how much you like eating dick?"

He looked at the banana and grinned. "I've never tried it. You want a trial run with me?"

"You're a sick mother fucker."

He laughed and threw the peel away. "I just came to tell you that Knight wants to have the teams drill today. We're up at nine on the dot."

"You could have sent a fucking text."

"But then I wouldn't have gotten to see Claire bear."

"You're still not going to get to see her."

"Aw, don't be like that. She's like a sister to me. A very hot step-sister that I wouldn't mind fucking if you weren't in the picture."

"Are you just trying to piss me off?" I asked, trying not to smile. I knew Hunter would never move in on my girl. He was trying to get a rise out of me and I wasn't going to give it to him.

"Seriously, though. Is everything good between you two?"

"Yeah, why wouldn't it be?"

"No reason, but Knight is flipping the fuck out. He's worried that you're not being careful enough with her. She can't ever know all the secrets we're trying to keep from everyone."

Chapter Nine

CLAIRE

*S*hit. I stayed as still as I could as I listened from the hall. The secrets they were keeping. I kept telling myself that I was making it all up in my head. There was no such thing as special powers or superheroes. They were just extraordinary men. They were really good at what they did. Although, if that was true, why would Knight feel the need to eliminate me? It just didn't make sense. And by the way Hunter was talking, it wasn't just Knight that was part of this whole thing. If they were all in on it, what was Derek hiding from me?

"Look, we have more to worry about with Cap and you than the rest of us," Derek said. "If word ever got out, you and Cap would be the first ones we had to worry about. Knight knows how to disappear better than anyone. You'd better make sure you have a backup plan. Have you talked to the guys from your old unit?"

"No. I thought I'd keep it a secret unless I absolutely had to. They don't need to know that he's alive."

"At some point, Knight's going to do something stupid and then the whole world will know about him."

Oh, God. This was worse than I thought. Knight must be the one that had all the power. Maybe the others just had minimal powers in comparison. But if Knight did something stupid, Derek would be exposed also. I didn't want that to happen. Whatever it was he was hiding from me, I wanted to be sure that no one ever found out. I liked Derek a lot. He was the first man that ever really got me and all my quirkiness. I had been able to relax around him. He made things easier the more time that went on. Whatever it took, I would make sure that Derek's secret never got out. I would do my part and protect them all in any way I could.

"He's not going to fuck up," Hunter said emphatically. "He wouldn't risk losing Kate for anything. We've got nothing to worry about. Just make sure that however much your girl knows, she also knows that it would be a very bad thing if it got out."

"She knows, but I can't keep bringing it up to her. The more we talk about it, the bigger the chance that something will be said that would implicate all of us. For now, she knows that Knight would be very displeased if she said anything. I think that's enough to scare her into staying quiet."

"You're okay with her being scared of Knight? She's your girl."

"She is and I'll do anything to keep her safe, but this isn't just about me. This is about all of you and if keeping her scared of Knight helps to convince her to stay quiet, I'll allow it for now."

"That's kind of harsh, but I respect where you're coming from. We'll see you at the gym. Nine o'clock. I'm not running extra drills because you were getting pussy."

I slid back into the bedroom and locked myself in the bathroom as Hunter left. I needed to take a few minutes to calm down and really think about everything that was going on. I jumped when Derek knocked on the door, bringing me out of my thoughts.

"Yes," I croaked out.

"Everything okay, Claire?"

"Uh, yes. Everything's just wonderful. Great. I just came in here to use the bathroom. You know, just...pooping." *Shit.* After he just licked my ass, I told him I was pooping.

"Okay," he chuckled. "I'll be in the kitchen. Take your time and use the Febreze under the sink."

"Alright," I shouted. *God that was so embarrassing.* I waited another five minutes for the embarrassment to die down, but then realized that the longer I stayed, the more it seemed like I was having bowel issues. I quickly got dressed and grabbed my stuff, determined to get out of there as quickly as possible.

"Where you going?" Derek asked with a twinkle in his eyes.

"Uh, home. Chickens. You know, have to feed them and water. Lots and lots of water. And chicken feed. And cleaning the coop," I said as I walked backwards, trying my best not to sound like an idiot, but failing miserably. "Off to feed those chickens." I jerked my thumb toward the door and made a clucking sound.

He stalked toward me with a devilish grin. "Right. You said that already. What are you really running from? Was that too weird this morning?"

"Running? I'm not running. And that," I pointed to the bedroom, "in there wasn't weird. It was perfectly normal and satisfying. Totally not weird at all. It was pleasant and...fulfilling."

"Fulfilling."

"Yes. Very good job. Well done." I slugged him in the arm and then cringed at my idiocy.

"Claire, it's alright to do what we did this morning. If it makes you uncomfortable, we won't do it again."

I cleared my throat, uncertain what to say. I still had mixed feelings about what happened, but that wasn't the reason I was freaking out. I had to get out of here.

"Right. Well, I'm glad it was good for you too. Tasty...and all." *Shoot me now.* I spun and ran out the door to the sound of Derek's laughter. I was so fucked when it came to him.

---

*J*hurried through my chores at home and quickly ran upstairs to shower. I was getting dressed when Lucy came into my room with a smirk on her face.

"So, Hunter tells me that you've been spending quite a lot of time with Derek."

"Well, that was kind of the point of having him help me."

"No, he was helping you pick up random men. He told me that Derek dragged you out of the bar that night."

"Okay, fine. He dragged me out of the bar. What does it matter?" I asked as I hurried around the room. "I'm dating again, which was the whole point."

"Not really. You're screwing him. That's not the same thing."

I pulled on my shoes and grabbed my keys off my nightstand. "Look, a few weeks ago, I wasn't with anyone. We're still seeing where this is going, and I'm fine with that. I don't need everything all mapped out right now. I just need..."

"His dick?"

"If you must know, yes. That's exactly what I need right now. And not that it's any of your business, but he makes me less nervous. I'm able to act like a somewhat normal person, which I'm taking as a good sign."

"Sure. It's always good to act like a normal person around the person you're fucking," she mocked me.

"Laugh at me all you want, but this is the best I've felt about myself in years. I'm finally happy and I don't care right now if it's not a forever thing. I'm just happy to not feel like such a loser all the time."

"Claire bear, you're not a loser. You're just..."

"So socially awkward that I scare away any man that comes near me? I know that, but thank you for clarifying it for me. Look, I have to get to work. Can we talk about this later?"

"Wait. Before you go, we need to talk about Dad."

I paused in the doorway and looked at her with worry. "Is he okay?"

"He's...This week hasn't been good for him. He's been really confused. I think we need to really consider what we're going to do with him soon. I start teaching in the fall and I won't be able to be here with him as much. You're already stretched pretty thin, and now that you're dating–"

"I'll be home more."

"No, Claire, you shouldn't have to give up any more of your life. You're twenty-seven years old. You've been taking care of Dad for years."

"We both have," I insisted.

"Yeah, we have. But we can't keep doing it. We're just not enough anymore. He needs more help than we can give him. I know that you don't want to take him away from his home, but it's not safe for him to be home alone any more."

I knew she was right, but it made me angry that she could come to this decision so easily. I just wasn't ready. I needed more time with him. Once he was in some home, I was afraid I would lose the last piece of him that I had left. What if he didn't remember me at all? What if he got so lost in his mind that I ceased to exist any more?

"Look, I'm just not ready for this. If you don't want to take care of him any more, I'll make sure that I'm home to be with him. I can't do this right now. I have to get to work."

"Just think about it."

"No. I'm not ripping him away from everything he knows until we absolutely have to."

I stormed downstairs and out the door. I just couldn't deal with any more of this shit right now. I needed to escape my reality and there was only one place I knew to do that, in a good book at the library.

I shoved my glasses up my nose for the tenth time in the last two minutes. It was hotter than blue blazes in the library today and the building was old and didn't have air conditioning. My sleeveless blouse was clinging to me and my pants were sticking to my thighs to the point that when I stood up, I thought I would have a wet spot. I maneuvered the fan yet again and hoped this time I would get more relief from the air flow. No such luck. Sighing, I went back to reading my book. It was slow today and I had already shelved all the books that had been returned and reorganized all the paperwork that had to be filed for the week. There was nothing left for me to do and the library didn't close for another two hours.

I was reading a mystery book that had me so wrapped up in it that I completely missed the men that entered fifteen minutes later. I looked up from my book and saw them sitting at a table, realizing that

I had completely zoned out. I made my way over to them and smiled at them as I approached.

"Good evening. Are you finding everything you need?"

One of the men looked me up and down like I was some kind of meat. The other glanced at me as if he didn't have the time of day for me.

"We're fine," the second one said dismissively.

"Okay, well," I glanced down at the books they were looking at and my eyes grew wide. They were looking at books about unique locks and keys. There was a book about safes as well. "If you need anything else, just let me know. The library will be closing in a little over an hour and a half. These particular books aren't allowed to be checked out, though."

The second man furrowed his brows and then gave me an assessing look. "We're not seeing exactly what we need. Maybe you could direct us towards what we're looking for?"

"Of course," I said with as much nonchalance as I could muster. "Are you looking for something in particular?"

The second man looked at the first and gave a slight nod. The first man smiled wide at me. "You know, we're really interested in historical artifacts and such. We've been looking into some ancient locks and haven't been able to figure out quite how they work."

I nodded eagerly, "Sure, I love history too. So, are you looking for any book in particular?"

"Actually, there is one that we'd really like to see, but it's no longer in print." The first man was doing his best to be charming and I used it to my advantage.

"You know, I can look up the book and see if I can find it for you. I have access to book dealers and collections that aren't easily accessible. I could look into it for you. All I would need is the book title and the author, if you have it."

The second man slid a piece of paper across the table to me and gripped my hand. I was a little alarmed by his tight grip, but tried not to let it show. "It wouldn't be so good if anyone knew we were looking for this. You know, other historians vying for the same information."

"Of course. You'll have my utmost discretion. I'll start looking into this right away and I'll let you know as soon as I find something, Mr.."

"Smith," the first man said. "John Smith."

"Mr. Smith. I'll just need a number to reach you at."

He scribbled a number down on a piece of paper and handed it over to me. I smiled as charmingly as I could and gave the first man a wink. "I'll get started right away. It was nice to meet you both."

The men stood up and walked out of the library, leaving their books on the table. I gathered them up and took them to the counter, then opened the paper and pulled out my phone.

"Hey, Claire," Derek's voice rang through the phone. "I didn't think I'd be hearing from you after you ran out of my house this morning."

"Uh, yeah, sorry about that. I have some information that might be useful to you."

"Information about what?"

"There were two men that were in here a few minutes ago. They were looking up old locks and keys. They weren't finding what they were looking for and they asked me to find a book for them that's out of print."

"Okay..."

"I thought this might have something to do with the bank robbery."

"Claire, you shouldn't go digging into this stuff. Sebastian has a handle on things."

"I'm not digging. I told the men that I would look into it and asked for a number to reach them at. I thought you might be able to use the number to track them or something."

He sighed into the phone and I got the distinct feeling that I was annoying him. "Claire, we contacted Nathan Kent and found out that the key that was in his box didn't go to anything. It's a key his grandfather had and the only thing that he had left from him. He was just keeping it safe while he was overseas."

"You don't seriously believe that, do you? That's the worst story I've ever heard. I mean, I would think a man in the military could come up with a more believable story than that. Besides, if they wanted into that box so bad, it obviously went to something."

"Claire," he barked at me. "I told you to fucking leave it alone. Tell the men that you couldn't find the book anywhere and leave it at that. Don't start getting involved in things that don't concern you."

I rolled my eyes and took a deep breath. "Derek, I possibly have access to a specific book they were looking for. If I can find it, we can get to whatever it is they want before they do. They obviously want it bad or they wouldn't have tried to rob a bank."

"Those men are in lock up. Whoever this is looking at locks is someone entirely different."

"Exactly! Which means that there are at least a few different people looking for whatever this is. If I can get my hands on the book, maybe we can find whatever it is they want before they do."

"Claire, do you hear yourself? You're a librarian. You're not a detective. Just stay out of this."

"Don't you at least want their phone number?" I asked in confusion. "You could track them or something."

"I want you to leave it alone. Don't get involved and don't try and figure this out on your own. Am I clear?"

I couldn't believe that he didn't even want the number of the people that were after whatever was in that box. And worse than that, he was ordering me to stay out of it as if I was some kind of idiot that couldn't take care of myself.

"Crystal clear. You're absolutely right. I'm just a librarian. I'll keep my nose out of it."

"Claire, that's not-"

"No, you're right. I have to go. I have books to shelve."

I hung up before he could say anything else and picked up the books the men had left behind. After putting them away, I picked up the piece of paper and started to research the book. I contacted a few collectors and antique book stores, hoping that I would have some luck. No one had access to the book, but a few knew which one I was talking about. They promised to let me know if they found the book. By the time I finished, it was an hour after the library closed and I was tired, sweaty, and hungry.

Lucy had sent me a message asking me to take care of the chickens tonight, so I dragged my ass home and changed into my work clothes.

I made sure all the chickens were fed and watered and after seeing that they were all in the coop, I shut it up tight for the night. In the morning, I would have to bring out a few more bags of feed and clean out the coop, seeing as I hadn't done it earlier this week like I should have. The grass also needed to be cut and there were weeds growing like crazy in the vegetable garden. It looked like I would be getting an early start tomorrow so that I could tackle all the projects that needed to be taken care of.

After I dragged my ass upstairs and showered off, I plopped down on the bed and plugged in my phone to charge for the night. I noticed that I had a few text messages from Derek, apologizing for being so harsh with me earlier and a voice mail from him. Again, he apologized and asked me to call him, but I was too tired. Or maybe I was just too pissy at the moment. I didn't feel like talking to him and I didn't want to listen to his apologies right now. My bed was calling my name, so I put the phone down and was asleep within minutes.

*A*lmost a week later, I was out in my vegetable garden, still weeding those damn weeds. When the crops came in, we would take them down to the farmer's market in town and sell them for additional income. It wasn't a ton extra, but it helped offset the costs of running the farm. Lucy usually handled gathering the eggs and delivering them to the grocery store in the mornings, which was fine by me because I much preferred to work in the garden than deal with people.

Dad walked out to meet me with a cup of coffee. I didn't really have time to stop right now, but I also didn't want to miss out on these moments with him.

"You work too hard, Claire bear. Why don't you take a break?"

I took the cup of coffee from him and leaned against a nearby fence. "I just want to get some weeding done. I've been neglecting my chores around here."

"Lucy says you have a man friend."

"A man friend?" I said with a grin. "Is that what people call it?"

"Claire, I don't want you to feel that you have to be here taking care of the farm all the time. I know that it's a lot to deal with and I'm not as helpful as I should be."

"I want to help out around here."

"I understand that, but you shouldn't have to give up so much of your life because of my dreams."

"I'm not giving up anything. I like to do this stuff."

"I know, but you have a full time job at the library, and-" He ran his hand over his greying beard and sighed like he had the weight of the world on his shoulders. "Claire, you and Lucy both know that I'm...I'm losing myself. The doctors say it's only going to get worse. I think it's time we start looking into other arrangements."

"No. Absolutely not. I'm not going to just ship you off to some home for other people to care for you."

"You don't have a choice. I won't do this to either of you anymore. You're both too young to be dealing with this kind of burden. It's not fair that you both put your lives on hold for me. You never went to college for anything you really wanted, and it's taken Lucy much longer than it should have to get her teaching degree. She should have been teaching for a few years now."

"Daddy, you know she wanted to get her masters."

"I know, but it wouldn't have taken her so long if it weren't for me. I want us to sit down this weekend and really look at our options."

"But-"

"Don't argue with me, Claire. I've thought about this a lot and I want to make this move before I'm too far gone. The one thing I don't ever want is to be a burden to you and your sister."

"Daddy, you could never be a burden."

He pulled me in for a hug and kissed the side of my head. "I appreciate that, but we both know it isn't true. Now, I want you to bring this fella around to meet me. I need to make sure he's good enough for my girl."

"He is Daddy."

"Still, I want to see for myself."

I grinned up at my dad, happy that for the moment he was himself and able to play the protective dad card. Soon, I wouldn't have these moments any more. He would be beyond my reach and the man I knew would cease to exist.

J was in the middle of a gripping thriller, sitting at a table in the library. The heroine was just about to enter the house where the killer awaited her. I sucked down some more of my Diet Coke and flipped the page, completely entranced in the book. *Don't go in there.* It was silly, really. The characters couldn't hear me and I couldn't change whatever happened in the book, but as I read on, I begged the woman not to be so stupid as to enter a house where her lights weren't working. She did anyway.

Lenora flipped the light switch several times and nothing happened. Walking into the room further, she stopped suddenly when she heard the floor creak off to her left. She knew this house well. Knew that there was one floor board that always creaked when you walked on it. She spun around and squinted into the darkness, not seeing a thing. She walked slowly over to the hallway where the creaky board was located, trying her best not to make any noise. If someone was still in the house, she would...

Well, she wasn't sure what she would do. She didn't have a weapon of any kind and no real way to defend herself, but she just couldn't bring herself to leave. In her mind, she could hear the terrorizing music that would be playing in a horror film right now. She knew she should leave. It was the only sensible thing to do, but she didn't turn around.

"Don't go in there," I whispered.

Lenora finally reached the hallway, but she didn't see anyone. There were four bedrooms down the hallway and each one had the door slightly open. She'd have to look in each one if she wanted to be sure there was no one there. Creeping down to the first door, she gently nudged the door open and peeked inside. The moonlight shining in cast an eerie glow around the room. The closet door was open slightly and she knew she wouldn't be able to move on unless she checked in the closet.

Taking a deep breath Lenora walked over to the closet and quickly flung the door open, jumping in a kind of karate stance as if that would be intimidating. There was nothing in there but Dad's old clothes. She shut the door tight and walked out of the room, glancing both ways down the hall before continuing. She stepped out and crept down to the next door on the right side. Quickly looking around the corner, she saw that this room was empty also. She had just taken a step toward the closet when she heard another creak from the hallway. She quickly ran toward the door, stepped into the hallway when-"

I screamed as a hand landed hard on my shoulder. Flinging my closed fist back, I heard the satisfying crunch of my fist hitting bone followed by a groan. I stood quickly and spun around only to be shocked to see Derek holding his nose and groaning while blood dripped between his fingers.

"Oh my God! I'm so sorry." I headed for him, but he backed up, obviously not wanting me near him. "I can't believe I did that. I was in the middle of this really exciting book and the woman was just about to find out who was in her house. Oh my gosh, it was so scary because she walked into her house and all the lights were out and she still went to see who was there. I mean, who does that? Why wouldn't she just call the police? Well, obviously because then it wouldn't be a very good thriller, but still. It was so scary and then you came up behind me and put your hand on my shoulder and it just totally freaked me out."

I blew out a breath and saw that Derek was staring at me through a bloody hand. I cringed and pointed toward the bathroom. "I'll just grab you some paper towels."

I hurried off the bathroom and grabbed a couple of paper towels and then went back for a few more. Then I thought that maybe they should be wet, so I went back and got a few more. By the time I got back to Derek, I had a whole armful of paper towels, both wet and dry. I set them down on the table in front of him and took a step back.

"Um, here are the paper towels. I wasn't sure if you wanted them wet or dry. I'm sure to soak up the blood you need dry, but then I thought that you wouldn't be able to really clean up the blood unless you had wet paper towels. So, I got you both. Wet and dry." I cleared my throat as he continued to stare at me. I started to get even more uncomfortable as the seconds ticked on and I played with my shirt. Still, he continued to stare at me. "Would you just say something already," I shouted.

He picked up the dry paper towels and tilted back his head,

squeezing the paper towels around his nose. Looking out of the corner of his eye, he smirked at me. "So, you hit me because of a scary book?"

I narrowed my eyes at him and threw my hands on my hips. "It was a really scary book and I was just about to find out who the killer was. You shouldn't have snuck up on me."

"So, you're saying I deserved this?"

"Well, yeah, kind of. Why didn't you just say hello or be a normal person and come around and sit on the other side of the table?"

"I actually have been here for about fifteen minutes trying to get your attention. I was saying your name and I did stand in front of you for about five minutes. I'm not sure sitting across from you would have been a good idea. I might have gotten a book to the face."

I opened my mouth to say something, but I had nothing. I was kind of embarrassed now that he had been trying to get my attention for so long and I hadn't noticed he was there. How many times had that happened with other people?

"Is your face alright?" I finally went with. There was really nothing else to say.

"My face is fine. I don't think you broke my nose. I think you just hit me the right way."

I cringed and bit my lip. "I really am sorry. I never would have hit you if I had known it was you. I thought that..."

He grinned at me. "Say it."

"I thought you were a serial killer," I muttered. He burst out laughing and then cringed when he started bleeding again. Shoving some more paper towels at him, I grabbed my book and stomped off to the circulation desk at the back of the library. He followed behind me and I looked at the clock, seeing that it was past time to close up for the night. I shut down my computer and made sure that everything was all set for the morning. Derek was standing by the desk waiting for me by the time I had finished. His nose had stopped bleeding and most of the blood had been wiped from his face.

"Are you coming home with me tonight?"

"Um, I think I'm going to head home for the night. Dad isn't doing too good and-"

"Look, Claire, I get that I pissed you off, but you don't have to lie to me about it and use your dad as an excuse."

"I'm not. I have been avoiding you, but I'm not lying to you right now. My dad is getting worse every day and now he wants to talk this weekend about his options. He doesn't want to be a burden anymore to Lucy and me, which he's not, but-"

I stopped talking because I was on the verge of breaking down in tears. Derek walked over to me and wrapped me up in his arms. I hadn't realized how much I needed to feel his arms around me and needed his comfort until right this minute. I fisted his shirt and pulled him in tight to me as I cried. He rubbed my back and let me cry until my tears were all dried up. When I pulled back, he wiped the tears from my cheeks and the look on his face melted my heart. No matter what he had said last week, this man truly cared about me. I could see it on his face. Even if this thing didn't last between us, I was grateful that he was here for me right now.

"You go ahead and go home. I'll see you tomorrow. How about I stop by in the morning before you go to work?"

"Actually, would you mind saying hello to my dad? Lucy mentioned that I was seeing someone and he wants to meet you before...before he can't remember you anymore."

"Sure. I'll be there by eight."

"Thank you."

He smiled at me and kissed me gently. "I'm beginning to think there's not a lot I wouldn't do for you."

Chapter Ten

DEREK

*A*fter I got home tonight, I realized that every fucking word I said to her was true. I really would do anything for her. If it made her happy to have me meet her dad before he got too bad, I'd be over there every day getting to know him just to see her smile. I knew that he meant everything to her, and if they did put him in a home soon, I knew she was going to need a lot of support. It was going to kill her to take him somewhere else and then stay on the farm without him. Maybe she would consider moving in with me so she wouldn't be so lonely.

"Crap." I really was screwed if I was considering asking her to move in with me just so she wouldn't be alone. I started looking around my house and tried to imagine what it would be like to have her here in my space. I didn't really have a lot of stuff. Most of my things were just pieces of crap I had picked up along the way the last few years. Not a whole lot meant anything to me, but the idea of her moving her things in here, in my house, that brought a huge ass grin to my face. I pulled out my phone and dialed Pappy's number.

"Yo, Irish, I'm about to sink into some pussy. This better be good."

"I need your help over the next few weeks with moving."

"Moving what?"

"Claire's things. I'm going to ask her to move in with me."

There was silence on the other end for a few seconds and then some rustling and I heard him talking to another person. "Baby, we're going to have to pick this up later. Irish has lost his goddamn mind and I have to go sort him out."

I grinned and agreed when he said he was on his way over to talk some sense into me. I pulled out some beer and was just bringing it into the living room when Pappy walked through the door.

"Okay, what the fuck are you talking about?"

I handed him a beer and explained. "Claire told me that she's sitting down with her dad this weekend to discuss his options. She doesn't want him to go, but he's insisting on it. I don't want her to be alone, so I'm going to ask her to move in with me."

"You're fucking crazy. If you don't want her to be alone, get her a fucking puppy."

"A puppy? Seriously? I think I love her."

"Well, stop thinking. That shit will get you in trouble. Look, I get that you like this chick, but look at what women are doing to the men at Reed Security. They're tearing the balls off the men that work there. Don't fall down that rabbit hole, man."

"I'd happily hand over my balls to Claire. She's fucking awesome. Just tonight, she punched me in the face because she was reading a book."

"What? Do you have a concussion or something? Because you're not making any sense."

"I snuck up on her when she was reading a thriller. She was so into it that she didn't hear me. I scared her and she punched me. It was so fucking awesome."

"You said that," he retorted.

"Look, I get that this is still pretty new between us, but I never thought I would meet a woman that made me feel so alive, and not because she's a good lay, but because she's cute and smart. She's this amazing person that is so awkward, but so adorable at the same time. And when she gets lost in her books, the look on her face is so..."

"Cute?"

"Exactly! She's just so fucking cute."

"And adorable."

"Yes! I'm telling you. I don't need any more time. I just know and Sinner was right. When you know, you know. And I'm telling you, I can just tell with this woman. She's just so...so..."

"Amazing?" he said dryly.

I nodded, not able to come up with any other words to describe her. Pappy groaned and chugged his beer. "You're so fucked. Yeah, I'll be here whenever you need me, but if her sister needs someplace to stay, don't think that I'm letting her stay with me. We may fuck, but I'm not on a suicide train like you."

"She can stay here for all I care," I said, not even caring that I was now opening my home to basically anyone in her family. "Hell, I'd probably move her dad in with me if it made her happy."

"Dude, slow the fuck down. You aren't even engaged to this woman. Can you imagine moving him into your house and then having him walk in on you when you're trying to fuck her?"

He was right. That would probably be too much for our relationship. Still, I was going to ask her to move in with me as soon as she had her plans with her dad settled.

"You're right, but I'm telling you man. She's the one."

"Yeah, I know. Another one bites the dust. Just do me a favor and let me tell Lola," he grinned.

"For you, I'll let you tell the whole fucking team."

He rolled his eyes and muttered something about me being pussy whipped as he walked out the door. I didn't give a shit. I was happier than I had ever been.

I pulled up to her house at 7:55 the next morning with donuts and coffee. I wasn't sure if they had eaten yet, but I didn't want to show up empty handed. Back in my hometown, everyone always kept a box of Entenmann's around in case anyone stopped by for a visit. It was just ingrained in me to be prepared with donuts. The coffee was really for me. I needed it to stay awake today. I was so excited about the idea of asking her to move in with me that I had hardly slept at all. I actually got up around one in the morning to start making space for her in my closet.

Walking up to her porch, I smiled as she stepped out wringing her hands together. I thought it was cute how nervous she was, more nervous than I was. Whatever happened with her dad, I wanted him to like me, but she would be mine no matter what he thought.

"Good morning. You okay?" I asked, squinting against the bright sun.

"I'm good. Everything's good. I'm just waiting for my dad to come downstairs. He's been up there 'getting ready' for a half hour now. I'm not sure if he's going to come down with flowers or a gun. It's most likely a gun since he'll probably want to intimidate you."

"Claire, relax. I'm not worried about meeting your dad. I'm sure he's a great guy and if he wants to shove a gun in my face to try and intimidate me, that's fine too. As long as it isn't loaded."

She relaxed a little and pulled me inside where her dad had just walked into the kitchen. Holding my hand out, I walked over to him and introduced myself.

"Sir, it's nice to meet you. I'm Derek."

He shook my hand and eyed me speculatively. "Harry. It's nice to meet you. Claire hasn't told me anything about you, but Lucy, my other daughter, has said quite a bit."

"All good, I hope." I chuckled and shoved my hands in my pockets when he just glared at me.

"How about we take a walk?" It wasn't a question and he grabbed one of the coffees I brought as he walked out the door. I grabbed one also and followed him out onto the porch. He walked out toward the chicken coop and stopped by the fencing. "Sorry about that. I just didn't want her to follow us out here."

I nodded, not sure where he was going with this. He turned to me and ran a hand over his face.

"Claire told me that we met one night when I wasn't quite myself. She said that I pulled a gun on you."

"Yes, you did."

"Sorry about that. Most nights, I'm just not..."

"You don't have to explain. I understand. Claire has told me all about it. She's pretty torn up over you wanting to make plans to go to a home."

"I know this is going to be hard for her, but it has to happen soon. There are too many days where I'm only lucid in the morning. I can't ask my girls to give up any more of their lives to care for me. It's just not fair to them."

I stood silently, not sure if there was anything I could say that would make him feel better about the whole situation. I happened to agree with him. If it were me, I wouldn't want my loved ones giving up so much of their lives to care for me.

"What's going on with you and Claire?"

"No bullshit?"

"No bullshit."

"I love your daughter. She's mine and I don't care how long it takes me, I'm going to prove to her that I'm the one for her. I don't think she believes in herself enough yet to figure out that I'm not going anywhere, but I'll do anything to make her see herself the way I see her. This is going to sound insensitive, but when she told me that you were going to discuss your options this weekend, the first thing I thought of was that I wanted to ask her to move in with me so that she wasn't lonely. I know this is going to be hard on her and I don't want her here by herself and moping around the house. I want her to come to me for comfort and I want to show her that she doesn't have to do this shit alone anymore."

"And what about her job? Her future? Is she just supposed to marry you and play the good housewife?"

"If she wants to, but I don't see Claire ever being a housewife." It popped out without a second thought and I realized in that moment that I did intend to make her my wife one day. "If she wants to keep the farm going, that's fine with me. If she wants to stay at the library, which wouldn't surprise me, that's fine also. She can go back to school or whatever it is that will make her happy."

"Just like that."

"Just like that. I know it's probably hard to believe because we haven't been together that long, but she caught me right away. We had a rocky start, but it just made it that much better to fight for."

He raised an eyebrow at me and shook his head slightly. "Son, I know I told you no bullshit, but that was one sappy ass answer. Let's not ever speak of this conversation again. Understand me?"

I would have started laughing if it weren't for the serious expression on his face. He said no bullshit and that's what I gave him, because if I couldn't tell her father how I felt, I didn't deserve to have her. He needed to know exactly how much I wanted her before he lost all touch with reality and there was no way I would let him slip away without knowing his daughter would be cared for.

I was late getting back to Reed Security after my talk with Harry. I didn't want to rush out of there after I told him how much his daughter meant to me, so I stuck around until Claire had to get back out and get to work. I pulled into Reed Security and swore when I remembered that Cap was having a meeting this morning and it had started a half hour ago. I hurried inside and headed straight to the conference room, only then hearing my phone chime with incoming text messages. Based on the number of chimes, quite a few people had been trying to get ahold of me.

"Morning, Sunshine," Cap said with a scowl as I entered. Everyone else was smirking at me, obviously getting that I wasn't late because I slept in.

"Sorry," I said as I took my seat.

"No problem. We were just going over assignments and since you felt that it wasn't important to be here on time, your team gets the shit assignment."

I flipped him off. Yeah, he was technically my boss, but I also owned part of this company. I'd take the shit assignment though, because it's what any of us would have to do if we were late. I wasn't going to pull rank to show the others up.

"Thanks, Loverboy." Lola scowled at me from across the table, but I could see the way her lips were trying not to flicker up into a smile. She had my back no matter what.

"Anything for you, Brave." She hated the name Brave, but we all called her that from time to time. Her last name, Pruitt, meant Brave and it perfectly described her best quality. Still, she didn't like it, so instead of it being a common nickname, we used it when we wanted to piss her off.

She flipped me off and we listened as Cap went over the details of our next assignment. We were being hired to watch over a woman and her two kids before the woman testified against her husband in court. He was some high profile New York attorney and she had already had multiple threats made against her. She was scheduled to appear in court next week.

"Right now, she's under police protection. You three, pack your bags. You're taking a one o'clock flight to New York and you'll pick her up at the station. From there, you'll be taking her and her sons to a secure hotel until the trial. Lola, she's not the most trusting of men right now, so you'll be her close protection agent. Derek, you know the drill. If it looks like this is bigger than we thought, let me know and we'll send in another team."

I nodded and picked up the file. If we were going to make our flight, we had to head out soon. "Let's meet back here in an hour," I said to Pappy and Lola.

"I'll have someone drive you to the airport."

We headed out and the first thing I thought of was letting Claire know that I would be out of town, but based on how much time I had before I had to be back, I might just have to give her a call. This couldn't have come at a worse time. With Claire and Lucy talking with their dad this weekend, I had wanted to be there for her, but I couldn't just opt out of a job because my girlfriend was emotional, as terrible as that sounded.

After packing for the trip and heading back to Reed Security, I made sure that we were all set for our trip and we hit the road. Cap had ordered Sinner to drive us, which was always an interesting ride.

"Is that a fucking wedding ring?" Pappy asked as he looked over the back seat at Sinner's ring finger.

"Yep," he grinned. "Ran off to Vegas last weekend."

"Why the hell didn't you have a wedding?" Lola asked.

"Cara didn't want one. The stress of thinking of planning one sent her into a panic, so we said what the hell and booked a flight."

"Congratulations, man." I patted him on the shoulder, happy that he and Cara had finally tied the knot. Whoa, Pappy was right. Since when did I start thinking shit like that.

"I can't believe you did it. You're so fucking stupid, tying yourself down to one woman for the rest of your life," Pappy said, shaking his head.

"You fucking knew I proposed to her. Why the hell would you think I wouldn't go through with it?" Sinner asked.

"You used lollipops," Pappy argued. "None of us thought you were serious. Who fucking does that with someone that they really want to marry? I mean, Lola, if a guy proposed to you with lollipops, would you take him seriously?"

"If a guy proposed to me at all, I'd probably shove the lollipops up his ass," she sneered. "But no, I wouldn't take that as a serious proposal."

"See?" Pappy argued. "You can't really think that any of us expected you to go through with it. We all know how you are with women. I just assumed that you'd get tired of her after a while."

"I fucking quit my job defending her," Sinner said incredulously. "At what point did you think, *Nah, he's not serious about her?*"

Pappy shook his head as he looked out the window. "Fucking perfect. Next thing you know, Irish will be asking Claire to marry him. He's already fucking moving her in."

"I haven't talked to her about it yet, but yeah, I fully intend on marrying that girl."

"Pussies. Every last one of you. Lola and I are going to be the only fucking single people left on the team all because you guys can't think with the right head. I mean, Lola, who's a girl, no offense-"

"None taken," Lola replied, not the least bit offended.

"-isn't thinking of settling down for even a minute with some dude. And she's got all those hormones and shit running through her. No offense."

"None taken."

"Women are born to be fucking baby whisperers and go all goopy eyed over any man that walks past them, and you still couldn't get Lola to settle down. No offense."

"None taken."

"Mark my words, you and Lola are going to settle down one day and when you do, I'm going to fucking laugh my ass off and rub it in that you've been pussy whipped. Or dick whipped in Lola's case," Sinner smirked.

"The day I hand over my balls to some chick is the day I hand in my man card."

"What about you, Lola? You really have no plans of ever settling down?" I asked.

"With who? Some douchebag that doesn't even know how to use a weapon? Or maybe I should hook up with one of you idiots, then we could constantly fight over who has the bigger gun, which will always be me."

"You're telling me there's never been a single moment in life when you thought you might want something more than a one night stand?" I asked.

"There might have been a time," she whispered. "But not anymore."

"Lola-"

"Can we fucking drop this conversation? So what? Sinner got married. That's on him to deal with for the rest of his life. If you want to get married? Go for it. Hunter and I will stay blissfully single, fucking whoever we want, whenever we want."

It was silent for a minute and a little uncomfortable. We all knew there was a time that Lola would have wanted the whole package, but she hadn't spoken about a man since she was almost scalped all those years ago. She'd been carrying around that baggage with her ever since, but she wore her scar like a badge of honor.

"So, have you and Pappy ever fucked?" Sinner asked, breaking the tension.

"You're such an asshole," Pappy said, rolling his eyes.

"You have. I can tell by your face!" I was totally shocked. "How the hell did I never know this?"

"Because we fuck," Lola sneered. "We don't make googly eyes at one another and if he ever tried it, I'd make sure that the only way he could please a woman was with his fingers."

We all cringed, knowing that with Lola, that wasn't just a threat.

---

*W*e'd been watching Mrs. Arnold and her two boys for three days now. The trial started tomorrow and even though we hadn't received any threats or noticed anything unusual, I had an uneasy feeling. I began pacing the living room in the hotel suite, going over everything that we knew and our plan for the next day. We had a solid plan, but there was something that just wasn't right. I couldn't figure it out though. How was I supposed to protect them like this?

"You have to stop fucking pacing. What's going on?" Pappy asked from his place on the couch. He was cleaning his weapons, preparing for tomorrow.

"I don't know. Something's not right. I can feel it, but I can't figure it out for the life of me."

"Let's go over what we know."

We spent the next hour going over everything that would happen tomorrow and spitballing ideas on what could go wrong. Any way we looked at it, there wasn't a single thing that wasn't covered.

"Derek, I know that you don't want anything to go wrong, but we have all our bases covered. If something does go wrong, we'll deal with it like we always do. It's not going to be because we aren't prepared though."

I sighed and sat on the couch, unable to relax. "We need another team. I want to change things up tomorrow. We'll send in a decoy first. We need to know for sure that nothing's planned for when we show up at the courthouse."

"Derek, we don't have time for this. To get another team in here and prepared for this at the last minute? Not to mention, you don't know that Cap even has a team available."

"Don't fucking argue with me about this, Pappy. I'm fucking telling you that something's not right and I won't send her in there until I'm sure nothing's going to happen."

Lola stepped up between us and looked me in the eyes. "I'll do it. We're about the same size. I'll need a wig, but it should work. If they're going to attack, they'll already know when we're going to show up, so they won't wait."

"You're sure about this?"

She smirked at me. "Do I look like the type to back away from a challenge?"

"Alright. I'll get ahold of Cap and tell him what we need. Lola, get whatever you need so that you can pass as Mrs. Arnold."

Pappy didn't argue with me anymore as we prepared for our new plan. Cap sent Alec, Craig, and Florrie in as a secondary team. I was placing their team with Mrs. Arnold because there was no way in hell I was letting Lola go in place of Mrs. Arnold and not be there to protect her. We stayed up into the early hours of the morning planning out a new strategy. We weren't letting anyone in on our plan in case there was someone feeding information to her husband.

By the time we were ready to leave in the morning, my gut was churning, which meant that I was making the right decision. Lola and I rode in the first car while Hunter went ahead of us and got into position in case I was right and there was an attack staged. We successfully tricked the cop that was driving into thinking that Lola was Mrs. Arnold. The real Mrs. Arnold went with Craig, Florrie, and Alec in the second car, but they were taking a different route and weren't showing up at the courthouse until we gave them the all clear.

As we pulled up, everything looked good and I began to think that I had totally misjudged the whole situation. But as soon as we stepped out of the car, gunfire erupted around us, causing us to take cover back inside the car.

"Drive!" I yelled to the cop in the front seat, but he didn't respond. It was then I saw the bullet hole through the windshield and his head lolling to the side. The back doors were flung open on both sides and Lola was dragged out along with me. I could see Lola struggling, fighting back as best she could, but the man held a knife to her throat and she was on the verge of losing touch with reality. Her eyes were distant and she was shaking in fear, something I thought would never happen to Lola.

Wrenching the arm from around my neck, I flung him into the car, pulling my gun and unloading a few shots into him. I held my gun on the man holding Lola and shook my head. "She's not who you're looking for," I said. The man looked at me in confusion, but then sirens were closing in on us as cops came flying down the alley, surrounding us within seconds. The cops cuffed the man holding Lola and I rushed to her side as she practically collapsed to the ground. I held her as she cried and blocked everyone from seeing her, knowing she would hate herself if she thought someone saw her break down.

I looked around the alley, noting that there were three other men that were lying on the ground dead. Hunter was rushing over to us with his weapon at his side. The cops pulled their guns on him and he dropped his gun instantly, concern showing brightly in his eyes as he stared at Lola in my arms. I closed my eyes as Lola shook in my arms and fought for control of my anger. I couldn't believe this was happening again. We had walked into an ambush and this time, Lola was the one paying the price. I couldn't lose it right now. Lola needed me to be strong for her. I swallowed down my emotions and when I opened my eyes, I saw the cops were letting Hunter through. He walked over, almost as if it was painful to do so, and knelt down in front of Lola.

"Lola, hey sweetie. Look at me," Hunter said.

Lola slowly raised her head and looked at Hunter. Tears slipped down her cheeks and Hunter held out his arms for her. She didn't hesitate going to him and wrapping herself around him. It was clear that whatever they had between them was a hell of a lot more than just fucking. He carried her to a police car that was waiting nearby and slid in the backseat, saying something to the cop. He looked back at me in question and I held up a hand, letting him know that I would take care of things from here. After I dealt with the cops, I was going to have to call Cap and let him know what had happened. I would also have to talk with him about Lola. It was clear to me that she needed more help than her team could give her, and after all this time, she needed to take some time to deal with her demons.

✮✮✮✮✮

"Mrs. Arnold testified yesterday without further incident and she's been released from police protection now that her husband is in prison," I finished telling Cap as we all sat in his office for our debriefing.

"Thank fuck that's over," Cap said, throwing his pen on his desk. "Alright, you guys will have a week off. Then we'll reassess where we're at. Lola, I don't want to put you on the spot, but I need to know where your head is at and I need to know what your team thinks."

"I'm fine," Lola said shortly.

"All due respect, but what happened out there suggests otherwise."

Lola's face flared with anger and a little embarrassment. "All due respect, but if you don't trust me out there, you should be talking to me about this in private."

Cap glanced at me and then Pappy. Leaning forward in his seat, he rested his elbows on his desk. "Lola, I don't know when you're going to get that you're not in this alone. Your team cares about you. Hell, everyone at Reed Security cares about you and none of us like seeing what's happening to you. What happened to you was..." Cap shook his head. "It would have fucked up any of us. It's been years and you still haven't done anything. Now, as long as you were dealing with it, I let you get away with going it alone, but what happened on the job could have turned out a lot differently, and no one blames you for that. But it can't happen again. You need to get help and until then, you're out of the field. You can still show up to work and train, but you won't be working with your team again until I know that you're fine."

"Will that be all?" Lola said defiantly.

"That's all. We'll see you in a week," Cap said with a nod.

We all got up and walked out the door, but as soon as the office door shut, Lola spun around and slammed me up against the wall. "You should have had my back in there. You're my fucking team leader and you just let him walk all over me," she sneered.

Lola was hurting and I didn't want to push her right now, so I spoke calmly. "Lola, we all know that you've been dealing with this shit for a long time. You need help. No one thinks that you're not capable, but the Lola that I saw outside the courthouse was scared and couldn't defend herself. What would you have done if Hunter and I weren't there?"

"One time. One time in all these years and you suddenly think I can't handle myself?" She stepped back from me, chest heaving and turned on Hunter. "And where were you? You couldn't stand up for me either?"

"Lola, you forget that I've seen you at your worst many times. You can't convince me you're fine. You need help, sweetie."

A look of hurt crossed her face and she stepped back further from us. "That was between us," she said almost brokenly. "What happened between us was never supposed to be talked about." She looked up at him defiantly, like she was fighting for her life. "Did you tell Cap? Did you tell him about all the times that you had to hold me when we were on a job and I panicked in the middle of the night? Did you tell him about all the times that I was too fucking scared to stay in my room at night by myself?"

Fuck. I had to really hold back to keep from fucking ripping Hunter's throat out right now. If he knew all this time how bad it was, he should have fucking told me. Now I was seeing for the first time how truly bad off Lola was and I knew that I should have said or done something earlier.

"I didn't say anything to anyone. I told you then and it still stands. Anytime you need me, I'm there. You don't have to put up a good front for me. I know the shit you went through fucked with your head and I'll always be on your side. But part of being on your side is knowing when I can't be the only one that's fighting to help you. You need to fight for yourself now."

"I don't need your help. You all think you know what I need, but what I need is to keep working and you just had me sidelined."

"Only until you get help, Lola. You could be back in the field in no time."

"Right," she snorted. "Because a shrink will look at me and clear me just like that."

"Lola-" Hunter stepped toward her, but Lola held up her hand and shook her head.

"Don't," she whispered. "I don't need you anymore."

She turned around and walked quickly to the elevator, leaving Hunter and I staring after her.

"Do you want to tell me why all this is just coming out now?"

Hunter turned to me, anger humming through his body. "Don't pretend you didn't know. You heard her screams when we were out on jobs. I was just the only one that went to make sure she was okay." He stormed off and for the first time in a while, I wondered how the hell I became a team leader.

Chapter Eleven

CLAIRE

hen I saw Derek walk into the library right before I was about to close up, I almost ignored him. He had been absent for almost a week without a goodbye or any explanation of what was going on. I had texted him, but he only responded with saying, *on a job.* On a job. Like that was any kind of freaking answer. Where was he? Was he in danger? Would he be gone long? All of these I thought were reasonable questions, but when he didn't even bother to elaborate further, I decided that I would wait to hear from him and then give him a piece of my mind.

Except here he was and he looked like someone had kicked his puppy. No, it was worse than that. He looked like someone had run over his puppy and then pulled out a gun and shot the puppy in front of him. He looked like he hadn't slept in a while and his shoulders slumped like he carried the weight of the world. Putting aside my anger, I walked out from behind the counter and met him halfway through the library.

"Hey, is everything okay?"

He huffed out a big sigh and pulled me into his large frame, practically squeezing me to him. I was scared now. Something bad must have happened to make him respond this way. Derek was a strong man and nothing ever really got him down, but whatever was going on with him was obviously too much to deal with at the moment.

"I fucked up," he whispered in my ear. "I finally followed my instincts and I was right, but everything went to shit after that. My team..." I felt his throat working hard to get the words out, so I just gave him his time and held on tight. "I think my team is falling apart and I don't know how to fix it."

"Is everyone okay?"

"Physically? Yes. Everything else is fucked up though."

"Do you want to talk about it?"

He didn't say anything and so I held him for a few more minutes until he pulled back and gave me a small grin. "Are you done for the night?"

"Yeah, I was just about to close up."

"Stay with me tonight?"

I really needed to be at home tonight. Lucy had wanted to go out and one of us was staying with Dad at all times, but I could tell that Derek needed me more right now. "Sure, just let me get my stuff."

I finished closing up, grabbed my things, and followed Derek outside. I followed him to his house, calling Lucy on the way and explaining that I needed to stay with Derek. He wrapped me in his arms as soon as we entered his house. When he carried me upstairs and gently laid me down on the bed, I pulled off my shirt and reached forward for his belt, but he put his hand over mine to stop me.

"Not tonight. I just need to hold you. Can we just..." He looked away, as if I would think he was weak for not wanting sex tonight. I pulled him down next to me, but he turned on his stomach and laid his head on my chest.

"What happened?" I asked softly.

"We were on this job a few years back and it went sideways really fast. Long story short, Lola was in the hands of a serial killer, about to be scalped."

"That's what the scar on her forehead is?"

"Yeah. Hunter was unconscious outside after having his head bashed in and I was unconscious with a gunshot wound. It didn't get as bad as it could have, but psychologically, it totally fucked with her head." His hand left small circles over my hip and he took in deep breaths. "I think I really fucked up. I saw that it was messing with her head and I didn't push her to get help the way I should have."

"You can't make someone get help, Derek. They have to want it."

"There were steps I could have taken though. As her team leader, it's my responsibility to make sure everyone on the team is at their best. It didn't seem to be affecting her job performance, so I let it slide. Then this week...I should have done something sooner. This job could have gone a lot differently."

I didn't know what to say to him, so I ran my fingers through his hair, hoping it would soothe him. It must have, because within minutes, he was sound asleep, his soft breaths puffing across my skin. I laid awake for a long time that night wondering how I could help him, but I really didn't have a clue. I didn't know exactly what was going on and I thought he must have been holding back out of respect for Lola. Besides, I didn't know anything about what it was like to be in a high pressure work environment. What sage advice could I give him? I drifted off sometime late that night with Derek still lying on top of me.

"Crap," I murmured as the lights went out in the library. That was the fifth time this year. Whatever was going on with this building, someone needed to fix it before someone got hurt. Luckily, there was no one in the library, so I made my way to my office and found the fuse box behind all the crap stacked up against the wall. I needed to find another place for it so that when this happened, I didn't have to go digging around. Better yet, I needed to get some glow in the dark stickies to place around the fuse box so I had a direct line to it.

Opening the box, I checked the switches, but they were all flipped. That was weird. I flipped them all off and back on again, just to see what would happen, but the building remained dark. The sound of a door creaking had me spinning around in fear. My heart pounded as I searched the darkness for the mysterious noise, but I couldn't find anything.

"Let's find that goody two shoes and get out of here," I heard a man whisper. I dropped to the ground and scurried against a nearby file cabinet.

"Just remember what Leto said. We don't hurt her. We need whatever information she's holding out on us," another voice said.

"Sure. I'll keep that in mind, but if she doesn't cooperate, I have no problem using more creative ways to get the information from her," the first voice said.

"You aren't going to tickle it out of her," the second voice said. I reared back in confusion. "You're so weird. That's not a real form of torture."

Tickling or not, that wasn't happening. When no one appeared in the office doorway, I crawled out of the office and over to the aisle that was closest to the front door, but a hand on my shoulder had me stopping in my tracks. Another hand was placed over my mouth and I jolted from the familiar touch.

"Don't scream," Derek whispered in my ear. "I'll get you out of here. You just have to do as I say. Nod if you understand."

I nodded and slowly turned to see his handsome face staring down at me. He grinned that devilish grin and held out his hand for me, which I immediately took. Pulling me to my feet, he kissed me hard and I would have gone boneless if it weren't for the urgency in his voice. "We have to keep moving. These men were serious. They'll tickle the information out of you."

He pulled me down another aisle as I wondered why Derek was worried about two men tickling me when he was a badass warrior, most likely a superhero. He could handle two men like that. We made our way over to the old marble stairs that led to the second floor and quickly made our way further away from the intruders.

"We have to get away from them. They can never know that you have one of the Horcruxes."

Horcruxes? What's he talking about? "Derek-"

He silenced me with a finger to my lips. "Not now. Right now we have to focus on getting out of here alive."

"But Derek-"

"Please, Claire. You have to trust me. I don't have a lot of faith in myself at the moment, but I need for you to trust in me now. I'd never let anything happen to you."

I nodded in understanding. After everything he'd been through, he needed this from me. I followed him over to the rooftop access and took a deep gulp as he flung open the door and ushered me onto the roof. He searched the side of the building until he found the fire escape ladder.

"Quickly, Claire. Start climbing down. I'm right behind you." I looked over the side of the building and shook off my fear. I was with Derek. This would be fine. Before I could step over, Derek jerked me to him and pulled me in for an earth shattering kiss that had me going weak in the knees. When he pulled back, I felt dizzy with lust.

"Go. Now," he ordered.

"You want me to go now? Now that you just gave me one of the most spellbinding kisses of all time?"

"Claire, now's not the time for this. We have to get out of here before the Nazgûl find us."

"Nazgûl?"

"Yes, Claire. Ringwraiths," he answered gravely.

I swallowed hard and stepped over the edge of the building, doing my best not to look at the concrete slab below us, and placed my foot on the first rung. Slowly, I started making my way down the ladder, but just a few feet down, the rung broke off and I slipped, flailing as I fell. I jerked to a stop in mid-air and looked up to see Derek holding onto my arm, smiling his charming smile.

"I told you I'd never let anything happen to you." He pulled me back up to the rooftop as if I weighed nothing and pulled me back into his arms. It felt safe in his arms and I never wanted to leave, but I knew we had to keep moving. He didn't need me breaking down on him right now. I stepped out of his arms and gave a slight nod.

"I'm ready."

"Claire, I'm going to throw you, but don't worry. I'll be there to catch you."

I looked over the edge of the building again at the concrete below. If he didn't catch me, we wouldn't have to worry about the Nazgûl getting their hands on me.

Turning back to him, I took his hand in mine. "I trust you, Derek."

He picked me up by the waist and tossed me over the building. I closed my eyes as the wind rushed by me in a flurry. I felt his love burning through me and knew that everything would be fine. Derek would never let me die. He would always be there to protect me. When I landed in a soft blanket of arms, I opened my eyes to see Derek smiling back at me. A red cape danced on the breeze behind him and a large S was emblazoned on his chest.

"I told you I'd catch you. I always will."

"My hero. My Superman."

Wetness licked at my pussy and I tried to clench my legs together, but something was prying them apart. Looking down, I saw Derek between my legs and I was lying on my bed. How did he get me here so fast? Of course, he was Superman. He could fly. I laid my head back down and relaxed into the bliss of him pleasuring me when I realized that it was early morning, but it had just been night time. I sat up, jerking my body from Derek's grasp and looked at him in confusion.

"What's going on?"

"Uh, if I have to explain that then I'm not doing this right."

"No, I mean. You-Superman..."

"Yeah, I heard you calling me that in your sleep. I'm not gonna lie. You can call me Superman anytime you want."

"No, I mean...well," I grunted in frustration. I couldn't seem to get my thoughts out. "What happened to the Nazgûl?"

"The what?" he asked as if we hadn't just talked about this or escaped their clutches.

"The ringwraiths," I said in frustration. "You know, they were chasing us for the..horcruxes."

Now that I said that, I heard how ridiculous it sounded, and apparently Derek thought the same thing as he raised an eyebrow at me. "Of course, that was two different books. That's why it didn't make sense," I muttered to myself.

"Yeah, that's why it doesn't make sense."

I snapped my eyes up to his and gave him my best bitch face, which was probably more like a smiling kitty. "Don't make fun of me. It felt so real."

"I'm sure it did. Now, can I get back to being Superman or would you like to go back to your fantasy world?"

"Hey, my fantasy world is pretty spectacular."

"I'm sure it is, but if you'd rather be there than here, maybe I should leave the two of you alone."

"No, no. It's fine. Really. I'm just having trouble waking up fully this morning."

He climbed over me and started kissing my neck and digging his erection into me. I wanted to be into it. I needed him so badly, but my mind was still replaying my dream and I couldn't focus. When he sighed and pulled back from me, I knew that he knew. It wasn't going to happen this morning.

"I'm sorry, Derek. I just can't focus."

"The whole point is that you're not supposed to focus."

"I know that, but my mind is somewhere else and it's just not going to happen."

He rolled off the bed and pretended to be hurt, but I saw him grinning at me. "It's fine, Claire. Go play with your imaginary characters."

"Stop. Don't be a jerk. I can't make my mind shut off like that. Haven't you ever gotten lost in a really good book?"

"It sounds to me like you're lost in more than one good book."

I shrugged. "Side effect of being a librarian. Besides, I don't really have time to hang around this morning. I have so much work to get done on the farm and no time to do it."

"What do you have to do?"

"Aside from the normal chores? There's a fence that's broken. The shed door is falling off its hinges. The chicken coop needs to be cleaned. I have vegetables that need to be picked for the market. Lucy has an early class this morning, so I have to do her egg run. The list is much longer, but that's the stuff that really needs to be done this morning."

"I won't keep you then, but I expect you to make it up to me in a very big way."

"I promise."

"Hey, how did things go with your dad last weekend?"

I got up and started getting dressed, not really wanting to talk about my dad, but knowing that I would have to tell Derek at some point. "Uh, he found a retirement home that he really likes. It's similar to a nursing home, but has a little more freedom for residents. They'll provide all his meals and everything, but he'll have his own little apartment. It's not much, but he said he would rather be there than..." I took a deep breath as I choked back my tears. Strong arms wrapped around me from behind and ran up and down my arms. I focused on anything from his skin tone to the thick, dark hair that covered his arms. He rested his head on top of mine as I calmed myself. He made it feel like it was okay to break down, like he would always be there to put me back together.

"Is there anything you need?" he asked.

"The one thing I need is for this to not be happening."

"I'm sorry, Claire. I wish I could change this for you."

"I know."

"It's just too much right now. I feel like everything's breaking down. I don't know what to do with the farm when dad leaves."

"Did he tell you what he wanted?"

"He said it was up to Lucy and me. He wanted us to do whatever we felt was right. He already had lawyers draw up the paperwork to make us his legal guardians. We're now in charge of everything regarding the farm and his care."

"He's making the right call, Claire. He needs to know that you have access to everything you need and that you have control of the situation."

"I know, but Lucy wants to sell off the farm. She doesn't want to deal with it anymore. She's going to be teaching next year and she doesn't want to have two jobs anymore. That would leave it all up to me."

Derek turned me around to face him and looked into my eyes. "What do you want?"

"I don't know. I don't want to let go of the farm. It feels like I'm letting go of my dad, but I'm not sure I can keep it all up. It's exhausting."

"Take some time to think it over. Whatever you decide, you have to make the decision for you and no one else. Your dad will understand if you want to let the farm go. I've actually been thinking, now that your dad is moving out, what would you think about moving in with me?"

My mouth dropped open and I couldn't speak. I hadn't been expecting that. All this time, I just assumed that this was something great, but that it would eventually end. Moving in together was so life altering. It wasn't a decision I could easily come to.

"I don't know what to say."

"Just say whatever you're thinking."

"Um, I guess that I wasn't really thinking that we were headed in that direction. Don't get me wrong, I love you," *Oh shit! Don't say that. Don't ruin this by telling him you love him. What the heck are you thinking? Quick. Fix it. Say something, anything to make that not sound how it really did.* "Well, not love, but really, really like. Like, like-like. A lot. Not to say that you're not lovable. I just don't want to freak you out with some love declaration when that's not what we are. I mean, I'm not the person that...I'm not the girl that gets the super sexy guy. I'm the girl that you have fun with and everything, but..." I swallowed hard and puffed out my cheeks to stop from rambling anymore. Derek just smirked at me and pulled me in close for a hug.

"Are you finished?" I nodded against his chest. "I love you, too, Claire. And I wouldn't have asked you to move in unless I thought you were the girl that got the super sexy guy. When are you going to realize that you are fucking gorgeous and you're the only woman I want in or out of my bed?"

"You love me?"

He pulled back and kissed me on the lips. "Silly woman, of course I love you. So, what do you think? Are you going to move in with me?"

"Can I think about it? It's not that I don't want to, but I need some time with everything that's going on."

"You can think about it all you want, but in the end, you will end up in my bed. You know how I know that?" I shook my head. "Because I fucking love you and there's no way this ends any differently."

He kissed me hard and I could feel his erection poking me in the stomach, but I didn't have time for more than a kiss if I was going to get all my stuff done this morning. Not to mention that I really did need to think about everything he said and I couldn't think straight with him inside me. I stumbled back out of his grasp and gave a shaky smile.

"I'd better get going. I have a lot to do this morning."

I left his house feeling a lot lighter about everything. No matter what I decided with my dad, I had options and for the first time in my life, I didn't feel so alone.

𝒲hen I pulled up to the house, it was still early. I got changed quickly and said a quick hello to Daddy. He was just sitting down to his first cup of coffee.

"Is Lucy still sleeping?"

"She's in the shower," he said as he opened the morning paper. He still insisted on having it delivered, even though most news could easily be found online.

"Okay, well I'm going to get started on some chores. Tell her I've got her deliveries today."

"No problem, Claire bear."

I headed out to the chicken coop and got to the task of collecting all the eggs from the coop. Then I started cleaning it out and laying down the new shavings. Once that was all done, I fed and watered the chickens. It was still early morning, but I was already sweating like crazy. I had several more things to do before I delivered the eggs, but I really needed a drink of water. Turning to the house, my heart stopped when I saw smoke coming from the direction of the house.

I ran as fast as my short legs would carry me and practically fell to my knees when I saw flames licking through the windows of the house. I looked around frantically, but couldn't see my dad or Lucy anywhere. My phone was still inside on the charger, so I had no way to call for help. Without a second thought, I ran inside to find my father and Lucy.

Chapter Twelve

DEREK

s soon as Claire left, I called Cap. There was no way I was going to let Claire work herself up over all the things she had to do around the farm today. I was going to take a personal day and if he didn't like it, he could shove it.

"We don't have anything going on anyway. In fact, how about a few of us come out and help?"

"Seriously?"

"Yeah," Cap laughed into the phone. "We'll head out there now. The guys'll be happy to have something different to do today."

"That'd be great. Thanks, Cap. I really appreciate it and so will Claire."

"No problem. We'll see you in a few."

Since I was going to be working on a farm today, I just threw on some clothes, not bothering to shower first. It was going to be a hot one, so there was no point in showering first. Heading to my truck, I threw a spare pair of clothes inside and headed for her house, stopping for coffee and donuts for everyone on the way. I was just outside of town when I saw traces of smoke filling the sky. Dread curled in my gut and I stepped on the gas, pulling up Cap's number on my phone as I sped toward Claire's house.

"Yo, we're on our way now."

"Cap, where the fuck are you? Do you see the smoke heading out of town?"

"Shit. Is that where she lives?"

"I'm still too far away. I don't know if it's her house, but it's pretty damn close."

"I'm calling the fire department now."

He hung up and I pushed it as hard as I could, desperate to get to her, needing to know for certain that she was okay. My tires spun in the gravel as I pulled down her driveway. Her house was engulfed in flames and I prayed that no one was inside. Jumping out of the truck and running to the house, I saw her father kneeling on the ground, bent over and coughing.

"Harry, where are Claire and Lucy?"

A coughing fit overtook him and he pointed inside. Running in the back door, I pulled my shirt up over my face and squinted through the smoke, trying to see if there was anyone in the room. I dropped to the floor and crawled as quickly as I could through the house. When I didn't immediately see anyone on the first floor, I made my way up the stairs to the second floor. I heard banging and quickly ran down the hall, to where Claire was gagging and hitting a door.

Pulling on her arm, I tried to get her to come with me, but she wouldn't leave. She shook her head rapidly, but after a strangled cough, she collapsed right in my arms. I knew that Lucy had to be behind the door and I prayed that the smoke wasn't as bad in her room. Claire would never forgive me if I let her sister die in a fire. I set Claire down on the floor and whipped off my shirt, wrapping it around her face to keep the smoke out of her airways as much as possible.

"Derek!" I spun around to see Pappy running toward me. "You have to find another way out. The downstairs is blocked now."

"Lucy's stuck in that room," I choked out as I pointed to the door Claire had been banging on. Pappy ran over to the door and gave a swift boot to the door, but it didn't budge. I picked up Claire, knowing that I had to get her out of there. She stirred in my arms and lifted her head, looking toward the door. I glanced in the same direction and saw Pappy lift his boot one more time and break the door in, disappearing inside. I pushed a door open on the opposite side of the hall and ran for the window. The window had swelled shut and I couldn't get it open. Setting down Claire, I picked up a small table and broke the glass out on the window. I picked up a comforter from the bed and cleared the glass away, laying the comforter over the ledge of the window.

I stuck my head out the window, breathing in the fresh air. If I passed out, I wouldn't do Claire any good. Cap and Sinner saw me and ran over to the ledge of the porch, waving for me to crawl out the window. Hauling Claire through the window, I crawled out on the porch roof to the edge where Cap and Sinner were waiting below. A coughing fit overtook me and I held tight to Claire, sure that I would drop her if I didn't get control of myself.

"Derek, drop her down," Cap yelled. I looked down one last time and held Claire out over the edge of the roof and let her go. Cap caught her easily and ran over to the ambulance that I saw waiting in the driveway. I turned back to the window that had smoke pouring out of it and covered my mouth with the crook of my arm. Running back to the bedroom door, I saw Pappy carrying Lucy out of the other bedroom and waved him over. I ran back for the window and crawled out, holding out my arms to get Lucy. When I had her securely in my arms, I moved over to the ledge like I had with Claire and dropped her down into Sinner's arms. By now, there was a second ambulance waiting in the driveway and Sinner ran with Lucy over to it just as the first ambulance was pulling away.

Hunter and I slid on our bellies over the edge of the porch, hanging on to the edge and then dropping to our feet. We just barely made it away from the house as flames took over the porch roof. If we had been just a minute later, Claire and Lucy wouldn't have made it out.

"You okay, man?" I asked as Hunter and I walked over to where everyone was gathered around the ambulance. The firemen were already working on putting out the flames, but the house would be a complete loss.

"Yeah," he nodded, coughing as he started jogging over to the ambulance. Burg and Lola ran up to us, keys in hand.

"Let's go," Burg said. "We need to get you guys checked out."

Lola drove me in my truck and Burg drove Pappy in one of the others. I was coughing the whole ride and felt like I was struggling to breathe, but what I really needed was to know that Claire was okay. My heart was racing out of control and it had nothing to do with the fact that I had just come out of a burning house. When we pulled up to the emergency room, I immediately ran to the desk to ask for Claire.

"Claire," I coughed more harshly this time, my lungs working overtime to get me some air. "Claire Grant. Fire," I choked out.

The nurse looked at me worriedly and ran around the counter, pulling on my arm. "Come on. Let's get you in a bed. You need a doctor to look you over."

"I need-"

"What you need is a mask on your face before you pass out. You were in that fire?" I nodded, still coughing and unable to speak. "Right. Well, I'll check on Ms. Grant for you." She shoved me down onto a bed and placed a mask over my face. "Now, if you promise to keep this on your face, I'll find out how she's doing, okay?" I nodded again and she gave me a little wink. "Good. I need someone to come over and check you out, so hang tight."

I let my eyes slide closed and let the oxygen do it's work, but it was short lived when I heard Pappy's voice coming from the ER desk.

"No! I don't need to be checked out," I heard Pappy yelling as he coughed harshly. "You need to tell me what the fuck is going on with Lucy Grant. I pulled her out of..." He started coughing again and I got up from the bed that I was currently sitting on with an oxygen mask on my face. I pulled the mask off and yanked the curtain open.

"Pappy, calm the fuck down. They have to get her stable. Sit your ass down and get some fucking air." I started coughing again and a nurse smiled gratefully at me as she ushered me back to my bed and replaced the mask. I was just as desperate to find out about Claire, but I also knew that they were doing everything they could for Claire and Lucy and we would only be in the way.

Hours passes as I slipped in and out of sleep. My body was exhausted and was begging for me to just pass out. The doctor came by and examined both Pappy and I and cleared us. We needed to stay for a few more hours, but the doctor said they would release us that night. The nurse came in and let us know that Claire and Lucy were doing okay and that they needed to stay overnight until they were cleared. If I could stay the fuck awake, I would have been bugging the nurse every five minutes for an update. Pappy wasn't quite as bad as me since he hadn't been inside as long, so he came to hang out beside me, promising the nurses that he would stay where he was.

"How can you just lay in that fucking bed when we don't know what the fuck is going on with them?" Pappy asked as he ran a hand over his bald head.

"We're in a fucking hospital. They're doing everything they can for them, so you just have to be patient."

"I thought you loved Claire. Why aren't you more worried?"

"I am fucking worried, but I'm also fucking tired as hell, seeing as how we were in a fucking fire."

Pappy stood up and started pacing in the small space around my bed, pushing the curtain out with his large frame. Every once in a while, he let out a small cough and then ran a hand over his face. Tension ran through his body and I couldn't figure out why he was so worried. I knew that he slept with Lucy occasionally, but as far as I knew, that's all it was. Maybe I was wrong.

"Is there something you're not telling me?" I asked as he continued to pace.

"Like what?"

"Like why you're so worked up over a girl you're just fucking. Are you *not* just fucking?"

He stopped and stared at me. "Why the fuck would you ask that? You know I don't do relationships."

"Yeah, I know, but you're acting like the love of your life is dying in the next room. We know they're going to be okay, so why are you freaking out so much?"

He plopped down in the chair and hung his head as if he was fighting some internal battle. "You remember what it was like when we thought Knight was dead. I don't ever want to feel that way again. And Lucy, I don't know what the hell we are. Fuck, this is so messed up," he murmured to himself.

I got that he was messed up because of what had happened with Knight, but I also didn't miss how he had just admitted that he and Lucy might be something more.

"You have a thing for Lucy," I said with a grin.

He looked up at me and scowled. "It's not like."

"Oh, that's right. You and Lola have a thing." He shook his head and stood up, resuming his pacing. "How does that work exactly? Do you ask Lola before you fuck Lucy?"

"You've got it all fucking wrong, man."

"Right. Because you're making this so clear."

"Look, Lola and I, we just...I was just there for her when she needed an outlet, but we haven't been together in a long time. It was never more than that with us."

"Are you sure she knows that?"

"Who do you think made the rules?" he asked.

I didn't argue that point because if there was one thing I knew about Lola, it was that she always set her own boundaries. If she wanted more with Pappy, chances were that ship had already sailed. Based on how he was reacting to Lucy being in the hospital, he was already in deeper than he even knew.

"So, tell me something. Did you ever call out Lola's name when you were fucking Lucy?" He flipped me off and scowled. "What? I'm just saying, their names are very close. Lucy, Lola. It could be easily confused."

"Fuck you."

"Does Lola know you're seeing Lucy?"

"I'm not fucking seeing her. We fuck. That's it."

"Uh-huh and now you're pacing my little curtained off area of the hospital, worrying your pretty little head off over a woman you're just fucking," I said smugly.

"Fuck," he said as he sat down. "What the fuck am I going to do? Do you think I should stop seeing her? Will that make it go away?"

I laughed and then started coughing again. "It's not the fucking plague, Pappy. You know, having feelings for a woman isn't the end of the world, contrary to what you've believed all these years."

"I didn't say I had feelings for her. Don't go spouting all that love crap to me. I don't do love. I don't do relationships. And I sure as fuck don't ever want to be in the position where I can't get a woman out of my head."

"Like right now," I smiled.

"Exactly," he said.

"Exactly," I agreed. He stopped and looked at me, only then realizing that he had just admitted that he couldn't get Lucy out of his head.

"Fuck you," he said as he threw back the curtain and stormed out toward the lobby. I burst out laughing, but quickly put my mask back over my face as another coughing fit came on. Still, I couldn't stop laughing as I thought about Pappy falling for a woman.

*W*hen the doctor finally said I was good to go home, I asked to be directed to Claire's room and only then remembered that her father had been pulled from that fire also. He hadn't taken in nearly as much smoke, but they were keeping him overnight because of his age. I wanted to check on Claire, but I also knew that she would be worried about her dad. I walked down to his room and stood in the doorway. He was lying in bed, staring out the window. I knocked and walked in, but he just stared at me. I thought for a minute that he didn't recognize me, but then he motioned for me to sit down.

"How are you?" I asked him as I took a seat.

"Fine. They just wanted to keep me overnight to be sure. How are Claire and Lucy?"

"They'll be okay. I was going to go check on them, but I know Claire will want to know how you are, so I stopped here first."

"Thank you for pulling them out of the fire." He shook his head and sighed. "I asked them to transfer me right to the retirement home. I already talked to the director over there and they have temporary housing for me until my apartment is available."

"You could stay with me. I have the space."

"I started that fire," he said dejectedly. "I got confused and I didn't remember that I had started making breakfast for the girls. It happened so fast and I couldn't even get them out. Claire pulled me out and then went back for Lucy."

I had wondered how the fire started, but now that I knew that he had started the fire, I wholeheartedly agreed with him. He was in no condition to be left alone anymore. Still, I felt bad for him. He was obviously taking it pretty hard that he had endangered his kids.

"You know I'll take care of both of them. I don't want you to worry about that."

"I know you will. Now, go check on my girls and make sure they're okay for me."

I nodded and stood, making my way to the door. "It's not your fault," I said as I turned back to him. "You didn't purposely start that fire. It could have happened to anyone. Lucy and Claire won't blame you."

"I blame me," he said as he rolled away from me.

I went in search of Claire's room and felt a huge weight lifted when I finally saw her with my own eyes. She was sleeping peacefully in her bed with one of those oxygen things under her nose. I sat down next to her and held her hand, finally feeling the enormity of what had happened today. If I hadn't shown up when I did, would she have left the house when she couldn't get to Lucy? Most likely not. She would have died in that fire and I would have lost my fucking mind. I never thought I wanted any kind of relationship with a woman before Claire. But Claire pulled me in right from the start and I'd been powerless to stop it ever since.

"Are you Superman?" she whispered from the bed.

I smirked at her when I looked up and saw her eyes looking dazed. That wasn't the first time that she had said something like that to me. It was fucking cute that she thought I was that badass. She wasn't like other women that saw only that part of me. She saw right through my outer shell and took care of the man inside. That was the dream, to have a woman love even the worst parts of you. Since we hadn't actually discussed our future beyond saying 'I love you', I wasn't completely sure that she wanted the same things as me, but I was willing to put it all on the line to have her.

"Not Superman, sweetheart. Just a man that would do anything for the woman he loves."

Her eyes drifted shut as a small smile touched her lips. I sat with her for a few more minutes, but since she was out, I wanted to go check on Lucy. I found out her room number and wasn't at all shocked to see Hunter standing in her room when I got there. The tension in the room was palpable and Hunter and Lucy were glaring at one another.

"Did I come at a bad time?"

"You can tell your friend he can leave. I don't need him coming in here and making demands," Lucy said angrily. She looked pretty good. Other than a cough here and there, she didn't look nearly as bad as Claire.

"Okay, let's skip that for a minute. How are you?"

"I'm fine. The door cut off a lot of the smoke and I put a towel under the door to block it from coming in. I certainly don't need some alpha male coming in here and telling me where I'll be staying."

I quirked an eyebrow at Hunter, but he was just staring at Lucy with his arms crossed over his chest.

"You don't have any place to go. Your fucking house burned down."

"She can stay with me," I said, hoping to appease them both.

"She's not staying with anyone but me. If you want Claire to stay with you, go for it, but Lucy will be staying with me where I can keep an eye on her."

"I don't need anyone to keep an eye on me. I'm an adult and I can take care of myself."

"You were stuck in a burning house and couldn't get out. I wouldn't say that's taking care of yourself," Hunter snapped.

"I was in the shower when the fire started. It's not like I knew there was a fire and didn't know whether or not I should leave the burning house. I didn't know the house was on fire," she shouted and then broke into a coughing fit. Hunter rushed over to place an oxygen mask over her face. She grabbed it out of his hands and glared at him.

"I can do it myself."

"Stop fucking talking and put it over your face."

I had to really hold back from laughing. I had never seen Hunter so possessive over a woman, but it was like something inside him snapped when he found out Lucy was in that building.

"Lucy, do you want to stay with me or Hunter?"

She started to remove the mask, but Hunter stopped her. "She's staying with me and that's final."

Lucy tried to pull the mask away again, but Hunter snapped his gaze to her again, giving her a look that promised death if she dared argue with him. I held up my hands and started backing away toward the door.

"Obviously, I've interrupted something here. I'll let you two work this out. Let me know what the plan is before I leave in the morning with Claire." I turned for the door, but then thought better of it. "Hunter." He turned to me finally and raised an eyebrow. "Welcome to the club," I said with a grin. He stepped toward me like he was going to beat my ass, so I hustled out the door.

Claire had been pretty out of it the rest of the night, but by the morning, she was awake and looking much better. She still had a little bit of a cough and a pretty bad headache, but the doctor said that was normal.

"You're sure that Lucy is fine?" she asked, still worried about her sister even though I had already told her at least ten times that she was fine.

"I'm sure. Hunter is taking her home with him and he'll watch over her."

"Why is she going home with him? Can't she stay with me?"

"I offered, but Hunter was pretty adamant that she stay with him."

"I don't understand. They don't have that kind of relationship."

"I think that's about to change."

"Why do you say that?"

"Nothing," I said, not wanting to speak too soon. I wasn't completely sure that Hunter wouldn't puss out and walk away.

"And you're sure my father is fine?"

"Yes, I went with him to the retirement home and made sure he was settled in okay. He was fine."

"Thank you for doing that."

"Don't you know by now that I'd do anything for you?"

"I'm beginning to see that," she smiled.

"Are you ready to go home?"

She nodded and I helped her out of bed, only then realizing that I hadn't thought of bringing her anything to change into. I scratched the back of my head, wondering what the hell I was going to do now.

"Let me guess, he didn't bring you any clothes." I turned to see Maggie standing in the doorway with a bag. She walked forward and held her hand out to Claire. "Hi, I'm Maggie, Sebastian's wife."

"Oh," Claire said hesitantly. "Um, it's nice to meet you."

Claire looked uncomfortable around Maggie and I didn't understand why until I remembered her first meeting with Sebastian. She had been holding out on handing over the key and he wasn't in the mood to fuck around. He had been kind of harsh with her and she hadn't really gotten to see another side to him. That would have changed yesterday when we were going to help around the farm, but that never happened.

"When he told me that you and your sister were in the hospital, I thought I should bring you and your sister some clothes and stuff to wash up. You can't rely on a man to remember that stuff. I just brought sweats and t-shirts. I figured that would be the most comfortable to go home in. Are you going home with Derek?"

"Uh..."

I hadn't told her that was the plan yet. It hadn't really come up.

"Yes," I answered for her.

"Don't let him walk all over you. All these men think that they can answer for us and tell us what to do. You have to put your foot down or that's the way it will be the rest of your life."

"Freckles, I think-"

"Since you don't really have anything, I'll go shopping and pick up some stuff for you and bring it over this afternoon. Maybe when you're feeling up to it we can go shopping for clothes. God knows I need some time away from my daughter."

"I can take her-"

"Then we can go for a massage. I'm sure that would feel great after everything."

It was like I wasn't even there. Maggie just continued to interrupt me any time I tried to talk. Claire just sat there in stunned silence.

"When do you have to be back to work?" Maggie asked.

"Um...I guess I need to find out. I hadn't really thought about it yet."

"She'll be taking at least a week off," I interrupted.

Maggie rolled her eyes and stared Claire down.

"I don't think I can take a week off and I think I'll be fine with just taking today to relax," Claire said.

"No. You were in a fire. You're going to be exhausted. You have no idea the toll that takes on your body," I argued.

"Sebastian was the same way with me. 'Maggie, it's not safe to do that'. 'Maggie, you need to take it easy'. 'Maggie, don't throw that grenade'."

"He actually said that to you?"

She shrugged. "Well, something similar on our wedding day. Sometimes, a girl's gotta do what a girl's gotta do. You know what I mean?"

"This may seem like a stupid question because I'm new to the group, but why were you throwing a grenade on your wedding day?" Claire asked, genuinely confused.

"Well, I'm a reporter and I was chasing down a lead and it just so happened that another security company was trying to protect someone that was involved in the same story."

"Wait, so you don't work for the security company?"

"Nope. I'm a freelance reporter. Well, I do work for the company sometimes, but it's usually helping with research."

"And your husband let you throw a grenade?" Claire asked stupidly.

"Well, not him, but Sinner."

"On your wedding day."

She nodded vigorously. "It was great. You should really try it sometime. Derek, I think you should take Claire to Reed Security to try out some toys. I bet it would be a real bonding experience for the two of you."

"I was thinking something more along the lines of taking her home to meet my family. You know, something normal," I said, slightly irritated.

"Normal is boring. Just hang with me, Claire. I know some girls that really know how to let loose and have some fun."

"I'm not sure that's a good idea," I muttered. The door opened and Sebastian walked in.

"Hey, how's it going?" he asked.

"Great," I said sarcastically. "Freckles here is trying to convince my girlfriend to go play with grenades and other fun toys at Reed Security."

"Umm, no. Maggie, you get a little too happy around grenades. Not to mention that you now think you're 'awesome' with a gun. I don't need someone accidentally getting shot."

"Ooh!" Maggie said excitedly. "We should get all the girls together and do the training course. It's so much fun and there are a lot more weapons to choose from since Knight took over."

"That would actually be great, besides the Knight part. I don't have that many friends and I'm a little awkward around people most of the time."

"You don't seem like you are."

"Well, you kind of came in and took over the conversation. Shit," she mumbled. "What I meant to say was that you talk a lot. I mean, you didn't stop talking enough for me to be nervous." She blew out a harsh breath. "I'm really sorry. Please don't hate me. That all came out wrong."

"It's okay. I got the gist. I dominated the conversation and it didn't give you a chance to be nervous. Totally get it."

"I'm going to take Claire home now so she can rest," I said, hoping Maggie would take the hint.

"How about this?" Maggie continued as if Cap and I weren't there. "You and I will go get Lucy and the three of us can go have a nice, relaxing day at the spa. After what you've been through, you deserve it. Sebastian can watch my daughter and Derek and Hunter can go get whatever you and Lucy need. You'll have to be specific, otherwise, you'll end up with all lingerie."

They walked out the door, leaving Cap and I standing in the room. "What the hell just happened?" I asked.

"My wife just took your girlfriend hostage," Cap muttered.

"That didn't really seem like Maggie. Since when does she go to the spa?"

Sebastian shook his head, eyebrows furrowed as he considered what I said. Then his eyes went wide. "Maggie has my keys."

"Yeah, so?"

"The keys to the Reed Security SUV. The back is loaded with weapons."

"Shit!"

We bolted for the door, hoping we could catch up to them in time to get the keys back before they decided to go blow something up for fun.

Chapter Thirteen

CLAIRE

$\mathcal{A}$fter getting Lucy her clothes, I had to sit down again. I was exhausted and as nice as a spa day sounded, I just wasn't up for it. I didn't have to say anything though. Hunter shook his head and gave a firm no when Maggie told him what we were doing.

"There's no fucking way either of them are going to the spa after what they just went through. Lucy's coming home with me and you're going home with Derek," he pointed at me. I just nodded. I didn't have the energy to argue with him.

"Excuse me, but I can answer for myself," Lucy sniped.

Hunter walked over to her and crowded her against the bed. "You just almost died in a fucking fire." He ran his hand over the side of her face and leaned in closer, lowering his voice. "Humor me."

I felt like an intruder in the incredibly intimate moment and turned away. Maggie huffed next to me and then Sebastian and Derek burst into the room, huffing after what seemed like an intense workout.

"Shit," Sebastian said as he bent over, breathing deep. "We thought we weren't going to catch you in time."

"Catch us before what?" I asked.

"Nothing," they both said quickly. Derek walked over to me and held out his hand.

"Come on. I'm going to take you home. You can go to the spa some other time with Maggie."

"Alright. Lucy, are you sure you don't want to come home with me?" I asked.

She looked at Hunter, but even I could see the pleading in his eyes. She shook her head and stood next to Hunter. "No, I'll go home with Hunter. I'll let you know what I'm going to do for a place to stay when I figure it out."

"I'll do the same."

We said our goodbyes and Derek and I walked down to his truck. I fell asleep on the way to his house and woke when he lifted me from the truck. I raised my head from his shoulder to protest him carrying me, but he shushed me.

"Just relax. I've got you."

I laid my head back against his shoulder and wrapped my arms around his neck. He carried me inside and back to his room, laying me down on the bed and covering me with a blanket. I had never felt so cherished until this moment. He laid down behind me and pulled me back into him, running his hand across my belly.

"I was so fucking scared when I pulled up to your house yesterday," He murmured against my ear. "I never thought that I would ever love someone the way I love you. I can't lose you."

I was so shocked by his statement that it took me a moment to respond. I rolled over and kissed him hard. "I love you, too. I'm sorry that I scared you. I just couldn't leave them in the house. I didn't have my phone on me to call for help, so I knew I couldn't wait."

I thought about what happened yesterday when he pulled me out of the fire. He had floated down from the roof with me. I remember looking up at him and then we were floating through the air. I couldn't deny it anymore. There were too many incidents in which the men of Reed Security seemed to have superpowers. I had to find out what was really going on if we were going to take this any further.

The problem was, I didn't know how to ask him. Anyone else would think I was crazy and Derek would just deny it. After all, it's not like he could really tell me without putting me in danger. At least, that's why I assumed he wasn't telling me.

"Derek, I need to talk to you about something and I need you to know that you can be honest with me."

"You know I will be. I would never lie to you."

"I know that, but this is different. This is something I know you don't want me to know, but there's really no point in denying it anymore."

He looked at me strangely, but nodded. I took a deep breath and decided to just go for it. "I know your secret." His brows furrowed, so I continued. "I know that you and other members of Reed Security have special..qualities."

"Well, yeah." I breathed a sigh of relief that he wasn't denying it. "In the military, I was a team leader. That's my strong suit. Sinner, Burg, and Cazzo were all special forces. They're pretty much trained in everything. Chance was a sniper. Hunter worked with explosives."

"Look, I told you that you don't have to lie to me. I already know."

"I'm not lying to you. I just told you...I don't understand what you're talking about."

"You do too!"

"No, Claire. You're going to have to be more specific. If that's not what you're talking about then you're going to have to spell it out for me."

"You, pushing me out of the way at the grocery store when no one was around. Knight, taking a bullet when he didn't have a bullet-proof vest on. You, going into a burning truck and coming out without a scratch on you." I was getting really worked up and my voice got louder and louder. "You floated off the roof with me when my house was on fire. I know. You're all super heroes!" I said in exasperation.

Derek stared at me for a minute and then burst out laughing. Anger flooded me. If there was one thing I didn't want, it was to be laughed at, especially by the man I loved. When I threw the covers off and stormed into the bathroom, he laughed even harder. I should have known this would be his reaction. I should have known that he would just make fun of me and pretend none of that stuff actually happened.

Why would I assume he would open up to me just because he said he loved me?

"Claire, come out, please," he said, still laughing.

"No. If I wanted to be laughed at, I would have told someone else. You were supposed to tell me the truth."

"Claire, I promise. No more laughing. Why don't you come out and we'll talk about this seriously?"

I wanted to believe him so badly, but I also knew how ridiculous this whole thing sounded. Part of me still thought I was going insane, but now that I had put it out there, it was time to find out once and for all. I opened the door and hesitantly looked up at Derek. He wasn't laughing anymore as he held out his hand to me. I took it and followed him over to the bed.

"Okay, Claire. You have my full attention. Do you want to tell me what made you think we all have superpowers?"

"Well, at the grocery store, when you pushed me out of the way, I looked around before you tackled me. There was no one there. You got to me so quickly." I shook my head and looked away from him. "Look, I know that alone doesn't sound like much, but that was the first time I suspected that there was someone out there that was more than what they seemed. I even went looking online for people with extraordinary abilities. There are plenty of known cases, so don't laugh at me like I'm being ridiculous."

"At the grocery store, I was following you out. I don't know why, but I did. I was behind you. That's why you didn't see me."

"What about Knight? I saw him get shot and the bullet just bounced off him."

"He was wearing a skinny vest. It's a new technology that we've been trying out. It's as strong as a bullet proof vest but thin like a shirt. It's still in the testing phases and no one knows about the technology."

Okay, well that sounded plausible, but why did it feel like he had all the answers? "But I overheard you two talking. He told you that you had to make sure that I stayed quiet or he would make sure I did. Then he threatened to make me disappear. You don't do that unless you have something to hide."

"Claire, that's something that I can't tell you. I can tell you that he's not who he appears to be, but if people ever found out his true identity, he would be in a lot of trouble and so would everyone at Reed Security that helped him. That's what we were referring to. There's nothing special about him other than he's highly skilled."

"But..." It still didn't make sense. "The fire in the truck...We flew off the roof of my house..."

"Claire, I climbed in through the back window of the truck to pull the man out. The fire hadn't reached that part of the truck yet. And I'm sorry to tell you this, but we didn't fly off the roof. I dropped you down into Cap's arms. You were pretty out of it, so it would make sense that it would feel like you were floating."

I sat there stunned. All along, I kept telling myself that there was a plausible explanation, but then something would happen and it would strengthen the idea that it was possible. I felt so stupid as I sat there with Derek. How could he possible see me as anything but an idiot after what I just told him?

"Oh my God," I whispered as I stood and paced the room. I was such an idiot. I had to get out of there before I made a bigger idiot out of myself. I'd stay in a hotel or a ditch if I had to. There was no way I was staying with Derek to have him snicker at me behind my back.

"Claire, calm down. It's fine. Now that you explained it to me, I could see how you would think that."

"Don't patronize me, Derek. I know what a fool I've made of myself."

"Look at me." I didn't and he took my chin and turned my face toward his. "You are not a fool. You may have a slightly overactive imagination, but that's one of the things I love about you. Who cares if you actually believed that? Do you know how fucking high it made me to hear you call me Superman? Who gives a fuck if you thought I was an alien? It doesn't fucking matter to me and no one else has to know if you don't want them to. I would never do anything to make you feel like an idiot. Well, I mean, after I laughed at you, but I seriously thought you were shitting me. Maybe you just need to spend less time at the library."

"Yes, I think it's quite possible I've immersed myself in too many books," I said, looking up at him and realized in that moment that he really didn't care. I was a bit of a whack-a-doodle and he really didn't care. He loved me, crazy and all. I shook my head in disbelief. This man was just too good to be true.

"Are you real?"

"Uh, I think we just covered this, Claire," he said in confusion.

"No, I mean, is it possible that you are really that great of a guy? That you wouldn't judge me for being...a little creative? Any other man would have run for the hills."

"Let me tell you something, after I saw you at the garden center and went back to your house with you, I couldn't get you out of my head. I was training with the guys and making a total ass out of myself because I couldn't concentrate. It hit me that after that first time I kissed you, I was totally fucked because I knew right then and there that you were it for me. I just felt it inside me. And when I told the guys that I was that fucked up over a kiss, they knew too. Sinner, Cazzo, and Burg all told me that I just had to accept my fate, that there was nothing I could do about it but hang on for the ride. I didn't want to accept it yet because I had never planned on having all that, but the more time that went on, the more I knew they were right. My point is that it would take a hell of a lot to make me walk away from you right now. I want you to move in with me and I want to have the whole package with you."

I couldn't believe this man. How did I get so lucky to be such a bumbling idiot and still keep this man's attention? "I want that too."

"Good, because I'm not ever fucking letting you go."

*A*fter a week of Derek refusing to sleep with me because he was sure I wasn't recovered enough, I decided to take matters into my own hands. I had a special surprise for him and I was pretty sure that he would go along with it since he had laughed at me when I first told him about my theory about the men at Reed Security.

I had stopped at a costume shop on the way home and picked up my order, then made my way home. Derek was already there, which was perfect for my plan. I walked in the door and scowled when he walked over to me and took everything from me and then ushered me to the couch.

"You need to put your feet up. I don't want you overdoing it."

"Enough! Derek, I love you, but this has got to stop. I was cleared by the doctor. I rested and took some time off work, but I've been back to work for several days now and I feel fine. I don't need you to baby me anymore."

He ran a hand over his face and sighed. "Claire, I just want to be sure you're alright."

"I know, but enough's enough. Besides, I have other plans for tonight and it's not going to work if you won't let me have any fun."

"What are you planning for the night?" he asked in concern. "I don't think you should be going anywhere. It's too soon for you to be going out."

"Derek, what I have planned is for the two of us and we are most definitely staying in."

He grinned and scooped me up in his arms. "I suppose I can get behind that."

"You have no idea how in character you already are."

"What are you talking about?"

I made him put me down and then walked over to the bag I had brought in with me, handing it over to him with a grin. He hesitantly took the bag and opened it, shaking his head as soon as he saw it.

"No. I'd do almost anything for you, but this is going too far."

"Please, Derek. It would make me feel so much better. Besides, if you're Superman, I can be Lois Lane and Superman always gets the girl," I said, batting my eyelashes at him. He sighed and trudged back to the bedroom. I did a little victory dance and then set the living room exactly how I wanted it for the scene. Then, I went back to the bedroom to get out my tight, black dress that Derek had gotten for me.

Derek was struggling to put on the costume and watching him get in tights was hilarious. "No self-respecting man wears tights. I hope you realize how much I love you."

"I do," I said with a grin.

He pulled the leotard up as far as he could, but the padding was getting stuck. "This fucking thing is too tight. It's made for pussies that don't have a muscular body." He started ripping out the padding and then pulled the leotard up the rest of the way. His dick was straining through the fabric and I had to say, he looked way better than any of the actors that played Superman. Last were the boots and cape. I sighed and watched him dreamily as he finished pulling on the outfit. "I look fucking ridiculous."

"You look so fucking sexy. I think you're going to get very lucky tonight."

I walked over to my closet and pulled out the dress, but he stopped me.

"What do you think you're doing?"

"I'm getting dressed for my part."

"Uh-uh. If I have to wear this ridiculous thing, then I get to choose what you wear."

"Which will be?"

He walked over to the closet and pulled out a gift box. "I've been saving this for you and I think tonight is the perfect night."

I opened the box and saw a sexy, lacy bra and panty set with garter belts and silk stockings. "This is what you want me to wear under the dress?"

"No. This is what I want you to wear. And that's all." I blushed as he pulled me against him and kissed me hard. "Get dressed before I change my mind and fuck you right now."

I quickly pulled off my clothes and stepped into the lingerie he picked out for me. I had never gotten any lingerie for myself and I had to admit, it made me feel sexy. Not comfortable enough to wear every day, but I would wear it for him if he wanted me to.

"So, what did you have in mind for me when you picked out this costume?" he asked. I led him into the living room where I had a dining room chair set up in the corner with rope and a gag. "In the chair," he growled.

I did as he said and sat down in the chair, spreading my legs for him. A rumble ripped through his chest as he stared at the apex of my thighs. He bent down and ran his fingertips up my calves, brushing behind my knees and then up my thighs. His knuckles brushed my sex, but he didn't linger. I quivered when he picked up the rope and tied one ankle to the leg of the chair and then the other. He leaned forward and placed a kiss on my stomach and then kissed up to my breasts, biting my nipples through the fabric of the bra. I panted as my pussy clenched with need. Then his hands were pulling my arms back and tying them behind the chair, making my breasts thrust forward.

"You look so fucking gorgeous like this. I may have to do this to you every night just so I can see your breasts on display for me."

My chest heaved as he lightly touched me all over, never giving me exactly what I needed to push me over the edge. I needed more. I needed him inside me, but I was powerless to make him give me what I wanted. What I needed. "Get me out of these ropes."

"Shh."

"No, dammit. This was supposed to be my fantasy."

He chuckled and picked up the gag off the floor. "It became my fantasy the moment you made me put on this ridiculous outfit." He pushed the gag slightly inside my mouth and tied it behind my head even as I protested. "I think before Superman saves the girl, he needs to have a taste of her first."

He knelt down in front of me and traced his finger over the edge of my panties. I tried to thrust my hips forward, but there wasn't any wiggle room. He slowly dipped a finger inside and slid it along the wetness between my legs. I moaned, my hips bucking every time he slid closer to my clit. I was panting hard and grunting my frustration every time he teased me.

"Just a taste," he grinned wickedly. He ran his nose over my panties and all I could do was watch and hope that he finally put his mouth where I needed him. He bit the fabric, nipping me in the process, then moved it to the side. His tongue flicked over my clit and I gasped as his tongue ravaged me.

"Mmhfph..ahhh" I panted. My heart was racing and my mouth was so dry. Stars burst behind my eyes as he sucked me into his mouth and made me come with a scream. He slipped a finger inside me and kissed up my stomach to my breasts and then my neck. He sucked the delicate skin into his mouth, practically devouring my neck as he thrust his finger into my slick heat over and over. I was sure I was going to have a heart attack as my second orgasm rushed through my body, but he didn't relent. He fucked me harder and harder, moving his mouth to my ear. I was clenched so tight around him, sure I was going to have another orgasm right then and there.

The door swung open and my eyes flew open to see Sebastian, Hunter, Mark, Sam, and four other men that I had never met before. Derek's head whipped around and he swore. I gasped as I realized that I was practically naked and tied to a chair and that eight men were staring at me. I was panicking, I knew that much. In fact, I was pretty sure that if I didn't die of embarrassment in the next ten seconds, I would have a panic attack so big that it would do the job.

"Uh, Derek? Why the fuck are you dressed like Superman?" Hunter asked.

"Can't you see? He's reenacting the movie," Sam said with a smile. "Well, the dirty version anyway. I think I would have remembered a scene like this."

"Those tights look like they're strangling your cock. Bad choice, man. Is there some kind of hole for you to whip it out," Mark asked as he leaned over like he was examining the material.

Derek seemed to snap out of it and stood up, blocking me from their view. "Stop fucking looking at my dick," he snapped.

Mark backed up with his hands raised. "I'm not looking to join in. Just curious about the outfit. I don't think Cara's into the superhero stuff, but it's not a bad idea. Keep it spicy in the bedroom."

"Just got married and you're already looking for ways to spice it up?" one of the other guys said.

"I don't need to spice anything up. I'm just saying, look at her. It's fucking hot."

I blushed furiously and Derek held up the cape to further block me. "You guys need to get the fuck out. Now."

"We're not trying to poach your woman. We're just saying, she's fucking hot," another one said. "I'm John, by the way."

I gave a slight wave with my hand still tied down at the wrist. "Nice to meet you," I said meekly.

Derek sighed and pointed around the room. "You know Sebastian, Sam, Hunter, and Mark. That's John, Chris, Chance, and Jackson."

They all said hi with huge grins and I gave another wave. "Uh, nice to meet you all. I wish it had been under different circumstances, but I can assure you this is not what it looks like," I shook my head furiously.

"Really? Cause it looks like he tied you to a chair and he's having his way with you," Chance said.

"Okay, well..." I chuckled a little. "Then, I guess it's exactly what it looks like."

"What are you assholes doing here anyway?" Derek asked.

"Poker night, remember? We just made the plans this afternoon," Sebastian said.

"Shit," Derek muttered as he ran a hand over his scruff. "Too fucking bad. Plans changed. Go to someone else's house."

"I don't know," Sinner grinned. "We could always stay here, catch a movie."

"Out!" Derek pointed for the front door and stepped toward them, leaving me open for all to see. I tried to squeeze my legs together, but I couldn't do it. The guys all laughed and backed out of the house.

"Clark! Save me," one of them yelled.

"My pussy needs sucking," another yelled.

"Fuck off," Derek slammed the door in their faces and I felt horrible. I had never imagined Derek would be caught dead in what he was wearing. He leaned his head against the door and his shoulders shook. I couldn't tell if he was laughing or crying.

"Derek, I'm so-"

"Don't," he snapped. He turned and stalked towards me, a gleam in his eye that I knew all too well. He was turned on. I looked down and saw his cock pushing hard against the fabric. My eyes grew wide as I realized that he was even more turned on than before. I swallowed hard as he picked up the chair, with me still in it and stalked toward the bedroom.

"What are you doing?" I yelped.

"Having my fucking way with you." He set the chair down and tore off the costume. "I think I'm a little fucked up because it fucking turned me on to know that they all thought you were so hot, but they couldn't have you. You're all mine and I'm going to make sure that you know it by the end of the night."

He pulled at the center of my bra until it ripped apart. His mouth latched on hard to my breast and he bit painfully at my nipple. It was so hot. His fingers ripped at my panties and then were inside me, pushing hard through my slickness. I came in a matter of minutes. He tore at the ropes and then threw me on the bed, crawling over me like a predator. I had no doubt that he was going to devour every inch of me tonight.

When he slammed his rigid cock inside me, I gasped at the near painful intrusion, but he didn't let up. He fucked me hard, bending my legs in ways I didn't know they would go. His hands pulled at my hair, kneaded my breasts, and strummed my clit until I was squeezing him so painfully that I heard him groan in pain. I couldn't help it though. He had done this to me. He had worked me up so much that I could only explode from the sensations.

When he flopped down next to me on the bed, we both stared at the ceiling, chests heaving from our hour long fuck-a-thon. I could barely feel my legs and my pussy was so sore that I wasn't sure I would be walking right for days.

"Do you think next time you could be Iron Man?"

"Are you fucking kidding me? I'm not putting metal anywhere near my cock."

"I don't suppose you would wear a wig and be Thor."

"I'm not wearing a wig, but I will bring my hammer down on you anytime you want."

Chapter Fourteen

DEREK

"*H*ow's your dad settling in at his new home?"

Claire had just gotten back from seeing him. She had gone every day since he was released from the hospital and every day she came home feeling guilty as hell that he was in there.

"He's okay. He says he's happy there, that it's a relief that he doesn't have to worry about hurting someone."

I pulled her into my arms and kissed her on the forehead. "He'll be alright, Claire. This really is the best thing for all of you."

"I know. I just don't like that he's not at home anymore," she said, wrapping her arms around my waist and squeezing me tight. I wished there was something I could do to make this easier for her.

"Have you and Lucy talked any more about what you want to do with the farm?"

"Lucy doesn't want it. She said that if I did, that was fine as long as I didn't expect her to work out there any more."

"What do you want to do? Do you want to rebuild?"

"Part of me says yes, but the farm is just so much work. I don't think I can keep up with both jobs for many more years, so I think now is the time to decide."

"Would you rather have the farm or work at the library?"

"I don't know. I just don't think I can make the decision right this minute. There's just too much to think about."

"You know, if you wanted, we could move out there and rebuild. You could design a house that you really wanted and I could sell this one."

"Uh, Derek, you just told me you love me. Don't you think that's moving a little fast? I mean, talking about moving in together is one thing, but building a house together is so permanent."

I pulled her against me and tilted her head up to look into my eyes. "I know that, Claire. That's why I suggested it. I told you, I knew a while ago that you were it for me. No amount of time is going to change that, so you take all the time you need to come to the same conclusion and I'll be here waiting for you."

I could tell she was having a hard time believing it, so I let it go for now. She would see eventually what I already did and then it would all be a piece of cake.

"I have a surprise for you," I said, grinning with excitement.

"You got the Thor costume?" she asked, her eyes wide and bright.

"No, my brothers are coming for a visit."

"All of them?" Her voice was full of panic and I couldn't help but laugh at that.

"Well, all but Josh. I told them that I had a woman and they didn't believe me, so I told them to come see for themselves. They're coming out on Friday."

"Friday?" she squeaked. "Uh...that's no good for me. I have...yoga with my sister and then we're going to a book convention on Saturday."

"A book convention?"

"Yep," she croaked. "It's a really cool one that I've been dying to go to."

"Really? I had no idea. What's the name of the convention?"

She cleared her throat and fidgeted with her shirt. "S-s-simmering, sexy, romance readers book convention."

"Simmering, sexy romance readers book convention."

She nodded in a roundabout way. "Sure. Yep. That's it."

"I'll have to look it up online. It sounds like something I might want to go with you to see."

"No!" she shouted as I walked over to my laptop. "You can't look it up online. It's not being advertised. It's a VIP thing. Sort of like a special club that you have to belong to. You won't find a word about it online."

"Well, I can still go with you. I'll call my brothers and they can come too. Maybe they'll get some pointers."

"No. It's not for men. Only women are allowed."

"That's not really fair. I think I want to talk to the person that's running this convention. Do you have the number?"

"There's no number."

"Let me guess. It's all a secret."

"Something like that," she said sheepishly.

"Claire."

"Yeah?"

"Why don't you want to meet my brothers?"

She sighed in defeat and sat down in the chair. "It's not that I don't want to, but you remember what I was like when I met you. What if I make a fool of myself and they don't like me?"

"How could anyone not like you? It's not possible. Besides, their opinions mean jack shit to me. If they don't like you, they can fuck off. But I'm telling you, they're going to love you."

"Promise?"

"I swear."

"Claire is really nervous about meeting you guys, so don't be a bunch of dicks when you get here," I told Joe. He was my youngest brother and the most likely to cause trouble for me.

"Why do you assume that we would give her a hard time? I'm sure she's great."

"She is great, but she's not the best with people until she gets to know them, so don't make her self-conscious."

It was the day before they were coming and I was starting to panic

a little that they would be terrible to her because they didn't understand how much she meant to me.

"I'm sure it'll be fine. Have some faith, man. We're your brothers.
We've got your back."

"That's what I'm afraid of," I muttered. "Look, I love this woman
and I plan on spending the rest of my life with her. Just, please don't
fuck this up for me."

"You what? Did you just say that you love her?"

"Yes, I did and I meant it," I said, rolling my eyes. Was it really so
hard to believe that I would fall in love?

"Whoa, I had no idea. I didn't know you were even interested in
that."

"I wasn't until I met her."

"You got it, bro. We'll stick to embarrassing childhood stories and
the story of you and Missy Tompkins."

"Don't you fucking dare," I yelled into the phone.

"Sorry, man. If we have to be on our best behavior, you've got to
give us something."

"That story's off limits."

"I suppose I could tell her about the tractor incident."

"Not that one either." I swear, it was like he wanted to find the
worst stories about me to share with her.

"Fine, then the condom story."

"Are you fucking trying to run her off?"

"Come on," he whined. "You gotta give me something."

"No. Just keep your mouth shut and be a good brother."

"You're no fucking fun anymore. Fine, we'll all be good little choir
boys and your precious Claire will never find out about you fucking
your math teacher."

I dropped my head into my hands and prayed that I could control
them when I was here. What the hell was I thinking? Claire had
nothing to be worried about, but I sure as hell did.

"I'll see you guys tomorrow. Just remember what I said."

I hung up before he could start debating the merits of telling her
the baseball story. Shit. I needed to find that photo album and hide it
before my brothers found it and came up with more stories.

*C*laire had her head buried in a book all morning, but I could see that she wasn't really reading. She was trying to distract herself from the fact that my brothers would be here in a little bit. It wasn't working though. Her nails had been chewed down to the nub and her lip was about to start bleeding from how she was chewing on it. I had thought about giving her a glass of wine, but that might just make things worse.

When two trucks pulled in an hour later, I got up and went outside to greet them. Claire followed me, but hung back. I wanted to pull her up close to me, but she didn't seem to want to get any closer. Maybe if she saw me interact with my brothers, it would make her feel more at ease.

"Hey, Will. It's good to see you, man." I pulled him in for a hug and was surprised when he squeezed me a little tighter than normal.

"It's good to see you. It's been too long."

"Yeah, I've been busy."

"So I've heard," he said with a smirk. "Don't worry. I won't say a word about the firecracker incident..unless she asks."

I swallowed hard as he walked past me toward Claire. I was so fucked. There was no way they were going to let that shit slide. Robert jumped out, still attached to his phone and didn't look up until he ran into me. A grin spread across his face and he quickly shoved his phone in his pocket.

"Sorry about that, man. I was answering some emails."

"How many cases are you working on right now? Got anything good?"

Robert was a lawyer in Chicago and was rarely seen without his phone in his hand. He was trying to move up in his firm, so he worked his ass off. I was actually surprised that he had gotten the time off to come here.

"I'm swamped, but when I found out that you had a woman, nothing was going to keep me back in Chicago. So, where is this woman?"

I turned and pointed to Claire, who was rambling on to Will. He had a grin on his face and Claire was blushing profusely, waving her hands around in the air. She had no doubt shoved her foot in her mouth and was trying to fix it. Robert rubbed his hands together and made his way over to her.

Andrew slapped my back and did some kind of funky dance that looked like a chicken on drugs. He wrapped his arms around me and slapped my back hard. This kid was always so full of life. He worked for some tech company, but he always had a pair of earbuds in and was jamming to some music.

"Hey, bro. I'm turnt to see your bae." I wrinkled my brows in confusion as he peeked over my shoulder. He punched me in the arm and let out a low whistle. "Damn, she's so hot, she's like my grandma's slippers."

"What? What the fuck does that mean?"

"It means her bikini photos are like a kale smoothie."

"What the fuck are you talking about? Speak English."

"It means she's quiche. Get with the times. Sorry, not sorry, she's on fleek and you're so basic. I can't even."

"You can't even what?"

"You know, man."

"No, I don't fucking know. Finish your damn sentence."

"Nice try, Hunty." He slapped my bicep and I looked at my arm and then back to him with a quirked eyebrow.

"I'm leaving now. When you've learned to speak English again, let me know."

I walked over to Eric and gave him a man hug. Finally, someone I could relate to. "Do you know what the fuck turnt means?"

He laughed and shook his head. "I don't try to understand him anymore. If you ignore him, eventually he speaks like a human just to get you to understand him."

"What the fuck kind of language is that? I didn't understand half of what he said."

"It's millennial speak. It's best to not try to understand it. You never will."

"How's the business going?"

"Can't complain. There's always someone that needs something fixed. I'm going to have to hire some new people soon. There's just too much work for my guys to handle the way we are."

"Sounds promising." Joe walked up and slugged me in the arm. Not one to be outdone, I turned and punched him in the jaw. He immediately dropped to the ground and then sat up rubbing his jaw.

"Dude, what the fuck was that for?"

"Is that how you greet people? You punch me, I'll fucking punch you right back, only I won't be as gentle. Normally, people just come up to me and say hi."

He grumbled as he walked over to Claire about not wanting to adult today. Whatever the fuck that meant.

"So, this is the girl, huh?"

"Yeah, she's the one. Try not to scare her off for me."

"You know me; I got your back." And he did. Eric was the one brother I could rely on to take me seriously when I asked him not to fuck this up for me. "Come on. Introduce me."

We walked over to Claire who had her brows furrowed as Andrew and Joe rambled on in some language I didn't understand.

"We didn't think he'd ever settle down, because duh," Joe said with a grin.

"You've seen him, the struggle is real," Andrew agreed.

"Uh..tots," she said uncertainly.

"Aw, you're givin' me all the feels," Joe said, pulling her in for a hug.

I pulled him off her by his shirt collar and threw him to the ground. "There'll be no feeling of any kind with my woman. Keep your hands to yourself," I growled. Claire laughed and I sent a chilling look her way.

"Feels just describes emotions, Derek. He was just saying that I was making him happy."

"Well, then fucking say that," I yelled at my stupid brother. "One day you're gonna get shot pulling shit like that."

Eric held out his hand to Claire and smiled at her. "It's nice to meet you, Claire. I'm Eric."

"Ah, I've heard a lot about you. Derek says that you're the normal one, the only one he can relate to." She looked at my other brothers with wide eyes and quickly shook her head, her face turning bright red.

"Shit, I meant that...I mean, you're a lawyer," she said to Robert. "And lawyers are generally pompous windbags that I wouldn't trust as far as I could throw," she rambled. "Not that you are! I'm sure you're very upstanding and work with kids or something. Not with assholes that hoard their money and steal from those that don't know any better. What kind of law do you practice?"

"I'm a corporate lawyer," Robert said in all seriousness.

She swallowed hard and looked to me for help. Robert threw his head back in laughter. "I'm just fucking with you. I'm a divorce lawyer. Not much better, I know, but it pays the bills."

"I'm really sorry," Claire said with tears in her eyes. "I really didn't mean to insult you."

"Hey, if you're going to be our sister-in-law someday, you're going to have to get a thicker skin. We all fuck with each other and that's just something you're going to have to get used to," he said as he wrapped an arm around her neck and headed for the front door.

"Sister-in-law?" she squeaked out.

"Derek's a fucking goner when it comes to you. Just accept your fate and ride the train to happy town." They disappeared inside and the rest of my brothers stood there grinning at me.

"What the fuck are you grinning at?"

"I like her," Joe said. "She's quirky and cute as hell."

"Yeah, it's about time you started dating someone with a personality," Will said. "Maybe we should clue her in on the kind of floozies you usually date."

"The Sugar Twins," Andrew said, pointing to me.

"Annabelle what's her face," Joe said.

"Three tits Tina," Will joined in.

"Saucy Sandy," Eric said dreamily.

"Alright, that's enough. You guys can stop all that shit. You're not saying anything to her about anyone I dated. Or anything I did as a kid. Or any stories that make me look like a dick."

"So, basically you want us to sit there and stare at the wall," Will grinned.

"Fuck off," I said, walking into the house, sure that when I got in there, Claire would already be hearing some terrible story about me.

*W*e all sat around the living room in an uncomfortable silence. Every time one of my brothers started to speak, I glared at them, letting them know that if they said anything negative about me, I'd fucking kill them. Claire was fidgeting next to me and was obviously uncomfortable.

"So, I'd love to hear some stories about you guys growing up together."

Andrew went to open his mouth, but snapped it shut when he looked at me.

"He was a good kid," Eric said, coming to the rescue. "He was very level headed and the day he joined the military, we were all so fucking proud of him."

Claire laughed a little and looked around the room. "Oh, come on. That can't be all you have to say. There has to be something better than that."

Will cleared his throat and crossed his ankle across his other knee. "You know how it is in a small town. Not a lot of trouble to get into. It was always pretty..."

"You know how it is with siblings," Andrew said. "You get into some crap, but it always turned out okay."

"I know that's not true. He already told me that you guys got into a lot of trouble." Claire looked around the room, daring them to tell her it wasn't true.

"Well, there was this one time we were over at the neighbor's house-"

"Keep your fucking mouth shut," I snapped at Joe.

"And Derek got the bright idea that we should take turns driving the tractor, insisting that our neighbor wouldn't mind if we plowed his field."

"Hey, what the fuck did I just say?"

"Shush," Claire waved a hand at me. "I'm trying to hear the story," she said excitedly. I grumbled and sat back in my seat, annoyed that the tractor story was being brought up. Joe leaned forward with a big grin on his face and continued.

"So, we all sat on the tractor wherever we could and Eric got the plow all hooked up. We took the tractor out to the field and were taking turns plowing the field up when the old man came running out yelling at us. Derek was the one driving, but the rest of us jumped off the tractor and took off back to our house. Derek tried to outrun the old man and just kept driving through the field, but the old man had called the cops as soon as he saw us out there. They came flying down the road, sirens blaring and ran out to the field. Derek was zigzagging through the field to try and get away from them. We all watched from the tree line as he continued to plow the field, trying to get away from the cops."

"What happened?" she asked with wide eyes.

"Eventually, he stopped the tractor and got down. He tried explaining to the old man that he just wanted to help out and plow the field."

"Aww, that's so sweet," Claire said sadly.

"Yeah, and it would have been if the farmer hadn't just planted the field," Joe laughed.

"Oh my God! You destroyed his crop?"

"Not really. It just didn't come up in straight lines that year," I grumbled.

She threw her head back in laughter and bounced on the couch with glee. "Tell me more. There has to be more!"

"There's the story of the Sugar Twins," Will grinned.

"No!" I barked at him.

"He was dating Melanie Cartwright and she had an identical twin, Melissa. Derek took Melanie's virginity in the back seat of his car when he was sixteen. Melissa was jealous because apparently, she had a thing for Derek also. She made sure to dress like Melanie and showed up for their date, telling Melanie that Derek had called and cancelled. After their date, Derek brought her back to the house and went to the pond behind the house. Derek liked to take Melanie back there to fuck her," he grinned.

I hid my face in my hands. This made me look so bad, but when I looked at Claire, she was laughing and covering her mouth with her hand.

"Anyway, Melanie came to the house looking for an explanation as to why Derek cancelled their date. We were all fucking confused because she asked where he was and we had just seen her go to the pond with Derek. She stomped back there and caught him fucking Melissa. We all followed, of course, when we realized what was going on. We didn't want to miss the show. Derek's standing with his pants around his ankles and his dick hanging out, insisting that he had no clue that she wasn't Melanie. Melissa was all sprawled out on the ground with an evil look on her face. Let's just say that relationship didn't last."

Claire turned to me with tears of laughter running down her face. "How did you not know?"

"They were fucking identical twins!"

"Still. There had to be something that was different about them. I can't believe you did that!" She was practically rolling around on the ground in hysterics and my brothers were laughing along with her. Sighing, I got up to grab beer for everyone. When I got back, I wished that I had stayed gone. Eric was knee deep in the condom story.

"So, there he is, little shithead of twelve, wanting to know how a condom works. Of course, he hadn't gone through puberty yet, so he didn't know you had to have an erection to get a condom on. He pulled it up over his soft dick and then wrapped a rubber band around it to hold it in place. He was worried it would slide off, so he wrapped it extra tight. When his penis started turning blue, he flipped out and called me in to help him out. I couldn't stop laughing and there was no way I was touching his dick. I ran and got my dad to help him. My dad sighed and then proceeded to help him get the rubber band off."

Claire sat there shocked, mouth hanging open. When she turned to me, she shut her mouth and her chest heaved. Her cheeks puffed as she tried to hold back her laughter, but when her whole body started shaking, I just shook my head and handed out the beers.

"What happened to 'I got your back, bro'?" I asked Eric.

"Sorry, I just really like that story," he chuckled.

This was going to be a long fucking night.

*C*laire asked Lucy to come over the next day so that she could meet my brothers. I knew it was a mistake the moment Lucy walked in the door. Her eyes immediately started checking out my brothers, sizing them up to see which one she wanted to sink her claws into. I didn't really give a shit, except for the fact that Hunter was fucking crazy about her and I didn't want one of my brothers to piss him off. Aside from warning my brothers off, there wasn't a whole lot I could do to stop it. If Lucy wanted to fuck someone, she would get it from someone else, if not one of my brothers. Still, I pulled Claire aside as soon as I saw her checking them out.

"You've got to tell your sister to stay away from my brothers."

"Why? You know how Lucy is. Do you think your brothers are going to get hurt or something? Because they don't really strike me as the type to care."

"It's not that. Hunter will go crazy and I don't want him killing one of my brothers."

"Derek, I know that Hunter is like a brother to you, but if Lucy doesn't want to be with him like that, there's nothing we can do to stop her. If she screws this up, it's on her. I'll talk to her, but in the end, it's up to her."

"I know, I just...fuck, I never thought Hunter would want a woman the way he wants Lucy. He would never give another woman a shot if Lucy trampled all over him."

She hugged me and rested her head against my chest. "I know. You can't make a person change, though."

I held her and thanked God that I had this woman in my life. She really was the best thing that had ever happened to me. I was just so thankful that my brothers were taking to her like their very own sister. I would sure hate to have to kill my brothers.

"So, Claire. Tell us how you met our dear brother," William asked over a beer later that afternoon.

"Uh, we met in the grocery store." Claire turned bright red and peeled at the label on her beer bottle.

"Yeah, so did he try to convince you that his cucumber was longer than the others in the store?" Andrew asked. Claire was taking a sip of beer and spit it out all over herself. I laughed so hard, because I remembered putting on a show for her specifically with a cucumber.

"I choked on a grape," she mumbled. "I was trying to work up the courage to talk to him and I choked on a grape."

"I knew she was watching me the whole time," I grinned.

"What? You knew?"

"Why do you think I was taking my time walking through the produce section? No one takes that much time to pick out fruit."

"But..." She stared with her mouth gaping open. "Did you see-"

"You staring at me with the two other women? Yeah. It was fucking adorable." I turned to my brothers, a huge grin splitting my face. "She was eating blueberries and watching me. I knew right then that I had her."

"You ass! I can't believe you knew all that time."

"I was just drawing you in, Claire bear."

"Claire bear, that's so fucking adorable," Will snickered. I expected Joe to make some snarky remark also, but as I looked around the room, I realized that he was missing. So was Lucy. Fuck. I stood and walked around the house, ignoring my brothers' strange looks. Claire got up and followed me with a quizzical look.

"What's wrong?"

"Your sister and Joe aren't here."

Claire looked around and shook her head, a look of disappointment on her face. The doorbell rang and I went to answer, cursing under my breath when I saw Pappy at the door.

"Hey, man," I said as I pulled it open.

"I brought beer. I heard your brothers were in town and I wanted to-"

He paused mid sentence as he looked over my shoulder. Claire and I turned around to see Lucy walking in the sliding door with Joe, holding hands and looking completely fucked. My eyes slid closed as I felt the anger burning through Pappy. I didn't have to look at him to know that he was on the verge of killing my brother. Lucy and Joe still hadn't seen Pappy and were headed for the front door.

"What the fuck are you doing, Lucy?"

Lucy gasped as she came to a stop by us. Joe looked between us in confusion. Obviously, Lucy hadn't told Joe that she wasn't exactly available. Lucy narrowed her eyes at Pappy and scowled.

"Don't worry about it. We aren't together and who I fuck is none of your business."

I saw Claire flinch next to me and Joe took a step back. "Whoa, Lucy, I'm just looking for a good time. I'm not getting in the middle of whatever the fuck you two have going on."

"We have *nothing* going on," she insisted. "Now, let's get out of here."

Joe took another step back, eyes flashing to mine for a brief moment, full of regret. Smart man. "Sorry, I don't poach what belongs to other men."

"I don't belong to anyone."

"Does he know that?" Joe asked. He shook his head and walked back in the other room. Lucy turned a glare on Pappy and crossed her arms over her chest.

"I hope you're happy."

"Why the fuck would I be happy that you're out screwing other guys?"

"Hunter, you need to get something through your head. We fuck occasionally. It's never been more than that and you can't just swoop in and change the rules when it's convenient for you."

"I flat out told you how it was going to be. I'm not fucking around on you and I expect the same courtesy."

"I never agreed to that and if you had it in your oversexed brain that we were going to have something different, that's not my problem."

Pappy turned to me, harnessing his anger so he didn't kill her. I appreciated that. "I'll meet your brothers some other time. I don't think it's a good idea for me to be around the man that Lucy just fucked right now."

I nodded and watched him walk out the door, pissed that Lucy and Joe had ruined what could have been a great night.

"You need to go, too, Lucy." Claire was angry, but she was doing a good job of hiding it.

"Why do I have to go? Joe and I both knew what we were doing. We're not teenagers, Claire."

"Then why are you acting like one? You can't just go around playing with people's feelings. It's obvious that Hunter thought the two of you had more."

"No, he told me what we were going to have. That's not the same as us coming to the same conclusion."

"I think you still need to go."

I could tell it hurt Claire to say that and Lucy was equally upset, but luckily didn't put up a fight. She walked out the door and didn't look back. Just like that, the great time that we were having deflated like a lead balloon.

Chapter Fifteen

CLAIRE

erek's brothers left last night and now I was back at work at the library, trying to catch up on some work from the last few weeks. With everything that had happened, I had fallen behind on paperwork and making sure that the library was in proper order at all times. I was in the kids' section on my hands and knees, sorting through books that had been shelved in the wrong spot, upside down, backwards, or lying on their covers. The whole section was in need of a good reorganization. I had my face plastered against the floor as I tried to reach a book that had been shoved under the bookcase when I felt like I was being watched. As gracefully as I could, I stood from my position and turned to see a man standing behind me. He looked familiar, but I couldn't place him.

"Ms. Grant. I'm not sure if you remember me, but a few weeks back, you offered to look into a book for me." I tilted my head, still trying to figure it out when he took a step closer. "It was a book about old locks and keys."

"Oh," I said, not able to come up with anything else to say in the moment. Now I remembered who the man was. He was the creepy one that kept looking at me like I was a hot dog on a summer day. Derek had told me not to help them. I was torn because I actually had heard back from one of my contacts that they may have a copy in their possession and to let them know if I wanted it. I hadn't responded because it had been right around the time of the fire.

Derek's voice was warring with my own need to find out what was going on, but in the end, I decided to listen to Derek. After all, I knew that was one of the most important things for him. Trust. If we didn't have that, I knew we would never survive.

I smiled kindly at the man and brushed the dust bunnies off my clothes. "I'm so sorry, but I haven't been able to reach anyone that had that book. They all promised to let me know as soon as they found something out. However, since it's out of print and it wasn't a best-selling book, I'm afraid the publishers didn't print up that many. It may be awhile before we come across one."

The man narrowed his eyes at me and took another step toward me. "It would be very bad if I didn't get my hands on that book. People's lives depend on it. Your life may depend on it," he said cryptically. Was that supposed to mean that there was some disaster on the way and if he didn't get his hands on the book, the world would cease to exist? Or was it a more generalized threat toward me? If I don't get what he wants, I'll end up dead? Both were situations I would like to avoid. I was in the middle of a good book and really wanted to get to the ending.

"Like I said, it may take a while to get it, but I have your number and as soon as I hear something, I'll be sure to let you know." I gave him my kindest smile that said I was being completely truthful with him, even though I had no plans to ever give this man what he wanted.

He nodded and took a few steps back before turning and walking out of the library. I finally let loose the breath I had been holding and leaned back against the bookcase I was standing by. I needed to call Derek and let him know that the man would be back for sure and he desperately wanted it. I made my way over to the office, abandoning the children's books that were still spread out in chaos over the floor. I'd deal with that later.

I picked up my cell phone and tried to dial Derek, but the call wouldn't go through. I didn't always have very good reception in here and a lot depended on the weather. Right now, there were storm clouds rolling through, so that was what was probably causing the interference. I went over to the landline and dialed his number, but after the second ring, all the lights in the library went out.

"Crap. Why does this always have to happen to me?" Someone needed to fix this building. I was tired of the lights going out multiple times a week, especially when I was the only one working at night. It didn't make me feel very safe, even though I was in a library and surrounded by books. Realistically what would happen? The books would decide to fight back? I shook the crazy thought from my head and went to my office to find the fuse box. When I pushed the crap stacked in front of the box to the side, I got a strange feeling that I had done this before. I shook my head and flipped open the fuse box. I really needed some additional light back here, like glow sticks or something.

I opened the box and noticed that all the switches seemed to be flipped exactly as they were supposed to be. I pursed my lips and went through each switch, flipping them off and then back on, just to be sure. When nothing happened, I felt a chill run up my spine. If that box was fine, what had made the lights go out? I ran through scenarios of scenes I had read in other books. *A powerful storm knocked a tree down and now the power is out all around town?* Very possible. *Someone cut the power lines to sneak in and return their overdue books from the last ten years?* Not likely. They'd probably just keep them. *There was a man on the loose reenacting the Michael Meyer movies?* It was Friday the 13th after all. I'm sure it's just a kid pranking me. *Killer in the library.* Now that one sounded eerily familiar, like a dream I had and it was now becoming reality.

I shook my head and went in search of a flashlight. I would just close up the library early and head home for the night. There was nothing I could do if the power was out. I grabbed my messenger bag and flung it over my shoulder, tossing my phone inside. I was just headed for the office door when I heard the front door creak open. I stood stock still as the door creaked closed and multiple footsteps clomped across the floor. It wasn't the smooth gait that Derek had. He was always stealthy when he walked, which was creepy since it made it hard to know when he was around.

As the steps got closer to my office, I started to panic. My heart was racing out of control and my body was shaking violently. It was hot in here. So hot that I thought I was going to pass out and then they would kill me. All over a stupid book that I could have gotten for them. It had to be them. No one cared about anything in the library enough to kill. Why did this sound so familiar though? I tried to put my finger on it, but then the office door started to open and I shoved myself under my desk. Luckily, it was very big and I was able to squeeze myself way into the back corner of it.

"Let's find that goody two shoes and get out of here," I heard a man whisper. "Just remember what Leto said. We don't hurt her. We need whatever information she's holding out on us," another voice said.

"Sure. I'll keep that in mind, but if she doesn't cooperate, I have no problem using more creative ways to get the information from her," the first voice said.

"You aren't going to tickle it out of her," I whispered. The conversation seemed to flow in my mind, like I'd heard it before.

"You aren't going to beat it out of her," the second voice said. I reared back in confusion. That wasn't what he was supposed to say. "Just as long as you remember what we're supposed to be doing here."

There was no way I was sticking around for a beating over a book. When they left the office and headed in another direction, I crawled out from underneath it and over to the open door. Peeking out, I didn't see anyone, so I got to my feet and slunk along the wall until I could reach one of the aisles of books. There were so many of them, it would be easy to get lost among the books, but I had been working here for a long time and knew this place like the back of my hand. I was just making my way down the first aisle when a hand landed on my shoulder and squeezed, followed by a firm grip over my mouth. I took in a deep breath and recognized Derek's familiar scent.

"Don't scream," Derek whispered in my ear. "I'll get you out of here. You just have to do as I say. Nod if you understand."

I nodded and slowly turned to see his handsome face staring down at me. He grinned that devilish grin and held out his hand for me, which I immediately took. He squeezed my hand tight and pulled me in for a hug, which for some reason, I thought would be a kiss. "I'll never let anything happen to you. We have to keep moving. These men are serious. They'll beat the information out of you if they get their hands on you." He turned before I could say anything and scanned the library for the direction the men had gone. He must have felt it was safe to move, because he started pulling me down another aisle at a slight jog.

While we zigzagged through the library aisles, I wondered why Derek was so worried about two men getting their hands on me when he was such a badass warrior. We'd already established he wasn't a superhero, but still, he was a highly trained killer. He could handle two men like that. We made our way over to the old marble stairs that led to the second floor and climbed them quietly as we distanced ourselves from the intruders.

"We have to get away from them. They can never know that you have access to the-"

"Horcruxes," I blurted out, then thought about what I had just said. Derek narrowed his eyes at me in concern.

"What are you talking about? What the hell are Horcruxes?"

"They're from Harry Potter. Voldemort created them so that he could never be killed. Harry had to collect all the horcruxes so that he could get rid of Voldemort. It was really a brilliant-"

He silenced me with a finger to my lips. "Not now. Right now we have to focus on getting out of here alive."

"But Derek-"

"Please, Claire. We don't have time to rehash Henry Potter right now. You have to trust me and let me get us out of here. I'd never let anything happen to you."

"Harry Potter," I grumbled as I followed behind him. I wanted to tell him that I had done all this before in my dream. Everything was playing out almost exactly as it had, which had to mean something. I could warn him what was going to happen next. But he wanted me to trust him and that's what I was going to do.

I followed him blindly, knowing that if anyone could get us out of this, it was Derek. After all, even if he wasn't really a superhero, he had been one to me so far. We made it to the rooftop access and I took a deep gulp as he flung open the door and ushered me onto the roof. I knew instantly that he was looking for the fire escape ladder, so I ran over to it and pointed down. "Here!"

He made his way over and gave me a quizzical look. "How did you know where it was?"

"Good luck, I guess." I didn't think now was the time to tell him that we were about to die, based on the fact that he had caught me in the dream.

"This thing looks pretty fucking old. I'm going down first to see if it'll hold my weight."

"Wait! What about the kiss?"

"What the hell are you talking about, Claire?"

"You're supposed to kiss me. Right here, right now. It could be our last kiss, Derek."

He grabbed me by the arms, but instead of pulling me in for a hot steamy kiss, he shook me a little. "Claire, snap the fuck out of it. This is not a dream. I am not Superman, and those men will kill us if they find us. We need to get the fuck out of here. Now!"

He started the climb down the ladder and I looked over. "Watch out for the seventh rung," I shouted. I sighed. The dream had been so much better. Being chased by people that were after Horcruxes and trying to escape the Nazgûl was so much more exciting than running from these men that didn't seem to want anything more than a book. How boring was that? Even dream Derek was so much better than real life Derek. There was an intensity to him in the dream that was dark and dangerous, but also passionate. Real life Derek was dark and dangerous, but didn't want to kiss me at all. I found that kind of disappointing. I guess it was the librarian's curse. You always want what you read about more than what's actually happening in real life.

Derek looked up at me and waved me down. I sighed and followed him over the edge, keeping my eyes averted from the concrete below. I already knew from my dream that the concrete was what freaked me out so much. I made sure to step around the seventh rung and held on tight as I made my way closer and closer to Derek.

Something flew through the window in front of me, hitting me in my arm and causing me to lose my grip. I screamed as I just barely gripped onto the ladder, my legs dangling in the air.

"Claire, just hold on. I'm coming to you," Derek shouted urgently. I could see him climbing fast to get to me, but there wasn't enough time. A large, gloved hand shot out of the window and grabbed on tight to my shirt, pulling me through the window. I tried to hold onto the rung, but my hands were sweaty and kept slipping. I fought for control, but the man had me half in the window by the time Derek was almost there.

"Claire, give me your hand," Derek said, reaching out to grab on to me.

I tried, but I was too far away. "This is the not the way it fucking happens in my dream!" I kicked my feet at the man holding onto my body, but he still wouldn't let go. "You were supposed to save me from falling to my death. None of this was in there."

"Claire, shut the fuck up," Derek said as he climbed higher up the ladder, trying to get a hold of the man grabbing onto me. My fingers slipped and the man pulled me the rest of the way inside. My stomach scratched along the glass that had been left in the frame and I bit my lip to keep from screaming.

The man was dragging me across the floor, not even giving me a chance to get to my feet. Derek burst through the window and started running for me. The man threw me into a corner and swung around, gun aimed right at Derek.

"Put the gun down," the man sneered, but Derek was holding firm to his own weapon. His eyes flicked briefly to mine, but then stayed trained on the man in front of us. I scurried back against the wall, only to run into the leg of something. I looked up to see I was leaning against an old card catalogue. I slowly stood and pulled out the drawer, removing it from the box entirely. The drawer was heavy and I had no doubt I could do some damage with it if I could get a good angle. Luckily, the man was still in a standoff with Derek and didn't see me sneaking up from behind. I kept my eyes trained on Derek, knowing he was the one I was drawing my strength from at the moment. When Derek's eyes widened, the man spun around and I nailed him in the face with the drawer. Blood gushed as I heard bone crack. I started gagging as the breaking bone reverberated in my ears. I looked down to see blood covering my shirt. I shook my head to try to clear the images, but they wouldn't go away.

"Claire. Claire!" Derek was shaking me, but I was still staring at the man whose face I had just bashed in. "Claire!" He slapped my face hard and I finally looked up at him. "We have to get out of here. Come on."

He started pulling me back through the library, which totally freaked me out. "Why are we going this way?"

"There were only two of them. We should be able to sneak past him."

We ran down the marble staircase and were about half way down when we heard a loud thumping noise. We stopped and through the darkness, saw the bookcases on the far end starting to topple into one another. Oh, no. All my books were going to be out of order. Derek gripped my hand tight and flew down the stairs, taking them a lot faster than my little legs would carry me.

"Come on, Claire!" he shouted. "We have to make it through before they all go over!"

We ran for the aisle right in front of us and were almost halfway through when the bookcase to our left started to fall over us.

"We're not going to make it. Turn back!" he shouted at me.

Books pelted us as we tried to finish running through and Derek gripped my hand tight and flung me on my ass across the floor. I went sliding out of the aisle just as the bookcase landed against the next and started to tip that one. Derek was still underneath there.

"Derek!" I ran for the bookcase and started shoving books out of my way, trying to find any sign that Derek was alive under there. I heard a faint groan and dug harder. After about five minutes, I saw his hand peeking out from under a book. I shoved more books aside and tried to lift the bookcase, but seriously, it was a lost cause. I wasn't strong enough to do that. Once I got enough books moved, I gripped onto his hand, set my feet, and started to pull. He slowly slid out from under the wreckage and when he was about half out, he shook off my hand and pulled himself the rest of the way out. Besides a cut over his eye, he didn't look too bad, considering. He laid back on the ground and took in deep breaths as I stared around at my newly destroyed library.

"This is going to take forever to get back in order."

"Priorities, Claire."

"Right. I should see if I can get some new bookcases out of this."

Derek sighed as he pulled himself up. "I meant that we should focus on getting out of here alive."

"Oh, right. That makes more sense."

He stood gingerly and swore as he patted down his pants. "Shit, my gun is buried somewhere under there." He gazed around the library as the dust lingered in the air. It was impossible to see anything, but when a shot pinged off the marble staircase behind us, he threw me to the ground and covered my body with his.

"We're sitting ducks here. We have to go back upstairs. You go first and I'm going to run directly behind you. If something happens to me, you run for your life and find a way out. Don't stop and wait for me."

He pushed me toward the stairs before I could argue, so I started running up the stairs, two at a time. I could feel Derek behind me, holding onto my pants as if that would keep me upright. When I wasn't going fast enough, he hauled me up over his shoulder and took off at an even faster pace.

"I have short legs," I yelled at him. "It's not my fault they don't move as fast as your gigantic beanstalk legs."

He smacked my ass and continued to make his way to the second floor. Gunshots pinged off the floor behind us and when I looked up, I saw at least ten men trying to climb over the bookcases to get to us.

"Holy shit. There's like a whole army of them," I gasped against the bouncing in my ribs. Derek pushed harder and didn't put me down as he ran in a different direction than before. He flung open an old, rusty door and slammed it behind us, only then setting me down.

"We're going out the window."

"Out the window?" I screeched. He flung the window open and looked from side to side at the outside of the building, He pulled his head back in and grinned. "Don't worry. There's a ledge you can walk on. Plenty of space. Absolutely nothing to be scared of." He glanced around the room and spied a piece of rope, brought it over to me and tied it around my waist.

"If there's nothing to be scared of, then why are you tying me to you?"

"Because, with the way you talk with your hands, you'll go flying off the building in the first five seconds."

"I just won't talk," I insisted.

He snorted and finished tying the other end of the rope to himself.

"Alright, I'm going to go first and you step exactly where I step."

"This is a really bad idea. We should just go down there and explain to the man that we don't have whatever he's looking for. I'm sure he'll understand and maybe I could even refer him to a few book collectors," I rambled.

"Sure. Because they came in here, guns blazing, because they were willing to talk it out. Let's go."

He climbed out the window and held his hand out for me. I hesitated. It wasn't that I didn't trust him, but I wasn't too fond of walking on the outside of a building.

"Hey, Claire, I would never let anything happen to you. Just trust me. I've got this," he smiled charmingly. What choice did I have? I wanted to trust Derek more than anything. I just didn't like the idea of plummeting to my death. I put my hand in his and squeezed tight as I stepped out onto the ledge.

"You made this ledge sound a lot bigger. This is barely big enough to hold my foot."

"Don't look down," he said.

"If I don't look down, I'm pretty sure I won't be able to see where I'm walking and then I'll end up in little bloody pieces on the ground."

Derek sighed and squeezed my hand reassuringly. "Look, we just have to make it to the other side of the building and then we can jump into that lake."

"The lake? That's not even close to the building. We'd need at least a running jump to even hope to make it. This isn't Italy where the buildings are built on the river."

"Jesus Christ, Claire. Would you fucking stop? I'm going to get us out of this, but I need you to do me a favor and shut up for the next five minutes."

I was a little hurt by that, but I shrugged it off, knowing he was right.

"Okay, step over this next piece. It's a little loose."

I was so lost in my thoughts that I really wasn't paying attention to which piece he was talking about, which was how I stepped directly on the piece he told me not to. The ledge crumbled under my feet and I started to slip, but Derek was there, gripping my wrist seconds later. His face strained as he held onto my wrist and clutched the wall behind him.

I took deep calming breaths, trying my best not to move a lot, knowing that would only make it more difficult for him to hold on.

"Claire, we're only going to have one shot at this." His voice was stretched thin and his arms shook, his muscles big and hard. Sweat trickled down his arm and I watched the way it slid closer and closer to my arm. Maybe I could lick the sweat if it got to my wrist.

"Claire! Stop fucking daydreaming and listen."

"Sorry," I blushed bright red.

"You need to swing one leg up to the ledge and pull yourself up. Ready?" I nodded, determined not to fuck this up. "Now, Claire." I swung my leg and just barely caught the ledge with my foot. I inched it further and further onto the ledge, well aware that Derek was using every ounce of strength to hold onto me. After I hooked my knee over the ledge, I was able to pull myself up the rest of the way. Derek was sweating and shook out his arm after the strain of holding me.

"You need to fucking listen to what I'm saying. This isn't a game, Claire. One of us could end up dead."

I was shocked. In my dreams, he had pulled me into his arms and told me he would never let anything happen to me. Reality sucked. I grumbled something about making sure I paid attention as he gripped my hand firmly in his and started walking across the ledge again. Dream Derek was so much better.

We made it to the corner of the building and very carefully rounded to the other side. I swallowed hard when I saw how far we had to jump. It was far, way too far to make it.

"There's no way we can make it, Derek." I turned to him in near panic. "This is crazy. We'll never make that jump! The fall alone will

kill us. We can't do this. I'll just stay up here and wait for help. I won't-
I can't. This is nuts!"

Derek grabbed me by the arms and gave me a firm shake. "Snap out
of it, Claire. You can do this. I'll be with you the whole time. This is
our way out. There are a whole handful of men down there very eager
to get what you have."

"But I don't have anything," I said on the verge of hysterics. "I'm a
librarian. They wanted a book that I don't have!"

"You must have found something or they wouldn't be here. Now,
think. Did you contact someone that could help you? Is there anyone
that had access to that book?"

"Y-yes, but I never told them I wanted it. I only inquired after it."

"Shit. That means that they've been monitoring your emails. They
know you can get them the book. That's why they want you." He
chewed his lip for a second and then looked back up at me. "We have
to get out of here where I can get to a phone or get you back to Reed
Security. We'll deal with it from there."

"So, we're really doing this? We're jumping to our deaths to outrun
men over a book?"

"I'm kind of surprised," he said with a smirk. "I would think a book
would be worth dying for to someone like you."

"Wait! You're going to catch me right?"

He looked at me quizzically and shook his head. "I'm up here with
you, Claire. How the hell am I going to catch you?"

"Superman caught me in my dream," I grumbled. I caught him
rolling his eyes at me. He took a step back, gripping my hand and
nodded once, leaping from the building and taking me down
with him.

"Oh, crap!" I yelled as we plummeted toward the water. When we
splashed down below, I tried to hold my breath, but the force of the
fall pushed all the air from my lungs and I found myself gasping for air,
but only coming up with water. A yank on my shirt had me moving
toward the surface and when I broke into the open air, I coughed until
all the water was free of my throat. Derek was looking at me in
concern, his hands framing my face.

"Are you alright," Derek asked.

I sputtered out another cough and nodded my head. "How long do you think we have?"

"Not long. We have to get out of here. We have to get to my truck without them seeing."

"Wait. Can you do something for me?"

"What? Are you hurt?"

"No. I need you to say, 'I told you I'd catch you. I always will.'"

"But I didn't catch you."

"For the love of baseball, just say it for me!"

He pulled me into his arms and looked at me adoringly. "Claire, I told you that I'd catch you in your dreams. I'll always do it, in or out of your dreams. You're mine forever, Claire, and nothing can stand between us."

He kissed me hard, his tongue slipping inside my mouth. This was so much better than what happened in my dreams. He definitely was the only man for me, cape or no cape.

When he pulled back, his eyes flicked over my shoulder and widened slightly. "We have to go. Now. We're going to have to swim, Claire. Are you a good swimmer?"

"Uh..."

"Hold onto my belt. Don't fucking let go, and for God's sakes, make sure you breathe."

I took a deep breath, seconds before he dove under the water and started propelling us away from the shore. He stopped every once in a while to make sure I came up for air and then dove back under, taking us further and further from the library. When we finally reached the shore on the other side, I was exhausted.

Derek tapped me and I didn't understand why, but then I looked at the shore and saw three men staring at us like they would rip us apart. I released Derek's belt and watched as he ran out of the water, taking on the first man.

The man had a knife, but Derek quickly disarmed him and put him in some kind of headlock as he flung the knife over into another man's chest. A third man came at him and I waited with baited breath as Derek just stood there with the other man in a headlock. I wanted to yell at him to do something, but I was just so mesmerized. When the

man got within striking distance, Derek kicked sand up in the man's
face and then spun around, still holding the other man around the
neck, and wrapped his knee around the man's neck, taking him to the
ground and then jerked his knee. The man went limp in the crook of
Derek's knee. The man that was currently in his arms was also limp
and I didn't know how to respond. Was it appropriate to cheer when
one's boyfriend just killed three people?

Derek dropped the two of them, walked over to the third man and
ripped the knife from his chest, and ran back over to me. "Come on.
There'll be more coming." He held out his hand for me and I eagerly
took it. He ran with me through the trees, further from the water and
my beloved library that was now in shambles. Branches scraped at me
and bugs bit at my skin, but I continued to follow Derek deeper into
the forest. He stopped in front of a thick, tall tree and gazed upward.

"This is perfect. You're going to go up there and hide. You don't say
a word. You don't try to help. You don't do anything until I come back
to get you. Do you understand?"

"But what about you?"

"There are more of them on the way. I have to figure out who's
behind this and finish this before we both end up dead."

I snorted because I saw what he just did. That was just crazy to
think that we would end up dead with him defending us.

"Claire, this is fucking serious. These men are trying to kill us over
a fucking book. That must be pretty damn special for them to come at
us so hard. I have to get this figured out or we're both dead."

"I'm sorry. I don't mean to laugh, but...you did see what you just
did, right? I think you lied to me about the whole Superman bit," I said
with a grin.

Against his will, a small smirk touched his lips and he pulled me in
for a deep kiss. "Now, get your ass up there and stay safe. I can't do
what I need to if I'm worried about you."

I climbed the tree, glancing down occasionally to see him staring at
my ass. I found a perch and waited, trying to see where he went, but he
had vanished into the trees and I was now left to wait it out on
my own.

Chapter Sixteen

DEREK

I shook my head as Claire made it up high enough into the trees to be unseen. I couldn't stop staring at that gorgeous ass the whole time. My cock was getting hard and now wasn't the time to be thinking about where I'd like to shove my dick. Now that these men were coming after her full force, I wished that I had taken the number she had gotten from them and ended this before it could go further. I had assumed that if she ignored them, they would move on. Stupid move on my part.

I slipped into the darkness of the tree cover and waited for them to come. It didn't take long. They barely made a sound as they passed, obviously trained professionals. I waited for them all to slip past me and then watched as the last man passed. He wiped the snot from his nose on his sleeve, leaving behind a green trail I could see from where I stood. Disgusting. Sneaking up behind him, I wrapped one hand around his mouth, cutting off any noise he would make and quickly slit his throat. I lowered him gently to the ground up against a tree so it looked like he was sleeping. He had a handgun that I quickly put in the back of my pants and moved on to the next guy.

The next two were whispering in Russian, a language I had picked up from some guys when I had been overseas in the military. I didn't remember a lot because it had been so long since I spoke the language. Grabbing the man on the right from behind, I quickly broke his neck and pulled out the knife that he had sheathed on his side and flung it into the second man's neck. He went down before he even realized he needed to pull his gun.

Yanking the knife from his throat, I wiped it on his clothes and tucked it into my belt. One of the men glanced over his shoulder and whistled, a signal for everyone to stop. I straightened myself against a thick tree just as he fully turned around and scanned where his men had just been. When he didn't see anyone, he started back toward me, signaling positions to the other men. As he passed the tree I was hiding behind, I pulled him into me and slit his throat, sliding him to the ground and wiping the knife again.

I could hear the others moving more quickly now, but I didn't have time to move into a better position. They were closing in fast now that their men were missing. Pulling the handgun from my belt, I held it firmly in my hand, keeping the knife in my left hand. I needed to wait until most of them were close to me or it would be too easy for them to get a shot off. When the first man stumbled past, completely missing the man lying on the ground, I let him keeping wandering on. The second man saw his fallen comrade and let out a low whistle to the others. As he ran up, I turned and shot him in the head and the man behind him. I whipped my knife into the man that had already passed me and watched as he slowly dropped to his knees and fell on his face. That left three that I needed to take down. I hadn't seen the asshole from the library yet and if he wasn't out here looking, that meant that he would be waiting for us in case we returned.

I closed my eyes and listened for the sound of rustling leaves or snapping twigs. One was off to the left, one down the center, and one down the right. These men were highly trained based on the way they were moving. They hardly made a noise as they moved closer and closer. The man on the left would reach me first and then the man down the center. The man on the right was a few seconds further behind. I would only have seconds to take all three out and if I made the wrong choice, I would end up dead and leave Claire all alone. I slowed my breathing as they closed in the last few feet.

I heard the swoosh of the knife and ducked, thrusting my knife high into the man's rib cage. I spun just in time to kick the other man back a few steps and fire a shot over his shoulder into the chest of the third man. The second man knocked the gun from my hands and pulled his own gun. I glanced over his shoulder, flinching slightly. He took the bait and I watched in slow motion as his eyes flicked over his shoulder. I slammed my hand into his wrist, grabbing the gun with my other and shooting him dead center in the head. As the blood trickled from his forehead, I let the adrenaline flow freely through my body. I closed my eyes and listened one last time, but I didn't hear anything. I had taken out all ten, but that didn't mean it was safe to go back to the truck. For all I knew, there were more men waiting there. Walking back over to the tree that Claire was hiding in, I was not at all surprised to see that she was already out of the tree. She bit her lip as she let her gaze rake over me.

"I guess you got them all."

"Why didn't you listen to me?"

"I...uh...when they all started going back toward you, I wanted to see you in action."

I couldn't help but chuckle. My woman was just too much sometimes. "We're going to have to keep going through the woods. I don't want to go back since I don't know what's going to be waiting for us."

"Where are we going?"

"There's a house not too far from here. The guy knows Sebastian. I'll give him a call when we get there, but we have to get moving. The sun's going to be setting soon."

I grabbed her hand and pulled her along with me through the forest. I did my best not leave a trail, but no matter how many times I told Claire to step where I stepped, she was like a herd of buffalo trampling the prairie grass. Finally, I stopped and hauled her up over my shoulder.

"What are you doing?" she whisper hissed.

"Trying not to leave a trail."

"And why do you have to carry me for that to happen?"

"Because if anyone is trying to track us, they'll find us within a few minutes."

"I'm not that bad," she huffed.

"Look, it's nothing against you. It's just the way nature is. Men are the hunters and women are the gatherers."

"That's a little sexist, don't you think?"

"Not at all. I see the way you hunt. You'd more likely give yourself a heart attack than actually kill the other person."

"Hey-"

"Quiet. We don't need to draw any more attention to us."

She huffed, but was quiet the rest of the way. It was well past dark when we finally made it out of the forest and to Sebastian's friend's house. I may have gotten a little turned around, but I didn't dare tell Claire. She would have teased me about stopping and asking for directions. I set her down at the tree line and stared at the massive house in front of me. We stayed where we were for a good ten minutes, but when I didn't see any signs of danger, I grabbed Claire's hand and led her to the log cabin in front of us. The flood lights flicked on when we entered the back yard and Ryan's frame was standing at the back door seconds later. As I got closer, he opened the door and stepped outside.

"Derek?"

"Yeah. Sorry to crash your house like this, but we had a bit of trouble and I need to get ahold of Sebastian."

"Sure," he waved at us. "Come on in."

We followed him inside and he handed me his phone, then went to the fridge for some water bottles. He also pulled out a dish and stuck it in the microwave.

"Hi, I'm Ryan," he said to Claire, handing over the water bottle.

"Claire. It's nice to meet you." She looked down at herself, a filthy mess and turned bright red. I shook my head and went to the other room for privacy, dialing Sebastian's number. The phone rang and rang, but no answer. I hit redial and waited again.

"This better be fucking good, Ryan. I haven't slept all week," his voice rumbled through the phone.

"Knee deep in pussy isn't a good excuse," I said.

There was a pause. "Who is this?"

"Derek, asshole. I ran into some trouble and had to stop at Ryan's house. I'm gonna need a lift back to Reed Security. We have shit to figure out."

"Goddamnit. Why can't this shit happen during the day? I was just about to go to sleep."

"It did happen during the day. I've been dragging my ass through the woods and fighting off trained killers."

"Seriously? Can't any of you keep your hands to yourselves for one fucking night? I just wanted some fucking sleep." He sighed into the phone, "I'll give Hunter a call. He'll take you back to Reed Security and I'll meet you there. How many people do we need?"

"Shit, I don't know."

"What is this about?"

"Nathan Kent."

"Fucking great," he growled. "I'll call in anyone that's available."

I hung up with Cap and went back to the kitchen, smelling some of the best food I had in ages. Or maybe it was just the fact that we hadn't eaten in hours and I was starving.

"You two look like you just went toe to toe with a grizzly bear."

"Something like that," I replied as he put a plate of food in front of me. I dug in without answering any further. Ryan raised an eyebrow in question, but didn't say anything else. His kid walked into the room a few minutes later with wide eyes. He had to be almost fourteen now. It had been a good three years since his mom had died.

"Whoa! Who'd you get in a fight with?" James asked as he sat down at the table, completely mesmerized by the blood splatter on my shirt.

Ryan shot me a look to keep my mouth shut. "It's not blood, kid. We were out paintballing. My team lost."

"I've been paintballing enough to know that's not paint."

"Had a run-in with a grizzly bear."

"There are no grizzly bears around here. Try again."

Damn, the kid was sharp.

I narrowed my eyes at him. This kid wouldn't let it go, so I decided to go with the truth. "Claire and I were being chased by men that wanted a library book. When they didn't get it, they tried to kill us. We had to jump off the top of the library and landed in the lake behind it. Then we swam across the lake and waited them out. I had to kill thirteen men with my bare hands before we hoofed it over here. Now I'm waiting on a ride back to Reed Security."

James stared at me in disbelief. "Fine. Don't tell me." He stood and walked toward the other room. "Killing over a library book, pfft," he muttered under his breath. I looked at Ryan and shrugged, going back to my food.

"That wasn't a lie, was it?"

I shook my head and he scrubbed a hand across his jaw. "Thank fuck his imagination isn't that crazy."

We finished eating and Pappy showed up a few minutes later, laughing his ass off when he saw us. "You two really know how to step in shit, don't you?"

I flipped him off and turned to Ryan. "Thank you for the food and phone. I appreciate the help."

"Any time, man. Just...clean up before you come over next time," he said with a grin. I shook his hand and headed out the door with Claire and Pappy.

"Cap said you ran into some trouble in the woods. Do we have bodies to clean up?"

"Thirteen."

"Thirteen? Jesus Christ, Irish. You're turning into Knight."

"Real funny, asshole. They would have kept coming after us. I had to stop them. Now we have to figure out who exactly is after Claire before they try again."

We drove to the other side of town and pulled into Reed Security. I was happy to see everyone waiting for us, ready to get to work.

"Alright, I contacted Sean and he got me the names of the men that tried to rob the bank." We walked over to the monitors on the walls in the conference room. "We're running known associates now, but I don't-"

"Hold it," I said, pointing at the screen. "This asshole was at the library. We need to look into him."

Becky typed in a few things on the computer and his picture, along with all the information she could get on him popped up on the screen. "Brian Mathers. He's a very popular fence, dealing mostly in ancient artifacts. He's been busted for some small time crimes, but never for fencing. He's suspected by the FBI in a number of robberies around the United States as well as a few international jobs."

"Alright, Becky. Let's set up something too good for him to resist. I want you to find something we can use to draw him out. We'll set up a meet and find out who's behind this job."

"Will do, bossman. I'll see what I can do."

"Cazzo, have you gotten ahold of Nathan Kent yet?"

"Nothing. I sent him a message when he was out in the theater, but either he hasn't gotten the message or he's still playing Army Ranger."

"We need to know what the fuck they're after. Everyone, pull any contact you have and get me in touch with Kent. We need to figure this out before someone ends up ten feet under." He turned to Claire, whom we all just remembered was still in the room. "Not that you have to worry about that. We're all professionals here."

She swallowed hard and gave a nervous chuckle. "Right, I knew that."

Cap sighed and jerked his head toward the door. "Irish, why don't you take her and show her your office?"

"Sure, Cap."

I led her out of the room and down the hall to my office, closing the door behind us. She spun around and shoved me up against the door. "That was so hot."

"What was so hot?"

"The way you killed those men." She backed away, shocked at what she had said. "That's so wrong. It shouldn't be a turn on, should it? I mean, I'm not turned on that you killed someone, well, thirteen some-one's, but the way you did it." She started fanning herself like she was on fire. "I've never seen anyone move like that. I didn't even get to see all of it because I was up a tree, but what I did see? Holy crap! The way your arms were flexing and I could see the muscles pulling tight when you did that crazy gun trick. I think I creamed my panties right there."

I slowly walked toward her, my eyes narrowing in on her luscious curves. If she wanted a predator, I could give her that. I would devour her like she was my last meal. "So, you like the way I move?"

I saw her throat work to swallow and a faint jerk of her chin. She took a little step back and right into my desk. Her face jerked around when she saw she was cornered. She gave a nervous laugh and crossed and uncrossed her legs. She was so damn cute. She wanted to play the game, but wasn't sure how.

I could feel myself swelling painfully behind my jeans, but I had to take my time and make sure this was good for her. She liked to play games and I liked to make her come. I shoved my body up against hers, my erection pushing into her stomach as she leaned further back breathing heavily. I ran my nose down her cheek, sniffing her as if she was my dinner. I let a low grumble escape from my throat as I latched onto the smooth skin of her neck, sucking hard and tasting the salt of her skin. I pulled her hands tight behind her back as I licked and sucked down her neck.

I stepped back quickly, whipping my shirt over my head and letting my muscles flex for her. She whimpered as her eyes roamed over my chest. My mouth was on her in seconds, my hands gripping her ass and hoisting her up onto my desk. Papers went flying, my computer crashed to the ground, and my mouth consumed her body. I ripped her pants from her legs and thrust her legs wide for my viewing. With a flick of my wrist, her panties were gone and her shimmering pussy was mine for the taking.

Her head banged onto the desk as I took her into my mouth. Her screams echoed around the room, but I didn't stop until every last drop was sucked dry from her. Her trembling body didn't have time to recover before I was shoved inside her, pummeling her as my body rippled from the force. Still, I wasn't deep enough. I climbed on top of the desk, lifting her hips to meet mine as I continued my assault. Her eyes rolled back in her head, but then she snapped her gaze to mine and shoved me backwards, flinging me off the desk and into my office chair. She climbed into my lap and straddled me, sliding down onto my cock with such force that I worried she had broken me. It was too good for me to care. The chair swiveled around us as she bounced on my dick. I pulled her shirt off and snapped off her bra, setting free her tits to bounce in my face.

I latched onto her nipples, pulling and tweaking with a need so primal, I felt like a caveman. She leaned further and further into my mouth, needing what I was offering. I heard the creak a second before the chair broke in half and we went sprawling across the floor. I was done letting her take the lead. I hauled her off the floor and shoved her up against the wall, wrapping her legs around my body. My pictures bounced off the wall and a few fell to the floor as I fucked her hard and fast. Her hand reached out and grasped onto the filing cabinet drawer and ripped it open as her orgasm tore through her. I thrust in one last time and was so keyed up that I shoved my fist through the drywall next to her head. She didn't even flinch, but latched onto my mouth, biting harshly into my lip. I spun around, sinking onto the ground next to the couch, breathing like I had just run a marathon.

She leaned her forehead against mine and her body collapsed into me. I pulled her in tight, needing to feel the beat of her heart against mine. A pounding at the door had me pulling the blanket off the couch and covering her nudity. No one would be seeing her like this but me. The door flung open and Cap, Pappy, Ice, and Sinner all stood in the doorway.

"Christ, Irish, there's a fucking couch right next to you," Cap snapped. I looked around the office and chuckled. The contents of my desk were scattered on the floor and my computer was broken on the ground. The chair was in two pieces and the filing cabinet was flung open. My pictures were hanging crookedly on the wall and lying in a broken mess on the ground. The couch next to us was in pristine condition.

"This is fucking hot. Cap, can I get an office so I can bring Cara in here? I have a few fantasies of my own to play out," Sinner smirked.

Claire buried her head in the crook of my neck and laughed.

"What did I tell you about women?" Ice pointed to me. "All these fucking women around here are turning the men into wild animals. Just the other day, I walked in on Cap in the training room, fucking Maggie on the rope, like it was a fucking sex swing." Cap's eyes snapped to Ice, obviously unaware that he had been caught. "Yeah, that's right. I saw, and believe me, I wish I hadn't. How the hell did you do that without getting rope burn on your junk?"

For the first time ever, I saw Cap fucking blush.

"Just keep your fucking mouth shut about what you saw."

"What's wrong?" Hunter asked, smiling. "Don't want everyone to know how kinky you and Maggie are?"

"No, I don't want Knight knowing that I used the training center."

Ice scoffed. "You should see what he and Kate do in there. Seriously? Does everyone use the training center for fucking?"

"We haven't yet," Claire piped up, only to bury her face in my neck again.

"Just one question," Ice asked Cap, crossing his arms over his chest in all seriousness. "Do you have to be in a committed relationship to use the training center? Because I think it's a little discriminatory to limit it to those that choose to have a chain around their neck. I like a good fuck as much as the next guy."

"Do you guys think you could leave us alone?" I asked.

Pappy turned to me with a smirk. "You didn't have any problem letting us hear you fuck her. By the way, based on the screaming, I'd give you a solid ten."

"I don't know," Sinner said. "Sounded more like a nine point five to me. Based on the destruction of the room, I mean."

"Based on the destruction of the room, I'd say you're paying for the damages," Cap said. "You have five minutes to get dressed and back to the conference room. Becky has something for us." He ushered everyone else from the room and shut the door. Claire finally looked up at me and I felt like my fucking heart would explode. She was so goddamn beautiful, but her "just fucked" look had me hard again less than five minutes after we finished. I was totally and completely fucked when it came to her.

"*E*veryone move into place," Cap said through the mic. We were in Philadelphia meeting up with Brian Mathers to fence the Imperial Regalia of the Holy Roman Empire. They were actually in Vienna, Austria at the Hofburg Palace, but Becky had let loose some intel on the Dark net that they had been stolen and it was being kept quiet while they were being retrieved.

Trying to choose one of us to go in as the seller was difficult since we all looked like ex-military. Since Lola was out for the time being, Florrie agreed to go in her place with Alec and Craig, her teammates, as her backup. The rest of us were there in case Mathers also had backup. Florrie was dressed in dress pants and a stylish suit jacket that she had rolled up slightly on her arms. We didn't need to keep Mathers' attention for long. The whole point was to corner him, make sure he was alone, and get him back to Reed Security where we could figure out what was going on.

"Florrie, you're up. Remember, we just need a distraction until we can capture him," Cap said. I watched through my scope as Florrie gave a slight nod and entered the abandoned warehouse. Alec and Craig were on either side of her in suits, looking every bit the muscle.

"Ms. Younge, I presume." Mathers held out his hand to Florrie, who went to place hers in his, but he kissed her knuckles instead. I could tell from my position that he was attracted to her. His leer was enough to send shivers down my spine. If it weren't for Alec and Craig standing right next to her, I would have demanded that we pull her out.

"Mr. Mathers, it's so nice to finally meet you. Shall we get down to business?"

"Why don't we go for a walk and discuss how you happened to come across such a priceless artifact?"

"There's no need to go for a walk. I wanted it and I took it."

He smirked and let his gaze wander over her body. "You really expect me to believe that *you* stole the Imperial Regalia of the Holy Roman Empire?"

"I don't expect you to believe anything. When you see it, the only thing you'll be wondering is how much I'll be asking for it," Florrie said smugly.

"By all means, please lead the way." He waved a hand in front of him for her to take him to the artifact. Craig and Alec walked on either side of them as Florrie led them outside the warehouse to the SUV.

"We're all clear, Florrie. This guy works alone. There are no signs of anyone with him," Cap said into the mic.

Mathers' hand came to rest on the small of Florrie's back and slid down to her ass. She spun and grabbed his hand, jerking it back as he collapsed to the ground in pain. "I would keep your hands to yourself if you plan on leaving here with them. Now, I need information and you're going to provide it. Get in the vehicle."

"What about the artifacts?" Mathers blustered.

She smiled evilly at him. "You mean the artifacts that I couldn't have possibly stolen? I didn't, but I am a trained killer, so unless you want to become the headline on the evening news, I'd get in the fucking truck." She released his hand and stood by as he rubbed his wrist.

Standing, he straightened his suit coat and tie. "There's no decency among thieves anymore. This used to be a gentleman's game."

"I'm not a thief, and a gentleman wouldn't grab a lady's ass," she said as she shoved him in the SUV.

I walked into the conference room at Reed Security to see Knight sitting at the table, glaring at Claire. She was obviously nervous to be sitting with him based on the stiffness in her shoulders. I wanted to kick Knight's ass for being so intimidating toward my woman, but he didn't know that she didn't really know who he was. It was time to set the record straight.

"Knight, can I talk to you for a minute?" He turned slowly and looked at me with narrowed eyes. "Now," I barked.

He stood slowly and followed me down the hall to my office that was still a disaster. He shook his head and leaned against the wall, arms and ankles crossed like he didn't have a care in the world.

"You have to knock that shit off. Claire isn't your fucking enemy."

"She's not my woman. How the hell do I know I can trust her?"

"How the hell did you know you could trust Kate? All she did was stitch you up, yet you couldn't leave her the fuck alone. You went to her when you wouldn't go to anyone else."

"That was different."

"Bullshit. You knew and I'm telling you that I know the same fucking thing. Claire would never do anything to hurt me and that includes doing something that would hurt one of my brothers."

He smirked and shook his head. "So, we're brothers now?"

I rolled my eyes at him and looked away. "Something like that. You work with us and I know you have my back no matter how bad you want to pretend you're still a lone wolf."

"If you say we're a fucking wolf pack, I'm gonna pull out my gun and shoot you."

"Look, I'm just saying that at some point you have to start fucking trusting people. Cap pulled you out of that fire and when he changed your identity, he put us all at risk. He wouldn't have done that if he didn't think he could trust you, and we wouldn't be standing behind his decision if we didn't trust him."

He still didn't look quite convinced, so I made a decision right then. "I'm going to trust you with something and I swear to God, if you say a fucking word, I'll turn you over to the military police myself." He nodded, knowing that it had to be something big. "She doesn't really know who you are. She thought...she thought you were a superhero."

"No," he shook his head in disbelief. "Nice fucking try."

"I'm serious, man. She saw you get shot in the bank and you didn't fucking die. Hell, you didn't even have a bullet hole. You were wearing that new vest, one that nobody knows about. She seriously thought that you were some kind of superhero and we were protecting your identity. I cleared up that part, but I didn't tell her your real identity. As much as I trust her, it's not my place to tell her that shit."

"So, she really thought I was a superhero?" A grin split his face, the first real smile I had ever seen on his face. "That's kind of fucking awesome."

"Don't let it go to your head."

"Too late. I already proved I'm bulletproof."

"Like I said, if it gets around that she thought that, you and I are finished. I love that woman more than my fucking life and I won't have her feeling like an idiot."

"No problem. As long as that's all cleared up, we're good."

We walked out of the office and down the hall to the conference room where everyone was seated. Cap shot us an irritated look.

"Now that the ladies are done gabbing, let's get to work. We have Mathers downstairs cooling his heels."

"I'll go-" Knight spoke up.

"No, Knight, we're not going to kill him," Cap cut him off. "Chris, I want you to go get everything you can from him."

"No problem." Chris cracked his knuckles and shook out his shoulders as he stood.

"What the fuck is going on with you guys? I said we're not killing him. This guy is a thief and based on the way he showed up to the meet, he won't last long in interrogation. Get what we need without leaving a mark on him." Cap slammed his folder shut and walked out of the office grumbling, "Suddenly, everyone wants to kill someone."

Twenty minutes later, Chris was back upstairs, having gotten everything we needed, and we were packing for Washington D.C.

Chapter Seventeen

CLAIRE

"This is so exciting. I've only been here once before and it was on a tour, so I didn't really have time to explore," I said to Derek as we walked through the doors to The Library of Congress. I stared in awe at the sheer size of it all. So many books and not enough time to look at all of them. I had put in a call to a friend of mine that had worked here for years. She had given me access to the restricted section, which was where the book I had been looking for was currently sitting. Apparently, there were some things in there that the government didn't want just anyone to read about.

I had to spend all of last night researching the library so that I would know where to go. My friend, Lizzie, had sent over all the information I would need on where to go and how to maneuver around the library without bringing too much attention to ourselves. Derek had also pulled up the schematics to the library with Becky's help and had been studying those for hours. It was too big of a library to just go in and wander around. We had to be sure that we could get around quickly and get out.

"Over here. She told me that I should meet her at the circulation desk."

I walked over and gave a huge smile when I saw my old friend from community college. "She had an uncle with connections and had always dreamed of working in the Library of Congress."

"Seriously?" Derek asked. "People dream about working in a library?"

I smacked him on the chest and gave Lizzie a hug. "It's so good to see you."

"You too. You certainly have done well for yourself." I wasn't naive enough to think that she was talking about my own job running a library. She was raking her eyes over Derek's body. I stepped in front of him, essentially blocking her view. "We'd love to chat, but we're kind of on a time crunch."

"Oh, of course," she smiled at me. "I think it's so cool that someone I know actually needs access to a book like that. Just keep it quiet. I'm not entirely sure I should be letting you in there."

"We'll be quick. I promise."

"I can't be gone from my position here. There's always someone that needs my help," she said as if her job was manning the Oval Office. "I wrote down the codes for you to get in, but you have to promise me you'll destroy them."

"I swear. Thank you so much for this."

Derek and I slipped away in the direction of the restricted section. We walked as casually as we could, trying our best not to draw attention to ourselves. It took us a good five minutes to get there and I quickly entered the codes to get in. When we were finally inside, I couldn't help the tear that slipped free from my eye.

"Are you crying?" Derek asked. I quickly swiped at my cheek and took a deep breath.

"Not at all. I just had something in my eye. Okay," I pulled out the piece of paper and began scanning the shelves for the number I needed. This place was huge and my fingers kept itching to reach out and grab all the books I could get my hands on. There were so many books to look through, aisles of books that were older than Derek and I combined. "Ooh! Here it is," I said, pulling the large book off the shelf. "But I don't know exactly what we're looking for. Did Mathers give you any-"

"I've been waiting for you."

Derek and I spun around to see a large, bald man standing at the end of the aisle we were in.

"Vanderhusing," Derek muttered.

"Who?"

"This is the guy that wants the book."

"And you came and got it for me," he grinned. "I haven't been able to get in here myself, but I've been keeping tabs on you, Claire. When my men told me that you might be able to find the book and then suddenly stopped talking with them, I knew you were on to something. It was sheer luck that I had already come here to try and find a way in myself."

"You can't be in here. It's the restricted section," I said dumbly.

His grin was maniacal and sent shivers down my spine. When he pulled a gun out, Derek stepped in front of me, holding me behind him.

"Put the gun down. You know you can't fire it in here anyway. You'll have security on you in seconds."

"Security is not a problem. I have security on my payroll, but even they couldn't get me in here. They can, however, give me enough time to get what I need. Now, you can either do as I say or we can do this the hard way."

As he took a step toward us, Derek stiffened slightly. The man's gaze dropped to the book in my hands and Derek knocked his hand away, kicking him backward into the bookshelf. Books rattled and fell to the ground and I screeched in horror when I saw the old books being trampled on by Derek and Van-what's his name.

"Derek, stop! You're ruining the books!"

"Do you want books or a boyfriend?" he asked as he ducked a punch and kicked the guy in the balls. I bit my lip and thought about his question. These were practically the Holy Grail of books. I didn't want them to be ruined. On the other hand, I loved Derek and I didn't really want to see him end up dead. His fist crunched against the man's face twice more before Vanguard or Vanderburg ended up in a heap on the floor. I stared at him numbly, mostly because there was what appeared to be an ancient copy of The Bible laying underneath him, pages torn from the frail binding.

"Claire, shove the book in your purse and let's get out of here."

I quickly opened my purse, but couldn't get the book inside. It was too thick and long for what I carried.

"You always have a book on you, but you didn't bring a purse big enough today?"

"A, I didn't plan on stealing a book from The Library of Congress, and B, I always carry a Kindle. They're teeny tiny compared to this thing."

He grabbed my hand and pulled me quickly back through the library, weaving in and out of aisles of books, around desks, and what looked like an employee only area. It seemed to take forever to get out of there, but he seemed to know exactly where he was going and somehow managed to sneak us out a back door without anyone realizing we had left.

"Derek, we can't just take the book from there. It's against the law. Besides, I'm a librarian. It goes against our code."

"Do librarian's really have a code, Claire?" he asked as he pulled me down the sidewalk. We were several blocks from the massive library and Derek was walking so fast that I could barely keep up.

"We could and we definitely should after this little excursion. Although, I'd probably be banned from any kind of librarian's club after stealing a book from the Library of Congress!"

"You want to say that a little louder? I don't think the policeman on the corner heard you."

I looked nervously around, sure that at any moment a policeman would step out and slap the cuffs on me. Derek whipped out his phone and quickly dialed, putting the phone to his ear. He pulled me down an alley, taking me through a maze of the city. "Cap, we're headed your way. We ran into some trouble. Vanderhusing was there...Yeah, I took him out for now, but-"

A sharp crack sounded and Derek threw me against a wall, crushing his body to mine. He had a gun out, aiming in the direction of what I now realized was a gunshot and fired off a few rounds. Pulling me behind him, we ran as fast as we could, taking cover behind dumpsters where we could, zigzagging through the alley. We ran out of the alley and into the street, darting into traffic just as the light was turning green. A car screeched to a stop just shy of hitting us and I glanced behind just in time to see Vanderhusing lift his gun. Instinctively, I raised the book to act as a shield and jolted as the bullet struck the book and propelled me backward. Derek caught me and tossed me to the side as he lifted his own weapon and fired a shot at the man, hitting him in the shoulder.

I lifted the book from where it had fallen on the ground next to me and saw a bullet hole in the center of the book. Flipping through the pages, I saw that it stopped at a metal plate that was inserted in the back of the book. Anger took over me and as Derek helped me to my feet, I rushed the man that was now whimpering on the sidewalk holding his shoulder. Derek picked his gun up and tucked it into his waistband, calling Cap back and asking for police assistance.

"You shot a book!" I shouted at the man. "What's wrong with you?" I kicked him in the side as my anger got the better of me. Derek wrapped an arm around my waist and hauled me back out of the way. I shouted over his shoulder, unable to control the rage inside. "Don't you have any respect? I'm going to get all my librarian friends together and we're going to take you down!"

"Claire!" Derek was holding me by the cheeks, trying to get my attention. My chest was heaving and I felt a little flush after all that had happened. "It's okay. It's just the adrenaline." I looked at him, not understanding his meaning until I looked down and saw that my arms were shaking uncontrollably. "You have to try and calm down, okay? I promise, he'll pay for shooting the book," he said in all sincerity.

I looked back at the man groaning on the ground that was now surrounded by several police officers. I nodded and tucked the book tightly against my chest. Derek pulled me in for a hug and rubbed his hands up and down my back. "Come on. We have to give our statement to the police."

---

*B*y the time we got to the police station, the adrenaline that had previously been coursing through my veins was wearing off and my nerves were settling in. Derek held my hand as we gave our statements, but then the detective got one look at the book I was still holding and decided that we needed to be questioned separately.

"Just stick to the story, Claire. Don't offer anything more and if they start asking questions, tell them you won't talk to them without a lawyer."

I nodded as an officer led me to a room that had a large window and a creaky metal chair pushed against an equally creaky table. I sat down and stared around the room that made my skin crawl, hoping it wouldn't be too long that I had to be in here. The book had been taken from me when the detectives realized that it had a bullet hole in it. Derek had decided to leave that part out since we had stolen the book. However, since I didn't have anywhere to put it, I had just held it in my hands, hoping that the detectives didn't realize something was amiss. Stupidly, I hadn't paid attention to what part of the book was facing out.

They left me stewing in that room for over an hour and the seat was getting more and more uncomfortable. Derek's words kept repeating in my head, *'Just stick to the story, Claire. Don't offer anything more and if they start asking questions, tell them you won't talk to them without a lawyer.'* I repeated it until I was sure that I could do exactly that. When the detective walked in the room, my heart jumped into my throat. This was it. I was sunk.

"Can I get you anything?"

"I didn't mean to steal the book," I shouted. "I went to the Library of Congress because I was trying to figure out what that man was trying to kill me over. I swear, I never would have taken it. I'm a librarian! We took an oath!" The man raised an eyebrow at me. "Okay, there's no oath, but I would never do something so...so heinous. I get mad when people don't return library books and I know this is so much worse. I swear to you on my life! But that man was chasing us and I didn't have time to think. I just had to get out of there and find out what he wanted so badly. Then he took a shot at me and I swear, I didn't mean to destroy library property, but it's a reaction, you know? When someone shoots at you, you duck or hold something up to block the bullet. So, that's what I did. The book was in my hands and I reacted, but if I hadn't, I would be dead right now. And you can't fault me for protecting myself. I only did what any other sane person would do!"

I was breathing hard by the time I finished my rant and the detective was just sitting across from me, staring at me with an expression I wasn't quite sure about. Was he going to lock me up? Would I go to prison? Did they send people to prison for stealing library books? I guess I should know that since I was a librarian, but sadly, I found myself uninformed on something that I really needed to know right now.

The door burst open and Derek stood next to a man in a suit. My eyes went wide and tears flooded my eyes. "I'm so sorry, Derek. I didn't mean to say anything, but he pressured me," I said, pointing to the detective.

Derek scowled at the man and took a menacing step toward him. "I told you that her lawyer was on the way. You shouldn't have interrogated her."

The detective stood and slipped his hands into his pockets casually. "I believe I said, 'Can I get you anything'." He shrugged as if that was all that needed to be said. Derek's eyes swung to mine and he raised an eyebrow in question.

"He makes it sound so simple, but you weren't here. You don't know the tone of voice he used!" I said hysterically.

"Relax, Ms. Grant. The Library of Congress isn't going to press any charges. When we explained the situation to them, they backed off right away. Well, with a little persuasion on your boss's part," he said to Derek.

"So, I'm not going to prison?" I said tearfully.

"No, Ms. Grant. We aren't in the business of putting hardened criminals like yourself in prison for book theft. However, I'm sorry to tell you that you've been banned from ever stepping foot in the Library of Congress again."

I slumped down into the chair. That almost seemed like worse news that going to prison. I hadn't gotten a chance to explore it and now I would never get the chance. The detective took in my defeated look and laughed. "Come now, Ms. Grant. It's not really all that bad, is it? It's just a library after all."

My gaze snapped up to his and I swear a growl erupted from my throat. Derek rushed over to me and hoisted me up by my elbow. "I think that's our cue to leave. Thank you for your help, detective."

He pulled me out of the police station and onto the street, pushing me up against the wall. "Claire, I'm never bringing you along on a job again. God forbid anyone ever got their hands on you, you'd crack in two seconds flat."

"I'm sorry. I'm not used to that type of intensity. I've never been questioned like that before."

"Yeah, it must have been rough to be asked if he could get you anything."

"Don't make fun of me. I'm not like you. I'm not trained in evasive..." I waved my hand around as I searched for the word. "Evasive anything. I'm just a librarian and I'm really not cut out for your life."

Derek pulled me in close and kissed me on the lips. "That's okay. You don't have to be cut out for my life. Just for me. And don't ever say you're just a librarian. You happen to be the smartest librarian I know."

"I'm the only librarian you know," I pouted.

"Who cares? I just hope–" He didn't finish his thought as his eyes caught something and he looked to the side. "Kent?"

A man with dark hair and brown eyes walked up to us. His suit was slightly rumpled and his tie was askew. Still, he was handsome and had a devilish grin.

"Hey, Derek. I haven't seen you in a while."

"We've been trying to get ahold of you. You have no idea the shit storm that's going on."

"I got your message, but I didn't have time to contact you. I only have two days leave to get this all sorted out."

"Well, we caught Vanderhusing. He's in custody now."

"Yeah, Lex Vanderhusing. He's been after me for quite some time now."

My eyes went a mile wide when he said the name. Lex. And he was Nathan Kent. Lex and Kent. It couldn't be a coincidence.

"What did he want from you, if you don't mind me asking?"

"There's an old family heirloom that I have hidden away. It's an

Emerald that dates back to the sixteenth century. My great-grandfather built a special box for it to keep it safe and gave me the key. That book he was after? It wouldn't have given him anything. I come from a line of locksmiths and he fashioned the lock and key in a special way. The key doesn't work like a regular key."

"Glad it's safe, man."

Kent reached out and shook Derek's hand. When he stepped toward me, I noticed he had a dark blue shirt on under his collared shirt. I swallowed hard and took his hand. "I'm Nathan, by the way."

"Claire," I whispered.

"Well, I have to get going. I still have to run by the *Washington Post* and drop off an article that'll keep Lex off the streets for many years to come." He pulled out a pair of glasses and slid them on his face. Derek said goodbye as I stood there dumbly. When Nathan turned, I saw a peek of something red slipping out the back of his suit jacket.

I pointed to Nathan's retreating form and slapped Derek on the arm. "Did you see that?"

"Claire, don't start," he warned.

"But how could you not see it? His last name is Kent and Vander-husing's first name is Lex! And he has an Emerald? Yeah right. You know Kryptonite was Superman's weakness and he kept it locked away too. And it was green! And then there were the glasses and don't tell me you missed the blue shirt he was wearing or the red that was sticking out. He was wearing a cape under his suit."

"Claire, do you know how ridiculous that sounds? There's no way he could fit a cape under a suit."

"He's Superman! He can do anything. Don't forget that he said he had to go to the paper. Clark Kent worked at the paper with Lois Lane. I wonder who his Lois Lane is?" I asked myself.

"I think you've had enough excitement for one day. It's time to get you home."

Derek led me back to the hotel where Sebastian was waiting for us, but my mind was only on Nathan Kent and how I could prove who he really was.

Chapter Eighteen

DEREK

I had left my keys to my house on my desk and had to go back into Reed Security. Pretty much everyone was gone for the day, but as I locked up my office, I noticed that Pappy was sitting in the break room drinking a beer. I walked in and took a seat across from him, waiting for him to say something. He had been quiet for weeks now, nothing like Pappy normally was.

"What's going on, man?"

He shrugged and took a swig of his beer. "Same shit, different day."

"Why don't you cut the shit and tell me what's really going on?"

"You want to know? I'm a little fucked up right now. Lola, one of my best friends, won't speak to me because she thinks I betrayed her. She's gone off on some fucking vacation and won't answer her phone. I have no idea if she's okay or if she needs me. Then there's Lucy. She won't talk to me either. She said I broke our pact, which was to stick to fucking and not get involved emotionally. Which I was fine with until she almost slipped through my fingers. Now my head's all fucked up."

"Look, as far as Lola goes, you can't help her if she won't help herself. She needs to get her head on straight if she wants to come back. I want to help her too, but she has to realize that she needs it.

Let her go off on her own, but be there when she comes back. She'll realize eventually that you're not trying to work against her."

"And Lucy?"

"You're going to have to show her that you can have something really great with her."

"But I'm not sure that we would. I mean, fuck, I don't want to let her go, but I'm not sure she's *the one*. Hell, I didn't even think that was a real thing until just a few weeks ago."

"You have to remember, their mom has been gone for a long time. She probably has some issues that you're going to have to work through."

"Did Claire?"

"No, but she's kind of nutty."

"That's one way to describe her."

"Hey, that's my woman you're talking about. Only I get to call her a nut. Speaking of which, I'm going to surprise her at the library. I have a new outfit in mind for tonight," I said, wiggling my eyebrows.

"You guys have a fucked up sex life, you know that?"

"Hey, I never thought I would be into role play, but with her, I totally dig it. The things that I've done with her-"

He held up his hand to stop me. "Save it. I don't need to know the kinky side of you."

"I'll catch you later, man. Good luck with Lucy." He nodded and I left, driving over to the library. Claire had been working late, reorganizing the library and getting it set back up the way she wanted. Sebastian had donated the funds for new bookcases that were sturdier and hired workers to help her get it back up and running. It was almost done because Claire was a machine when it came to organization.

It was three weeks after we had been to Washington D.C. and I was still trying to convince Claire that Nathan Kent wasn't actually Superman. She had let it go the past couple of days, but I could still see the wonder in her eyes. I had to find a distraction soon or she was going to drive me crazy.

She had decided not to keep the farm after everything that had happened. Since Lucy didn't want any part of it, she decided that she just wanted to live the peaceful life of the town librarian. Somehow, I couldn't see her living the peaceful life now that she'd had a taste of adventure. Her father was doing great in his new home and Claire was more relaxed knowing that he was safe and she didn't have to make sure someone was always there looking after him. I was just happy that she wasn't so tense all the time.

I stepped into the library and my eyes zeroed in on Claire. She was busy at the circulation desk, sorting through books. I snuck up to the second floor balcony and rigged up my rope and pulley that I had gotten specially for tonight. In my Batman outfit and mask, I climbed over the edge of the balcony with the rope and slid down to right in front of her. She jumped back in surprise and then a grin lit up her face.

"Care to take a ride in my BatMobile?"

PREVIEW OF HUNTER

LUCY

"You're going home with me," Hunter snapped at me from the foot of my hospital bed.

"I am not," I insisted.

"You don't have anywhere else to go."

"I'd rather sleep in the gutter," I sneered.

"Why can't you just accept my help?"

"Because you're not offering, you're demanding."

"Who fucking cares? You need a place to stay and I have it."

"That's besides the point," I said, coughing harshly as my chest burned from the smoke that was still affecting me. Hunter had pulled me from a burning building, which I was extremely grateful for, but now he seemed to think he could boss me around. He stormed over to my bed and forced the oxygen mask over my mouth. I breathed in the air and relaxed into the bed. I just wanted some fucking sleep, but that wouldn't be possible with him standing over me and staring at me with fury in his eyes.

When the coughing subsided and I could breathe easy again, Hunter sank down into the chair next to me and ran a hand over his bald head. Sighing heavily, he looked up at me and for a moment, I thought he was going to go soft, but then his brown eyes turned harsh and he stood up, pacing around the room.

"This is ridiculous. You don't have a place to stay and I have plenty of room. Besides, I already fucking told you that things were going to change between us. You might as well accept that now." He leaned his large frame back against the wall, crossing his arms over his chest. His muscles in his arms bulged and stretched his shirt tight across his massive chest. I almost started fanning myself at the sexy sight of him, but that would just prove to him that I wanted him.

"No," I said firmly.

I stared at the sexy hunk of a man across from my hospital bed and refused to give in. He was the most gorgeous specimen God had ever put on this planet and by far the best I had ever had in bed. I wanted him so badly, but I absolutely refused to give in to his demands to go home with him today. If I did that, I knew it would be that much harder to hold onto my heart.

Hunter thought that I was the same as him, out for a good time and nothing else. To some extent, that was true. While I was working my way through my masters degree, I had no intention of dating anyone that might cause a distraction. I had been working too hard and too long to deal with complications when I was so close to my dream. I was starting to teach at a college outside of Pittsburgh in the fall and there was no way I was messing it up. Since it was my first year, I needed to be doing my job just as well as all the other teachers if I wanted to stick around.

In reality, I was like every other woman. I wanted to find someone that made me happy and settle down with a family. Hunter was not the man to do that with. He had always been a good lay, but I saw his wandering eyes at the bar and I took it for what it was. Hunter was a man with a voracious sexual appetite that one woman could never fulfill. So, as much as he stood in front of me and insisted that I would be going home with him to be taken care of, I couldn't let my heart believe that he was serious. Hunter was the one man I wanted and the one man I knew would destroy my heart.

But then something happened. Suddenly, everyone was in my room, trying to make demands on where I go. Hunter was fussing over me in an angry, brooding kind of way and when he insisted I go home with him, I couldn't refuse again. The look in his eyes as he caressed my cheek had me melting right then and there.

"Humor me."

I wanted to argue. I wanted to tell him that if I humored him, I would end up a gushy puddle at his feet on the floor. But I couldn't deny him, so I nodded and let him take me home. He carried me down to his truck, which I thought was way over the top, but gave me such happy feels that I let him do it without argument. When he walked around to the other side and got in, he seemed slightly less angry, but I noticed that his knuckles were still clenched on the steering wheel. It was almost as if he was angry with me.

"Did I do something to make you mad?" I asked.

His hands tightened on the wheel some more and he didn't say anything. I shrugged and stared out the window. There was nothing I could do about his brooding mood. My head slipped against the window as the scenery went by. I hadn't gotten a wink of sleep last night with Hunter pacing my room and hovering over me like I was about to die. I had been in a fire and had some smoke inhalation, but I had been cleared and was fine. All that excitement had worn me out though and I was asleep before we reached the edge of town where his house was located.

When we got to his house, I jerked upright, wide awake in two seconds. I quickly got out of the truck before he could come around and get me out. I had to keep my distance from him.

"Lucy, stop!"

I turned and looked at Hunter, who was running to catch up to me. "What?"

"You shouldn't be-"

"Walking? I'm fine, Hunter. I had smoke inhalation, not a broken leg."

"You're so damn stubborn. Why won't you let me help you?"

"Because I don't need it. I'm fine and I don't need someone hovering over me." I sighed and looked longingly toward the door where a bed waited for me. "Look, I'm tired. Can we just go inside so I can go to sleep?"

His eyes softened and he nodded. "Yeah. You can have the guest room."

I nodded, not wanting to show the hurt on my face. The guest room. This was why I had to guard my heart from Hunter. He had demanded all night that I was his and he would take care of me, but then he took me to his house and put me in the guest room. Hunter definitely wasn't ready to let a woman into his life.

He led me up to the guest room, which I knew all too well. Whenever Hunter and I had sex, we came to this room. He never let women into his room. It was his sanctuary and he didn't want it tainted. I ripped off my clothes, not wanting to sleep in sweatpants and a t-shirt and crawled under the covers.

"What are you doing?"

"Going to sleep," I said with a yawn.

"I see that, but why did you take off your clothes? We're not having sex, you know."

I glared at him, "I know we're not having sex, but I want to be comfortable. What do you care anyway? It's not like you sleep in here."

I rolled over before he could say anything and closed my eyes. I heard him walk around the bed and go over to the other side. Sinking down on the bed, my eyes flew open when I felt him making himself comfortable.

"Why are you here?"

"I'm just making sure you're okay."

"I'm sleeping, Hunter. There's not much that can happen to me in here."

"Look, you don't have anyone else to look after you. Why do you have to bust my balls over this?"

I sat up and leaned back against the wall. "If you really felt it was that important to watch over me, why did you put me in here where you don't sleep?"

His brows furrowed and he shook his head slightly. "Because this is the guest room."

"I know that. But why did you put me in here instead of in your bedroom?"

"Because that's my bedroom."

"Exactly. You can leave now."

"I'm not-"

"Yes, you are or I'll go stay in a hotel. I don't need you to watch me sleep or sit here and make sure I'm breathing. I just want to be left alone and since we only have sex, there's no need for you to do anything more than give me a place to stay."

A growl rumbled through him and he shifted on the bed into my space. "How many fucking times do I have to tell you that you're mine?"

"If I was really yours, I wouldn't be in the guest room where you fuck all your random hookups."

"It's the guest room," he exploded. "You are a guest, the last time I checked. Guest. Room. Understand?"

"Perfectly." I flipped off the covers and picked up my clothes. There was no way I was staying here. He just didn't get it and I didn't have the energy to keep explaining it. How hard was it for him to understand that I didn't want him in my space?

"What are you doing?" he asked incredulously.

"I'm going to a hotel."

He ripped the sweats from my hands and held them away from me. "You're not fucking going anywhere."

I smirked at him and walked downstairs in just my t-shirt. I had no problem going to a hotel in just my t-shirt. Sure, it would be awkward, but right now, I would do just about anything to get away from Hunter.

"Lucy! Fucking stop!" He raced after me and spun me around, hauling me up over his shoulder. "I told you that you weren't going anywhere."

"And I told you that I wasn't staying here!"

"Stop being so damned difficult. I'll stay out of your fucking room."

"Now wasn't that simple?"

I let him carry me upstairs and put me back in the room, glad when he plopped me on the bed and walked out of the room, slamming the door behind him. I was finally able to drift off and get some sleep, knowing that at least for the moment, I had successfully kept Hunter at bay.

*W*hen I woke up, it was after dark and I was starving. I got dressed and went downstairs to find some food in the kitchen. Hunter was in there, brooding at the table with a beer. His eyes raked over my body as I walked in and I could see the hunger there. It couldn't happen though. Now that I knew exactly what Hunter wanted from me for the moment, I knew I had to stay away from his bed.

"You hungry?" he asked.

"Starved."

"Sit down. I'll heat up some dinner for you."

"Thanks."

"So, I was thinking that I could take you shopping in the morning for whatever you need. Maggie dropped off some stuff for you earlier, but I'm sure it's not enough."

"I'll need to swing by the bank tomorrow and get out some money."

"That's not necessary. I can get you whatever you need."

"Hunter, we're not together. You need to get that through your head. I appreciate the place to stay, but I'm not going to let you buy me new things."

"Why can't you let me fucking help you?" he said, slamming his hand down on the counter. "You're so damn stubborn. I'm trying to show you that I want to be there for you and you just can't fucking let me in."

"Am I really supposed to just believe that all the sudden you want me for more than a quick fuck? That's all we've ever been, Hunter. I was in a fire and now you want me?" I shook my head at him. "I don't think so. It doesn't work that way."

He walked over to me and sat down in front of me, pulling my hands into his large ones. He stared at them for a minute and I saw a flash of a vulnerable side to Hunter. "My best friend was in a fire and I thought he was dead. When I saw your house on fire...you can't imagine how fucking terrified I was. And then I saw you passed out on the floor and I could have sworn my heart was going to pound out of my fucking chest. It was like seeing Knight dying in that building all over again. Only this time it was worse because it was you and I didn't even have a chance at something real with you. That's all I want is a fucking chance."

I was speechless. I didn't think Hunter would ever say something like that to me. We had never had any deep, meaningful conversations or anything that was remotely serious. This was a new side to Hunter and it gave me hope that just maybe we could have something more.

He leaned back in his chair and ran a hand across the stubble on his jaw. "Sorry," he said with a chuckle. "I know that's not really our thing, personal stuff, I mean. I just wanted you to know that I am fucking serious about this thing between us. I don't know the first fucking thing about how to be in a relationship, but I want to try with you."

He looked up at me and I could see it in his eyes. He was serious and I was finally ready to give him the chance he was asking for. "Okay, let's try."

A faint smile touched his lips before he stood and placed a gentle kiss on my forehead. When he turned away to get my dinner from the microwave, I couldn't help but place my fingers to the spot he had just kissed. It was so tender and so unlike Hunter and made it all the more special.

I ate quietly and then let Hunter lead me back upstairs. This time, he took me to his room, seeming to struggle with actually letting me in there as he opened his door. The room was masculine and cold, exactly what I would expect from Hunter. There were no signs of life in his room other than a few pictures on his dresser from his days in the military.

His bed was huge and looked like the only thing he truly cared about in the room. There was a fluffy comforter that looked so cozy I could wrap myself up in it and sleep for days. I walked over, running my hands along the comforter and sank down onto the mattress. A sigh escaped my lips when I was enveloped by the comfort of the soft mattress. It was heaven. My eyes slipped shut and that was the last thing I remembered.

A strong arm was wrapped around my waist, pulling me back against a hard body that I knew to be Hunter's. I smiled dreamily as I thought about what he said to me last night. He wanted to try. Things were finally looking up. I was going to be starting a job in the fall and I now had a man that truly cared about me. Someone that I found myself equally attracted to, but never thought I would have something more with.

The sun was shining brightly through the windows and putting me in the best mood I'd been in for days. I stretched my arms above my head, ready to relax back into the comfort of the bed when I felt a sharp bite over my exposed nipple. I had gone to bed last night in clothes, but this morning I was naked. When had that happened? Hunter was watching me intently as he laved my nipple and sucked it hard into his mouth. I moaned and thrust my chest up higher into his mouth.

His hand slipped down my stomach, gliding smoothly across my skin and dipped down beneath the covers. I shuddered when his fingers slipped through my folds and pinched my clit. My eyes drifted closed as he pleasured me and brought me to orgasm. Hunter knew exactly how to take my body from zero to sixty and always gave me an ending with fireworks.

His lips trailed up my breasts to my neck as he slid between my legs. His erection pushed at my entrance as he rocked against me. I moaned as I begged for him to thrust inside me, but he just kept teasing me, making me wetter with every thrust.

"Hunter, get inside me."

"I don't think so. I wouldn't want you to overdo it. You just got out of the hospital," he teased.

"If you don't get inside me now, you'll never have another chance again," I threatened. His eyes narrowed at me as he pushed inside me to the hilt. His cock moved slowly inside me, thrusting in long, hard strokes that had me splitting apart in seconds. I bit my lip as I felt my body clenching around his. He threw my legs up over his shoulders as he started pounding me harder.

My eyes rolled back in my head as pleasure washed over my body. I would never find anyone that could give it to me the way Hunter did. His primal need for me matched mine for him in every way.

"Fuck me harder, Hunter. Give me what I need."

He pulled out and pounced on me like a tiger. "I'll fuck you the way I want to and you'll take it."

"Then stop talking and do it."

He flipped me onto my stomach and gripped onto my hips, pulling me up against him. I felt his rough hands spread my ass cheeks as his dick rubbed against my ass. "If you weren't just in a fucking fire, I'd be a lot rougher with you."

"I'm fine," I insisted. "I can take it."

"Not today."

He slapped my ass and pushed hard inside me. He was pounding me so hard that he had to hold me up. Normally I could hold my own with Hunter, but I wasn't quite myself today and now I could see why he was going easy with me. He pulled my body up against his, kneading my breasts as he kissed my neck. He sank down onto the bed with me in his lap and continued to thrust up into me. It was gentler than what we normally did and so much more intimate. When his hand slipped down to my pussy, it didn't take long for me to come again for him. He followed me over the edge and then held me tight to him as we both came down.

"Hard enough for today?"

"Yeah," I said breathily. We laid back down on the bed, both of us slipping in and out of sleep throughout the day. When I was awake, I couldn't help but stare at him and wonder if this was real. It felt like it was a dream. Just yesterday, we were nothing to each other. How did this all happen so fast?

By the time late afternoon rolled around, I was tired of being in bed. I slipped out of bed and was making my way to the bathroom when he snagged me around the waist.

"So, you're staying?" he asked as he held me to his chest.

"Yeah, I'm staying." He nipped at my ear and I batted him away. "But you could at least give me a drawer so that I don't have to have my stuff in a bag on the floor," I said, pointing to the bag he had put in the corner that was full of things Maggie had brought for me. I pulled out of his grasp and made my way to the bathroom, blowing him a kiss over my shoulder. I almost stumbled as I saw him looking intently at my bag with a strange look on his face. I didn't want to think about what that meant. Everything was fine. I was just letting my mind go crazy, thinking about what ifs.

I showered, taking my time to scrub the remnants of the fire off me. I should have taken a shower when I got home yesterday, but I was just too tired. After drying off, I walked out of the bathroom to an empty room. I grabbed my new bag of clothes and pulled out a pair of shorts and a t-shirt. Maggie had packed me everything a girl could need and after finishing up, I headed downstairs to see Hunter staring out the window. I slipped my arms around his waist, but he stiffened when I kissed his shoulder.

"Something wrong?"

"No," he said shortly. "What do you want for dinner?"

His mood was different than before, darker and I couldn't help but wonder what had happened in the short time I had been upstairs cleaning up. I stepped back from him, a little uncomfortable with this new tension and shoved my hands in my shorts. "Uh, I'm fine with whatever you want."

"I have to run into the office for a little bit. I can just pick up a pizza on the way back," he said, but he wouldn't look at me.

"Sure. I can just hang out here."

He nodded and picked up his keys, leaving without saying good-bye. I tried to watch TV and I tried to read, but I just kept going over what had happened this afternoon. He had asked me if I would stay, or had he phrased it differently? Maybe he hadn't been wondering if I would stay, but wondering when I was leaving. That's not what his body language suggested, but maybe I was reading him all wrong. I dissected every word, every move since I had come here yesterday for the rest of the night. Hunter wasn't back by dinner time, so I made myself a sandwich and flipped through the channels some more.

When eleven o'clock rolled around and he still wasn't home, I decided to go to bed. I had to go check out the farm tomorrow and talk to my sister, Claire about what our next steps would be. When I woke up in the morning, Hunter still wasn't there and I was beginning to think I had made a very bad decision in letting him into my heart.

*C*laire had picked me up and we drove out to the farm together to see how bad the damage was. The house was in shambles, barely anything left standing. We walked through the burnt interior and found some picture frames that hadn't been totally destroyed, but there was nothing left of the photos that were once in them. There was no upstairs, which meant that all of our things had been destroyed. After ten minutes, there was no point in looking anymore. There was nothing to find.

We went to the chicken coop and took care of the chickens, but at this point, I just didn't have it in me to do anything with them any more. What was the point?

"Claire, I think we need to just sell the chickens and put the farm up for sale. I don't want to deal with this any more."

"I don't think I can make that decision right now. There are too many things to consider."

"Well, if you want the farm, it's all yours, but after everything that's happened and with Dad no longer here, I just don't see the point. I'm going to be starting a new job and the last thing I want is to be driving out here to do upkeep on a farm we don't even live on anymore."

"Alright. I'll take care of the farm from now on until I make a decision."

A truck pulled in the drive and Claire and I watched as Derek and Hunter got out of the truck. Hunter stalked toward me with his sexy swagger that had my insides lighting on fire, but the closer he got, the more I realized that he wasn't happy. My eyes flicked to Claire, who obviously was seeing the same thing as me.

"Why the fuck did you leave the house?" he snapped at me as he got closer.

"Excuse me?"

"You fucking heard me. I got home and didn't know where you were."

Claire scurried off to Derek and they quickly made themselves scarce. I crossed my arms over my chest and glared at Hunter. "The last I checked, I don't have to tell you when I'm doing something."

"You could have some fucking common courtesy and leave me a note or something."

"Like you did last night?"

His eyes narrowed at me. "I was working and I told you I would be."

"Right. You also said that you would be bringing dinner home, but you didn't call and you didn't come home."

"See, this is why I don't have relationships. I go to work and then have you nagging me when I don't come home on time."

"I'm not nagging you. I don't really give a shit if you don't come home because you're working, but you don't get to yell at me when you just did the same thing to me."

He ran his hand over his head and started pacing in front of me. "Look, we just need to take a step back here. This is too...fuck, I don't know. I don't know what the hell I'm doing here. One minute, just fucking, and the next, the next there's this expectation for more and I don't know how to deal with that."

"Hunter, let me ask you something. Did you stay away last night because of the whole drawer thing?"

He looked up at me and I could see it in his eyes. It had totally freaked him out. "It was just too much. I should have talked to you about it, but I'm not used to having to discuss shit with someone else."

"You know that I wasn't asking for more, right? You asked me to stay with you and I just wanted someplace to put my things."

"I didn't..." He rubbed his hand along the back of his neck and sighed. "I didn't know. I just thought it was moving really fast and it freaked me out."

I nodded and looked over to where Claire and Derek were walking around the house. I wanted what my sister had. I wanted a man that would cherish me the way he obviously did my sister and didn't have to second guess or hold back because of fear that I wanted more than a drawer. I would never get that with Hunter and that was clear as day. He was a great guy, but he just wasn't ready for a relationship.

"Can you take me back to your house and then to a hotel?"

He looked up sharply at me in confusion. "You don't have to go. I know I kind of freaked out, but that doesn't mean you have to leave."

"Yes, it does. Hunter, we're great together, as fuck buddies. I like you, but when I start dating someone, I don't want there to be all this second guessing. I don't need someone to ask me to move in and offer me everything within the first month, but I need to know that he's ready for a future together."

"I'm trying, Lucy. Shit. I told you I've never done this before."

"I know and I'm not faulting you for that, but you asked me to come stay with you and you freaked out after one night together. You didn't even want me in your bedroom."

"Fuck, Lucy. You have to give me time to adjust. This is all new to me."

"I know, but I don't want to go through an adjustment period. I don't want to always be wondering what you're thinking or if you're freaking out. You just said we need to take a step back and we haven't even been together a day. I'm sorry, but this isn't going to work with us."

I walked toward his truck without another word. I didn't want to stand there and argue about what was going to happen between us for the next hour. It was clear to me that even if Hunter wanted to try for more, he just wasn't equipped to handle a relationship yet.

I got lucky and found a small apartment over the laundromat in town. It wasn't much, just a one bedroom apartment, but it was all mine. It needed some work, but I didn't think that was going to happen, especially considering how cheap the rent was. Still, since I was starting a job in just under a month, I couldn't be picky about where I was going to be staying. The college where I was going to be teaching was about a half hour from me. I didn't want to move to Pittsburgh and the rent would have been higher there anyway, so this would suit me fine. Besides, Claire was going to be staying with Derek and my dad was in a retirement home now, so it wasn't like there were other people to get an apartment with at the moment.

The apartment had been vacant for some time, so they agreed to let me move in right away. I wanted to paint the walls and spruce it up a little, but that would have to wait. I didn't even have any furniture yet. I had a little in savings from working since I was seventeen, but it would only be enough to get me by until my first paycheck, I hoped. The only thing I really needed right this minute was a bed to sleep on. I could get a futon for the time being. It wouldn't be the most comfortable, but it would work.

I set my bag of clothes and bathroom products that Maggie had bought for me in the corner of my bedroom and sighed at how pitiful it looked. Grabbing my keys, I locked the door behind me and headed for the closest Walmart to get the cheapest futon, sheets, and pillows I could get. I didn't really need a blanket yet because it was still pretty warm outside.

By the time I got my all my stuff picked out, I realized that I didn't have any towels or washcloths. I also didn't have dishes. There was just so much that I was missing that you don't really think about until you need it. I picked up the cheapest dishes I could find and the basics for the kitchen, not spending more than $200 on all of it. My total bill was much higher than I wanted, but there wasn't much I could do about it.

An employee helped me load the futon into my car and I drove slowly home since it was sticking out the trunk. When I pulled up to my apartment, I groaned at the prospect of dragging the futon up the narrow stairs by myself. I hauled the rest of the stuff inside first, knowing that as soon as I attempted to take the futon, I wouldn't want to do anything else.

I took the huge box out of the trunk and pushed it across the side-walk to the entrance door. With a little maneuvering, I was able to get it through the door and started pushing the heavy box up the stairs. I was about halfway up when I lost my footing and started to fall backwards. I tried to grasp onto the railing, but my fingers just brushed it before they slipped away. My eyes went wide as I realized I was about to be crushed by my own futon, but then I hit a hard chest and arms wrapped around me to grab the box, preventing it from sliding down further.

"Thank you so much. I'm sorry-" I stopped when I turned around in the massive arms and saw Hunter standing behind me with a smirk. "You."

"Me. What the hell are you doing?" he asked.

"Moving in."

"To this dump?"

I squirmed to get out of his arms, but I was trapped between him and the box. "It's my dump. Can you let me go?"

He lifted one of his elbows for me to squirm out from under and then he started pushing the box up the stairs as I did my best impression of a wallflower. When he got to the top of the stairs, he looked at the two doors and then back at me in question. I snapped out of my haze and rushed up the stairs to let him into my apartment. When I opened the door, I tried not to let my embarrassment show. Yeah, it was a piece of crap.

"You can just slide it in and I'll take it from there."

"I'll help you set it up. Where do you want it?"

"The bedroom," I pointed to the only other door in the place and he started pushing it over.

"This place is a rat trap. I can't believe you're staying here."

"It's what I can afford for now."

"You could have fucking stayed with me."

"Hunter, you do remember how that went, right? You, freaking out over a drawer?"

He opened the box and started putting together the futon. "I may have fucked up, but you're still mine, and the next time you fucking need something, I expect you to ask for help."

"I'm not yours. That's not how this works. Do you even understand how to be in a relationship? You don't normally have to demand that the other person is yours."

He abandoned the futon and walked toward me with a glint in his eye that I knew all too well. "I don't have to demand that you're mine." He took a few more steps, backing me up until I had nowhere to run.

"You know as well as I do that you will always be mine. Your body knows it. Now we just have to wait for your head to catch up."

I shook my head slightly and glanced around for some way for me to escape. I couldn't resist Hunter and if he had his way with me, I would fall back into his arms. "We were never more, Hunter," I whispered. "It would never have worked."

"Then I need to remind you what you're missing."

His mouth latched onto mine, sucking my bottom lip into his mouth and biting gently. When he pushed me up against the wall, I was powerless to resist him. The truth was, I craved him and his touch. If I had any hope of not falling under his spell, I was going to have to go out and find someone else to give me what I needed.

ALSO BY GIULIA LAGOMARSINO

Thank you for reading Claire and Derek's story. There's still more to come further down the line, so keep reading. The Reed Security gang will be back in Hunter's story!

Join my newsletter to get the most up-to-date information, along with new content in the Reed Security series.

https://giulialagomarsinoauthor.com/connect/

Join my Facebook reader group to find out more about my obsession with Dwayne Johnson!

https://www.facebook.com/groups/GiuliaLagomarsinobooks

Reading Order:

https://giulialagomarsinoauthor.com/reading-order/

To find the individual series, follow the links below:

For The Love Of A Good Woman series

Reed Security series

The Cortell Brothers

A Good Run Of Bad Luck

Made in United States
Orlando, FL
30 October 2024

53294068R00150